If you could travel to any place and time in history, what would you do? For Isabel, Suresh, and Nathan, three teenagers in Ms Sullivan's high school English class, the answer is: 1613 when Shakespeare's Globe Theatre burned down. Nathan intends to ensure that all of Shakespeare's plays burn down with it, so students will never have to study Shakespeare again. When they land in 1592, losing their time travel device during the journey, they are stranded in Elizabethan London with no return in sight. Now they must grow and adapt to survive, or die. In the process, they reckon with historical figures such as Francis Drake, John Dee, Walter Raleigh, and a young up-and-coming Shakespeare. Filled with intrigue and the volatile history of its time, *Killing Shakespeare* is a fantasy that examines life, love, literacy, and their importance to us.

Praise for Koom Kankesan

The Panic Button

"Lucid, confident and immensely engaging, Koom Kankesan's *The Panic Button* presents a fresh and frank new voice that opens a fascinating window upon Tamil culture while retaining a warmth and humour that is universal. Recommended."

—Alan Moore, author of *From Hell*, *Jerusalem*, and *The Great When: A Long London Novel*

"Kankesan's prose is occasionally overwrought, but it is also witty, with lots of verve and frank descriptions of contemporary life: the marketing scams, office sex and genuine post-adolescent confusion."

—Susan Swan, *The Globe and Mail*

The Rajapaksa Stories

"Absolutely hilarious! Koom Kankesan introduces us to a new Rajapaksa whom we won't forget for a long time."

—Lenin M. Sivam, filmmaker of *1999* and *A Gun and a Ring*

"I laughed until my head hurt . . . with his scandalous and hilarious imagination, Koom Kankesan enthralls the reader. His clever and quirky style is just an added bonus."

—Niromi de Soyza, author of *Tamil Tigress*

The Tamil Dream

"Engaging and frequently gripping."

—Chester Brown, author of *Louis Riel* and *Paying for It*

"Koom Kankesan's *The Tamil Dream* is a rich, rewarding and very timely novel about Sri Lankan refugees in Canada . . . A universal story with deep insight into the abyss between two worlds, this is a major work by a massive talent and a book you will never tire of recommending."

—John Higgs, author of *Stranger Than We Can Imagine: An Alternative History of the 20th Century, Watling Street,* and *William Blake vs. The World*

killing Shakespeare

KOOM KANKESAN

MAWENZI
HOUSE

We acknowledge the support of the Canada Council for the Arts for our publishing program. We also acknowledge support from the Government of Ontario through the Ontario Arts Council, and the support of the Government of Canada through the Canada Book Fund.

Cover design by Julian Dwyer
Illustration by Gordon Johnson from Pixabay
Author photo by Koom Kankesan

Library and Archives Canada Cataloguing in Publication

Title: Killing Shakespeare / Koom Kankesan.

Names: Kankesan, Koom, author.

Identifiers: Canadiana (print) 20240363841 | Canadiana (ebook) 20240363957 | ISBN 9781774151624 (softcover) | ISBN 9781774151631 (EPUB) | ISBN 9781774151648 (PDF)

Subjects: LCGFT: Novels. | LCGFT: Time-travel fiction.

Classification: LCC PS8621.A55 K55 2024 | DDC jC813/.6—dc23

Printed and bound in Canada by Coach House Printing

Mawenzi House Publishers Ltd.
39 Woburn Avenue (B)
Toronto, Ontario M5M 1K5
Canada

www.mawenzihouse.com

to 'Miskatonic' Mike Shea,
for his kindness and friendship

NATHAN

Molten sunlight streams in like liquid fire through the grade eleven classroom windows, feeling warm on my cheek and neck. Outside on the green football field, a large black crow struts about pecking for worms. Everything glows, even Ms Sullivan at the front of the classroom: tall, bony, olive-cardiganed, red hair partly grey as it straggles around her glasses, calling us to attention and pecking our brains for knowledge. Right now, that crow has more freedom than we do—what I wouldn't give to spread my arms and fly away. Suresh posted a video on TikTok last week wondering why Sullivan's already old and not married. Could it be because no one can bear to hear her droning on about Shakespeare? She's handing back our essays now. If Suresh hadn't taught me how to make mine better using Bard AI, I wouldn't have even finished it.

There's Isabel right at the front of the class, sitting up straight, her long hair tied into a judgmental knot. We used to be friends but now it doesn't feel so close between us. Maybe it's because I didn't get a chance to say anything to comfort her after her father passed away last fall. I got busy with the football team—we were in provincial finals. What can ya do? Out there on the field, empty now and filled with golden sunshine, is where I intercepted the fourth quarter pass from Carver High, crowds in the stands cheering, going wild around me. I scored a touchdown and we beat Carver by three points.

"Nathan Shimura . . . this is really an interesting essay, I must say," Sullivan's screech compels me to turn my head. "I'm wondering how much of it you actually wrote? Any of it?"

1

I don't like hearing my name, at least not the condescending way Ms Sullivan says it. "Nathan, let's test what you actually know. Your essay focuses on the contrast between Hermia and Helena. How would you characterise Hermia and Helena's relationship in *A Midsummer Night's Dream*?"

She's looking for a fight; I'm happy to give her one.

"I would characterise it as a massive waste of time," I reply. Some "oohs" and gasps from the class, but mostly laughs.

Sullivan asks me to stand up. She's going to try and humiliate me. When I don't move, she screeches: "To the front of the class!"

I get up, but really slowly, like. Like I couldn't be bothered not to. Shuffle up to the front. The truth is that if I don't, she'll call down to the office. Another suspension and it's real trouble. My mother's threatened to move us to Japan with my dad. I'd hate that even more than this boring class.

Walking up to the front, I pass Suresh, all dressed in black, his cellphone out. He's tall, taller than me, but hunched over and awkward. If he just played sports, if he used his height, he'd make more friends and wouldn't have to hang around me all the time. All he'd have to do is join one team. Any team. He's playing with his phone on the desk, angling it as if it isn't actually on, but I can see the red light blinking. Is he livestreaming? I'll give them all a show.

"Nathan, is there something you want to say?"

"Like what?"

"You used ChatGPT, right? This essay was written by AI."

"Prove it." I fold my arms.

"It's so obvious. Who do you think you're fooling? Teachers aren't stupid. Just like you have a fingerprint, everyone has a writing voice and rhythm that is uniquely their own. An expression of their soul. I can tell this isn't your voice. I can tell this isn't your work. Let's see if you can explain the content."

"Maybe I got a tutor to help me," I sarcastically reply.

"And maybe you cheated. A tutor's not supposed to do the work for you. You know that."

Silence. I won't give her the satisfaction of seeing me sweat.

"Did you even do the reading, Nathan?" Why can I not think of anything to say? "Communication is what our whole civilisation is based upon." The sound of her voice, relentless, like a coat hanger dragged across the radiator grill. That's not communication. "And that is why we read William Shakespeare. Honestly, your whole generation . . . " Students murmur but no one says anything. Except Suresh. Awkward, hunched-over Suresh agitatedly driving his hand up. Mugging for his own livestream.

"Yes, Suresh?"

"Why are we forced to read Shakespeare? You're the only teacher who's teaching it this year. His writing is sexist and racist. It's prejudiced towards the British Empire which colonised a lot of the world, including Canada and Sri Lanka—the two countries I've lived in."

People are really getting into the show. The expression on their faces, sneering amusement, like those emojis of people eating popcorn. I can't let Suresh have all the fun.

"Look," I say, unfolding my arms, "you ask us to read something written hundreds of years ago, boring and useless, no relation to real life. Then you give us assignments and we do the work. You try and find some way not to give us any marks. That's not fair."

"I didn't say I wouldn't give you any marks." She's backtracking now and almost steps back on her orthopaedic shoes before catching herself. She remembers why she was angry in the first place. "Unless you cheat. And you definitely did cheat. It's not true we don't get anything from reading. Just because you and your friends don't want to try." She turns to Isabel. "Isabel, prove him wrong. Find something in the play that characterises the relationship between Helena and Hermia. Quote it to our friends Nathan and Suresh just to show them how wrong they are about literature, please."

Isabel fingers the lilac scrunchy holding the knot of her hair, as if she's signalling me. She's too embarrassed to look directly at me but I can feel the heat in her face, just four feet away. We were good friends last year. What happened? Is it because her father, who taught English at the University of Toronto, was an old friend of Sullivan's? Is that it? What could I do? I had problems with my own father.

Isabel speaks quietly but fiercely, her tongue clicking, as if reprimanding me:

"How happy some o'er other some can be!
Through Athens I am thought as fair as she.
But what of that? Demetrius thinks not so;
He will not know what all but he do know.
And as he errs, doting on Hermia's eyes,
So I admiring of his qualities."

"Thank you, Isabel! The show's over, people," says Sullivan. "Today's performance is cancelled because Nathan cheated. He gets a zero. Nathan, you can go sit down—all the world's a stage but you're not a serious player, it would seem."

"But—"

"Go sit down. Thank you for caring, Isabel."

My fists are tight—I could put one through the cinderblock wall. Care. What does that word even mean? It gets tossed around like a football. My father never says he loves me. Even on the phone, far away, working in Japan. I'm not really like him. But I'm not like my mother either. Sullivan's supposed to care about her students, but I don't think she does. She

4

cares about Shakespeare, so she expects all of us to care about Shakespeare. She only cares about Isabel and other people who repeat what she says back to her.

As if to vex me further, her coat hanger voice cuts through my thoughts. "Now, we've been reading *A Midsummer Night's Dream*, which was probably written between 1590 and 1596. It would have been performed in The Rose and some of the other theatres south of the Thames river. But in the sixteen hundreds, Shakespeare was rich enough to be a partner in his own theatre—the Globe! Does anyone know what happened to the Globe?"

Nobody replies. Suresh puts up his hand again. I notice he's still livestreaming.

Sullivan doesn't even bother to let him speak this time. She just points to a poster of the Globe Theatre behind her desk. As if to say his thoughts aren't worth hearing.

Suresh wants to be my friend. I guess he's my friend though it's one sided. He did tell me about Bard AI. He must have done something further to his essay so he didn't get caught. Or maybe Sullivan just wanted to humiliate me in particular. Probably both. I'm getting mad now. I'm not even sure who I'm mad at more: Sullivan or Suresh or Shakespeare.

Sullivan's still pointing at the poster behind her desk. Something has to be done about her. She'll just stand there pointing expectantly at the dumb poster—how is that communication? Who cares? The poster, faded, like an old historical drawing on parchment, mocks me. A cutaway of The Globe with raised stage and galleries for rich people.

Sullivan's staring at Isabel with a plea on her face that seems to silently say "These people." Isabel can read the room and even she doesn't want to answer. When the silence becomes unbearable, Isabel whispers quietly: "It burned down, Ms Sullivan."

Flames leap in my own mind. "Yes, that is correct, Isabel," says Sullivan, "what your dad taught you has served you well." The other students aren't paying attention, they're on their cellphones. What's happening? My own phone pings. Suresh has gone mad and is scrawling insults in block letters over the livestream—THIS SCHOOL'S SO GHETTO!—and he's tagging me.

"In fact, the Globe burned down in 1613 during a production of *Henry VIII*," continues Sullivan. "A loose spark from a cannon that was fired as a prop—that's how successful the theatre was—they had cannons for props!—and the theatre burned down. Shakespeare's plays were meant to be acted, not read, and if some faithful person hadn't saved those theatre scripts, the world would have forgotten all about him. You wouldn't be here studying him now."

I groan. Everybody groans.

That's the reaction she wants, she's enjoying this. She's actually enjoying torturing us. And still she continues: "The plays were recovered, but Shakespeare died three years later in his hometown of Stratford-upon-Avon. Relatively little is known about his personal life. He must have been a special man, a wise and ambitious man. We should all learn from this. I've been telling you to put your cellphones down, seize life's opportunities to learn, think, grow. I have some handouts to give you. Nathan, make yourself useful and distribute them for me?"

She sticks her head into the classroom closet. Inside are shelves stuffed with textbooks, novels, plays, other useless junk. She's gone all the way in, and a key from her bunch is stuck in the lock. Flames continue to leap inside my brain. So what if I'll get in trouble? Maybe she should find out what it's like to be held hostage, trapped, like we are. An hour of glory is easily worth a week of punishment.

I can hear the crowds on the football field cheering as I walk around Sullivan's desk. The warm, spring sunlight on my helmet, padding, and face as I move calmly, as if it's the most natural thing to do. Suresh is still livestreaming and I'm in plain view, centre stage. I intercept the football thrown from Carver High and am running in the opposite direction now. No one can touch me. While Sullivan's bent over, pushing the grey and red hair out of her face, I close the closet door on her and lock it with a very satisfying click. I turn the key. Going for the touchdown. Removing the key from the handle, I approach the window, open it, pull my arm back and throw the ring as far as I can onto the field. The keys feel cold before the ring sails from my hand like a cannonball shot to the rafters, like an arcing football, dark green lanyard trailing through cold spring air. Touchdown.

ISABEL

By the end of day, fear and lethargy have overcome me. Not relief as everyone rushes out of school, drowning out the din of the bell, but fear. I must pick up the classwork and handouts that Nathan's going to miss while he's suspended because no one else will. They're his friends on social media but when it comes to the real world, where are they? This isn't the way I wanted to begin talking to him again but what can I do? I've got to comfort Ann Sullivan too. She and my mother go all the way back to teacher's college and Sullivan idolised dad almost as much as I did. We all did. Sullivan regularly visited him in hospital and sometimes we sat around him together.

When I arrive, she's the only one in the English office; she must have been holed in here all of the last period, provided substitute coverage for her final class given what happened. I can see she's been crying. Her mascara's runny, mixing with her foundation which is one good reason not to wear makeup.

7

"Why didn't you go home?" I ask. "Do you want mom to give you a call?"

She ushers me in. "I can't. I've got to have another meeting with them about what happened. Come in, Isabel. Close the door behind you."

"What's going to happen to Nathan? Is it too late? If they suspend him or worse, expel him, I know it's going to be really bad, Ms Sullivan. You have to stop them."

"Why would I *do* that? What about what he and the rest of them do to me? He's not the only one cheating, you know. At least half of them use AI. They think copying and cheating is doing work; that's what it's come to. Talk to your mother—she understands."

"Pushing them harder isn't going to make them like Shakespeare more," I say. "You're not going to get anything out of them this way."

"Hah!" she laughs as if spitting out the words. "I'd be *happy* if all I got was the silent treatment. Why would they think I *wouldn't* like that? But Nathan's the worst of them. This'll be his second suspension and schools really don't like handing out suspensions anymore. Or any consequences at all."

"There's more to him than you think."

"Isabel, I didn't know you cared. Are you *sweet* on him?"

Ann Sullivan's question takes me by surprise. I've known her practically since I was born. She's like an aunt to me which makes taking her class both uncomfortable and easy. The work's easy but seeing her this way's not; we've never discussed intimate feelings, never really spent a lot of time alone, though I like her. I feel sorry for her. She went through teacher's college with my mom and neither expected their jobs to turn out as difficult as they have been. It was her friendship with my dad that really made her take a proactive, academic interest in me.

Over bottles of wine, all three of them would complain about how worse things were getting. Students didn't read anymore, they weren't real students, and an A didn't mean what it used to mean.

"I'm not really friends with him anymore," I say. "Or he's not with me. Something happened last year after dad died."

"You're telling me that you were friends with Nathan? The boy who shoved me into the closet and locked it? He's a socio-path. They all are. You bet your boots he's getting suspended."

I feel badly for her but she also sort of brings this on herself. "Nathan's not stupid but he is volatile. He had a pretty rough time with his own family," I inform her. "And then the pandemic—it affected us all—I don't think many of us recovered."

"The pandemic, the pandemic. Always the pandemic. You and I went through the pandemic too but we don't act like that. What is it with kids today? Your whole generation— your cohort's out of control. And you think you know every-thing . . . it's this pandemic of infantilism and idiocy we should worry about! I'd love to see one of you try and hold down a job in the real world. Why am I telling you? You're one of the good ones." She removes her glasses and dabs the corners of her eyes with the edge of her cardigan.

"He understands things, Ms Sullivan. He's just really sensi-tive, touchy about his reputation . . . if you're going to single him out in class, he'll respond aggressively. He gets triggered easily. But he was nice for a while before dad . . . "

"Oh, you mean he was there for you? I had no idea. You never said."

Now it's my turn to dab my eyes. "Anyway, I first got to know Nathan in grade seven. I was sitting in the music room by myself at lunch, feeling sad after dad first got the diagnosis.

I was playing something sad, a nocturne by Chopin I think. I was playing it really slowly with just my left hand, my right hand was wiping my eyes and brushing away my hair. Nathan came in and when he saw it was me, he sat down beside me on the bench. He did it without being awkward or aggressive. He picked up his right hand and gently accompanied me on the nocturne. He knew it and he did it very well, slowing down the tempo, to match mine. He never said a thing, but for the first time, I didn't feel things would be as bad."

"I can't believe he knew Chopin."

"His father made him take lessons when he was young. Forced him to. My dad was demanding but his dad was something else altogether. We became friends. You know I was never that good with the piano but he was great. He just hated it because his father made him do it. There's something about music and athletics that resonates, something about rhythm and muscle memory, harmony. His parents fought all the time and then his father left for a job in Japan. Something in robotics. Nathan never sees him, except on WhatsApp."

"I know, I know. I've heard. Why don't you talk now?"

"We talk. We all talk. You know how it is. It's just . . . it changed during the pandemic, like everything else. My mother still wouldn't let me use social media, even after dad died, and I was cut off from the rest of them, except for the online classes. It was all so convoluted. Nothing was easy during the lockdowns. Nathan's an only child too; we'd walk over to each other's houses sometimes in the evening; he's also alone with his mom now. His father sends them money, but he really makes them plead for it, even though he makes like, what, five hundred thousand a year or something?"

"You're going to make me feel guilty, and I don't want to feel guilty," says Sullivan, looking crestfallen. "Does any of this justify what he does?" Her neck droops and her red-grey curls fall all over her olive cable-knit cardigan. "He's the instigator— he pushes the others—they wouldn't be half so bad without him. It's like they all derail the class whenever I push them to challenge themselves, they just can't handle it. Did they just not mature at all during the pandemic? Was that it? Did they devolve? They can't read anything longer than a paragraph or write anything longer than a sentence."

"What are you going to do? Nathan's in real trouble here."

"What *can* I do at this point? I'm human too. He's out of control. Either they get him out of my classroom or I'm going to the newspapers. I don't care what it does to my career. This isn't teaching—I don't know what it is. Since we've come back from the pandemic, all they do is fidget with their cellphones or fight. None of them has been able to sit down or function in a classroom."

"Not me, Ms Sullivan. I was never allowed to have one, remember? Dad would only allow me to read books."

Sullivan puts a hand to her chest, a kind of antiquated gesture. "I know. The academic world lost a great champion in Adrian. It's the reason you've turned out so great. You're his daughter."

"It may seem like that, but it didn't feel so great. I was isolated. He force-fed me books whilst slowly dying, like I was some sort of experiment. All those academic accolades and he still wasn't happy; he wanted to be a playwright or poet or novelist himself; he expected me to carry the torch."

"Well, we all do, that's natural."

"And yet, I miss him more than ever. Those crammed hours of reading and discussion as he got sicker by the month. Towards the end, he collapsed. And still he wanted to only talk about books. Books, books, books! He felt there was so much yet to discuss and write about. I humoured him out of guilt, Ms Sullivan, because I loved him and he was dying."

She doesn't know what to say. To tacitly agree would be to betray her dear dead friend, so she turns around and reaches up to a shelf of books above her desk. From the messy stack of mouldy paperbacks and hardbound volumes, she picks a grimy white jacketed book with pink lettering on it: the favourite and most recent of the books my dad published with UTP, the University of Toronto Press: it's called *The Internet of Dorian Gray*.

My dad was an English professor at U of T. His love and enthusiasm for literature and books dominated our lives at home. He was always talking books and ideas. He had me reading when I was three; I was not much older when he was reading Regency and Victorian novels to me; before I reached ten I was reading novels on my own. It was a very cloistered existence. Now that I look back, it wasn't a normal way to grow up. That might explain why I never got over losing my dad.

My mom put up with his constant pushing, our tense closeness which at times excluded her; she was a casual reader and admired my dad as much as I or Ms Sullivan or his students did. But his intensity could be too much for her.

I run my finger along the spine of Ms Sullivan's copy of *The Internet of Dorian Gray*—dad's thoughts encased in paper, as though he's a mind more than a body now, pure mind speaking to us across time. The book is about digital technologies eroding intelligence and philosophy and thinking and discourse and civility and empathy and everything else good in the universe. The technology of reading versus the technology of the internet. I read it in draft before his colleagues at university did. The effort on that final book might have killed him. I think now of his own spine, buckled and twisted as he lay in the hospital bed, the cancer eating away at him. His bitterness and hatred of the modern world eating away at him. I wish I could take his book and squeeze the loving, human part—my dad—out of it and leave the rest, all the ideas, with Sullivan. I return the book to her so she can place it on top of the books on her shelf, the shelf a monument to everything he stood for.

Sullivan would come to visit him in the hospital when he was so debilitated that he had stopped speaking, and she read Shakespeare to him. Sometimes she and my mom and I would read different parts and dad would smile dimly through the morphine.

Still, I love reading so he did something right. I love Shakespeare. If I could go to dinner with anyone living or dead, it'd be Shakespeare. I'd be a writer like my dad wanted but I don't really know if liking books and understanding them is enough. What would I write? Someone like Shakespeare is chosen isn't he? Special, perhaps by circumstances beyond his own life. Not destiny, but perhaps the right combination of genes and circumstances and willpower. I don't think I have all that. I'm just a teenager who likes reading.

"Well, I know they want to get rid of teaching Shakespeare here," mutters Sullivan bitterly as she fishes out extra copies of the handouts on the characters in *A Midsummer Night's Dream* and their complications and trysts and gives them to me to pass on to Nathan. She's old-school that way—makes actual handouts instead of simply putting everything online. "And I know I'm one of the last ones hanging on but they can't make me stop. There's a war on culture and reading, Isabel, a war on intelligence and complexity. *I'm* not about to throw out the baby with the bathwater. I'm not going to let them kill Shakespeare, not while I've still got my breath and am still teaching . . . Isabel?"

"Yes?"

"It's all over social media, isn't it? The clip of Nathan pushing me into the cupboard and locking me inside? Everybody's seen it?"

I shrug. "I haven't." This is true but she's right—everybody else has.

SURESH

"How happy some o'er other some can be!
Through Athens I am thought as fair as she.
But what of that? Demetrius thinks not so;
He will not know what all but he do know.
And as he errs, doting on Hermia's eyes,
So I admiring of his qualities."

Scrolling through the pdf of *A Midsummer Night's Dream* on my phone as I walk home, I go over the passage Isabel read aloud in class. I like the sound of her voice, the way her tongue clicks at the end of every line, emphasising every other syllable like the clip of a horse's hooves as it gallops along. She dresses plainly compared to other girls but she has a very fine, oval, symmetrical face like an elliptical mirror, framed by long auburn hair. There's something about that symmetrical face: a lot beneath the surface, like a lake. A gift of koinophilia from her European ancestors. Me on the other hand: what you see is what you get; my speech reveals my thoughts in typical Tamil fashion—you can read my emotions because they're framed on my face. The part she read for example, about unrequited desire, is as true for me as it was four hundred years ago.

I understand the play is old and a classic but there are newer things to read. Sullivan doesn't reply whenever I ask her why we aren't reading newer things, and this always bothers me. Is it because she herself doesn't read anything new? Does she dismiss me because I'm brown? Or is there some other reason? Perhaps it's me—perhaps I'm not smart enough to grasp the ideas. That's nonsense. Studying literature isn't like studying physics. Physics is much more difficult.

It's true, we did use Bard AI to do the assignment, but I fed my own ideas into the platform and this saved time. I don't know about Nathan. You have to find some way to game the system these days or everyone and everything will take advantage of you. Life hacking is the only way to survive. If we had taken lots of notes, done hours of research and then spent many more hours writing it all up, it's not as if we'd have anything new to add. What can you say about Shakespeare that hasn't been said? It's just a closed circuit with us handing Sullivan her own thoughts.

Much of what we do in school seems like a waste. Biding time until we go to university and even then, you've got to get through undergrad before being allowed to do your own research. I need more stimulation. Talking of time and closed circuits, I've always wondered: what exactly is time? Is it a thing or just a sensation? Does it belong in the domain of physics or the domain of poetry? Is it a closed circuit as some physicists believe, essentially predetermined, or does it flow continuously, unpredictably forward like the wind?

Someone calls me. "Suresh, always with your head glued to your phone!" I recognize those clipped words—Isabel!

I turn around and she strides towards me, auburn hair shining as the spring sunshine gives it a coppery hue. She carries class handouts. "Where are you going?" I ask.

"To Nathan's. I'm giving him the handouts from Ms Sullivan's and Mr Bonaventure's classes."

"Can I join you?"

She looks to the left and right, as if she's unsure, then says "Okay, hurry up, then."

"If you don't want me to come, just say so."

"Did I say that?"

We begin walking, falling into step, leaving the vicinity of Leonard Cohen Collegiate and the surrounding apartment buildings, crossing the wide avenue of Markham Road and continuing west along Ellesmere. "I have a bone to pick with you, Suresh," she finally says. "Why did you livestream what happened today?"

"It needed to be shown. What we go through. It's different for you—you're white and Sullivan likes you, but maybe not the rest of us, some of us get treated like shit by her. You've seen how it is—you're her pet."

She wheels around, upset, begins to put a hand to my shoulder as if she's going to push me away, then thinks better of it. "That's probably what got Nathan suspended, you know? The evidence they used against him. Was it worth it—for the likes? And I'm not Sullivan's pet. She's known my family since I was born."

"That's what I mean. Connections." She steps back, widening the distance between us even more. It's so obvious I like her. I'm just being honest with her—why does she pull away when I try to get close and have a real conversation with her? Is it not a good thing that I share my thoughts?

"Suresh, I haven't seen the livestream, but I heard about it. I'm not allowed to have a cellphone. Is it true you wrote 'This school's so ghetto' over it? Why? Why post that? It only spreads fire, and creates trouble for everyone. It doesn't actually change things. Suresh, don't you have any empathy?"

That hits hard. We continue to walk in silence.

"Nathan lives on a nice street, doesn't he?" I try my best to thaw the ice as we turn onto Dolly Varden Boulevard. The house, with a mixture of exposed brick and white siding, has a prominent garage and driveway, large bay window, gleaming red tiled roof. It's definitely not a bungalow. There's a Re/Max "For Sale" sign swinging on a post on the lawn.

Isabel's noticed the sign too, for she seems surprised and her words come out slowly as she watches the creaking sign swing in the wind: "With the money his father makes, they should be living in a mansion on the Bridle Path."

"Do you live in a bungalow?" I ask. "I live in the Tuxedo Court apartments."

She keeps nodding her head, looking at the sign, barely registering me. We stand like this, until Nathan sticks his shaggy dark-haired head out the door and asks us what we're doing there.

"Nathan, you'd better not be going outside! You're grounded!" comes a booming voice from within the house. His mother.

"I brought you some handouts," whispers Isabel, still in shock.

"It doesn't matter now," he whispers back. "You might as well come inside." Nathan's only five foot nine—I'm actually taller but the way he moves, leaning his firm jawed face over the doorstep, then pulling back in one graceful sweep before he can stumble and fall, makes him seem as if he's dancing, dodging through life. His status and grace give him a confidence I'll never have.

It's my first time inside Nathan's home, and when I see how much space they have within (it's so deceptive when you look at these houses from outside), the luxurious thick cream carpet, the artificial smell of lavender, the fabric on the couch—silky jade and crimson—nice and new and which people actually sit on, not covered in plastic like ours, I feel intimidated. Maybe I shouldn't have come.

"So you're the one who took the video? You two were working to sabotage his schooling together?" his mother bellows at me. She stands in the living room, arms folded, a small Asian woman wearing an applique vest who looks as if she never leaves the house, bobbed haircut with sharp pointed ends, and a voice that cuts like a school's fire alarm. Much smaller than Nathan—how on earth did he come from her?

"Mom, chill," says Nathan. "I'm just going to go outside and talk to them for a few minutes." He's sweating.

"No, you're not! You are *not* leaving this house!"

Nathan takes Isabel's arm and pulls her towards the stairs leading up to the second floor, his head hung as if bracing for another volley of shouting from his mother. I follow them up the cream carpeted stairs while his mom just glares at us. As we climb, I glance at the family photos on the wall. When younger, Nathan's hair wasn't as long or shaggy; he had a swoop to it, almost a Beatles haircut similar to his dad's. His father seems to be a typical Japanese businessman in the photos: heavy, often wearing suits, shellacked helmet of hair and thick rimmed glasses. But Nathan doesn't wear glasses or contacts, as far as I know. His father's teeth are prominent, not quite buck toothed but getting there: his jaw isn't firm like Nathan's. There's a kind of displeasure in the doughy features of his dad's chubby face. In one photo they're all standing outside this house, his father apart from his wife and son. How old is Nathan in that photo? Eleven, possibly twelve? He's already taller than his parents.

"Your mother's a real dragon lady," I say as we enter Nathan's room.

"Shhh," Isabel puts a finger to her lips. "She might hear you."

"Don't shush me!" But I'm lowering my voice because Isabel could be right. "Damn, Nathan, you have your own bathroom as part of your room? Why's your mom selling the house?"

"She'd already been thinking about it, moving us to Japan," he whispers back. "But it was the suspension today that made up her mind. She phoned her real estate agent friend and when I came home, there was the sign on the lawn. Now it's just time.

18

I'm grounded till she figures out the details."

Isabel gives Nathan the handouts. "The house will probably sell quickly if she wants it to," she says.

The handouts go from Nathan's hands into the trash. "Doesn't matter now. My life's fucked." He starts rubbing his hands over his face, then pulls at his shaggy hair. I've never seen him like this. Usually he's completely laid back and cool.

There's real sympathy in Isabel's blue eyes for Nathan. Sympathy or empathy? So much seems to be communicated between them without words. They have a story of their own; that's why she hesitated when I asked if I could come. They don't want me here. Is it true what she said, that I have no empathy?

"Suresh, how many likes did you get on that video?" asks Nathan.

"Over a thousand and more than three hundred shares. I'm sorry."

"Fuck it. Let's have a look."

"Why can't you pull it up on your own phone?"

"My mom confiscated it as part of the punishment, along with being grounded."

I don't want to open the video with Isabel here because I know she will disapprove but at the same time, I can't resist. It's like a massive itch inside my head that I must relieve. If I don't check my phone every few minutes, I start to get headaches. Is Isabel right—would they have looked at the video at school, or would Sullivan's word have been enough to suspend Nathan? If Isabel's right, will I be in trouble next? Yeah, it's up to two thousand likes now, a lot more views, and the comments are still pouring in, mostly supportive. Sullivan is not popular, and I've posted about her before. These can't all be people from our school; people who don't even go to Leonard Cohen Collegiate are watching and pumping us up. It does spread fast as fire, like Isabel says.

Even Isabel can't resist watching the video with us, though she pulls a face. She was there in the classroom. It's rewatching yourself and feeling good that's the real pleasure; the phone glows like treasure in the palm of my hand. "I think you should erase it," says Isabel. "You've had your fun. Why leave it up there?"

"I've got two moms and neither is any fun," Nathan shakes his head. "Okay, Suresh, let's watch it one more time and then we'd better delete it, like second mom says."

"Why? What are you afraid of, Isabel?" I ask, "You're not afraid of a bunch of teenagers on TikTok are you?"

"Oh, I am, and you should be too. They've got the Chinese government behind them," comes her dry reply.

The upload is erased and I show them my account to prove it. We stand around in silence; I'm left with an empty feeling.

"What are you two doing on the weekend?" Nathan asks. "I can't leave the house."

"Groceries with mom," replies Isabel. "We might visit dad's grave afterwards."

"Oh." Another awkward silence; a lot of heaviness radiating between them.

"Well, I'm having a party!" I say to lighten things up. "Here's the invitation." I take out a stack of cards I've printed in fancy Papyrus font and give one to each of them:

You are invited to:
A Time Traveller's Party arranged by—
Suresh Kandasamy
Football Field, behind Leonard Cohen Collegiate
2222 Ellesmere Rd, Scarborough, Ontario, M1G 3M3
Canada
Saturday April 20th, 2024
1:00 PM

"What is this? Why a party, behind the school, on a Saturday afternoon?" asks Isabel.

"And why are you holding on to a stack of these invitations?" asks Nathan. "Shouldn't you have given them out by now?"

"This is no ordinary party," I tell them. "It's an experiment with time. If you read carefully, the invitations are for people in the future, people who can time-travel. I'm copying an experiment that Stephen Hawking did. Hawking, the famous physicist? I was going to send the invitation out on social media but it occurred to me that a digital invitation would probably be deleted. Paper and cardboard, on the other hand, will last longer. If people from the future find one of these invitations, and if they can time-travel, they'll attend the party and prove to us that time-travel exists."

"Did anyone come to Stephen Hawking's party?"

"No. He used this method to prove that travelling backwards in time isn't possible."

"Or maybe no one from the future wanted to attend his party," says Nathan. "Seems kind of lame. You need fun for a party. Drinks. Vapes. Music so people can groove. Leave it to me—I'll get people out there."

"No, it's not that kind of party," I interject. "It's for time-travellers, not just people we know."

"You sure? One word from me and a ton of people will show up. We're heroes now."

Isabel punches Nathan lightly on the shoulder. "You're not leaving the house, remember? You're already in enough trouble as it is."

"I'm already grounded, second mom. How much worse can it get?"

NATHAN

I can't take it. Feel like a caged animal. Saturday comes, and I *must* leave the house.

Grabbing Suresh's invitation, I stuff it inside the sleeve of my spring jacket. Isn't hard to climb out my bedroom window which faces the street. My mom's in the back, clipping her rose bushes. I can hear her shears *clip-clip-clip*, sharp and metallic as stones being thrown into a bucket. Her voice sounds like that when she's upset at me, which is more and more often these days. I drop like a cat with my soft-soled Jordans onto the garage's red tiled roof. The tiles clink against each other and give, but don't break, as I pad over to the drainpipe and shimmy down. It's fun to break out of jail. I pull up my hood and walk down Dolly Varden.

I don't know who's going to be there—Suresh didn't want to spread the word. He and I first met in grade seven when his family moved here from Sri Lanka. He was serious, with a very stiff Tamil accent. He's shot up in height since then and lost most of the accent, but there's still something different about him, as if he doesn't know how to be a kid. He's an adult role playing the life of a kid. And not an adult from today but from yesteryear, my father's generation—formal, unsure. It's funny, he doesn't know what to do with his hands while he talks and swings them against his thighs. And he always dresses in black. Sometimes he pauses before saying anything, as if gauging whether it's right, whether it's safe. Other times, he just blurts out whatever's on his mind in an excited voice. I told him to try out for basketball; his height would be an asset and it's not as rough as football or hockey, but he never did. An odd duck.

It's pleasant and freedom feels good. The sun on my face feels good. I arrive at the school's parking lot to see Suresh and Isabel already there. Beyond them is the football field onto which

I threw Sullivan's keys. There are other people too, around a number of cars. Adults milling, kids I don't recognize.

"What's going on?" I ask.

"Saturday morning language classes," says Suresh. He's wearing a black hoodie and black jeans, so he looks like a large hunched-over crow, plodding towards me, gripping the grass with his talons. That's cruel, I know.

"People rent the school to run the language program," he says. "I used to be forced to go to Tamil classes here, but then everything changed during the pandemic. Looks like they started up again."

"You just couldn't stay away?" Isabel turns to me, pitches her sharp nose and crosses her arms. She's wearing a white blouse with a very large patterned collar and stonewashed blue jeans. Neither she nor Suresh dress normally.

"Well, neither could you, second mom," I reply.

"I came because I knew you couldn't resist. You heap trouble on top of trouble." There's a note of affection in her voice though. She shakes her head as if she wouldn't expect anything less. I'm glad she's here. Maybe it's the last time we'll all see each other, and perhaps she knows it too.

"Why don't we walk to the field?" I suggest. "Get away from all these people." If we had a football, we could throw it around. There's a person behind us. He's not following us, but in an odd way he's noticeable and he just seems to be there. We all sense him and turn at the same time. A man with a scraggly beard and thick rimmed glasses wearing a dark suit and a thin gold tie. He's holding something in his hands that glints in the sunlight like pale fire. It has wires trailing off it. Are we in trouble?

He's dressed as if from another time, a time of sharp thin suits and bowl haircuts. He puts the band of fire onto his head and does something with the wires, pressing them to his temples. It is only then we can see what it really is, offset against his dark hair: a thin platinum crown with a red gemstone in it. The man closes his eyes and his whole figure shimmers and flickers. And he's gone! The spring sunshine fills in the space where he just stood. Did the others see this?

Suresh taps my shoulder and coughs into his fist: "Turn around." Isabel and I wheel, and there's the man again. For a split second, I have the picture in my head of my dad, then myself, but the man doesn't look like either of us. Does he? Maybe in the glasses, he resembles my father a little but this man's face is much more gaunt. In fact, his whole body just shimmers in that tight suit as if it is all one with the crown; he slithers across the grass at us like he's sliding his feet, not trusting the ground, and slowly removes the headpiece. I feel a pull towards it. I want that crown.

How old is he? Is he a youth or a very old man? His movements are exaggerated and awkward like an old man's but the power they suggest . . . there's something strange about his face and eyes. His skin is too pale. He slithers right up to us and halts abruptly.

That crown in his hands. It looks like platinum, a single ring of metal gleaming in the sunshine. Suresh points to the gem wired to the outside of the crown, blinking like some electronic ruby. "Is that a transistor?" he asks. This guy's vanishing in and out of reality and Suresh is asking if the red thing's a transistor.

The man holds the crown in one hand and fishes something out of his pocket. A card. He holds it up and in a strange wavering voice says, "I have come a long way to find you."

We all stare at the card. Suresh's head snaps back. He didn't expect his little stunt to work; of course, none of us did. But there the card is, with Suresh's invitation, in Papyrus font.

You are invited to:
A Time Traveller's Party arranged by—
Suresh Kandasamy
Football Field, behind Leonard Cohen Collegiate
2222 Ellesmere Rd, Scarborough, Ontario, M1G 3M3
Canada
Saturday April 20th, 2024
1:00 PM

I remember my own invitation tucked in my jacket sleeve and pull it out. It's identical: they *are* the same invitation. Suresh holds both invitations up. A smudge from a Sharpie marker lies on both of them in exactly the same place, the upper left corner. The only difference is that the stranger's card is more creased—it looks older, handled and worn. Suresh takes a photo of the two invitations side by side. "*This* is definitely going on Instagram," he says.

We realise we are staring at a bona fide time traveller.

"It was very difficult to find you . . . " he wheezes. His knees buckle and he collapses on all fours. The crown drops and I catch it before it hits the ground.

"You travelled using this?" asks Suresh.

The stranger nods, "It uses alpha waves. Time travellers hone an intense kind of meditation and thought control before they're allowed to venture into the waves of space and time."

"What if somebody sees you?" asks Suresh.

"I'm not sufficiently dressed to pass as a teacher at your school?"

"You're only about sixty years out of fashion," I reply.

Isabel watches, says nothing, suspicion in her eyes.

"Give me back the device!" The man lunges for the crown, he's up on his thin knees and that slithering motion brings him close, elbows jumping out, arms almost around me. He's

25

quick but we're on a football field and I have the crown cradled in my left hand like a pigskin against my chest, protected, safe as a newborn baby. I feint to the side, dodge his interception. He growls and lunges again. Before I know it, my right arm's extended, hand curled into a fist, making contact with his jaw, cracking it. That is a *very* firm jaw. The hair on his beard feels strange against my knuckles which are sore and bruised. No blood. He definitely doesn't look like my father now, collapsed on the ground.

What just happened?

Suresh and I look at each other. The same thought flashes between us. We each grab the stranger by a shoulder and help him sit on the grass. He feels weird, not like muscle and soft flesh, but hard bone. Small and light, he's surprisingly powerful; the way his body jerks in a jaunty way gives me shivers.

Isabel looks at me like I'm crazy, but Suresh is intrigued. Where do my sudden rushes of energy and inspiration come from? Sometimes it's anger. Occasionally just excitement. But always instinctual, difficult to explain.

"Nathan, what are you thinking?" asks Isabel, folding her arms, lips pressed tightly.

I hold the crown up to the stranger and ask, "What's this? How does it work?"

His eyes, colourless and thin like the uncooked white of an egg, open slowly, flicker, then grow large. "You must be careful with that . . . you don't know what it will do."

"Why don't you tell us?"

"It can take you anywhere in time if you know enough about the place."

"So you can't go forward?"

"I could," says the stranger, "but you couldn't. You wouldn't know what to expect." He seems to be smiling now even though his face, pale and strange, hasn't changed expression. He doesn't seem tired.

"Stay here."

I lead the others away from him, keeping my eye on the stranger. When we're far enough away, I hold up the crown between us: "What do you think?"

"You're not seriously thinking—" sputters Isabel.

"Why not?" I reply.

"You could go back to before you got suspended," suggests Suresh, "and change events. Your mother wouldn't be mad at you."

"That's small! She was going to move us anyway. Just a matter of time. Let's think bigger. Let's go big . . ."

"How big?" asks Isabel.

"Shakespeare's time. You heard the guy. We know enough about it. If we visualise it, we can journey to the time the Globe Theatre burned down, then return before he realises we're gone."

"It's wrong, Nathan," says Isabel. "Suresh, don't listen to him."

"Come on," I say, waving the crown in front of them like a trophy, careful not to hand it over, "we can visit Shakespeare. Wouldn't you like that, Isabel? Aren't you just a little bit curious what your favourite writer's like? Seeing one of his plays in person? *I'd* be curious."

"Why are you suddenly so interested in him? You hate everything we've been studying."

I shrug. "You know me too well. I want to go back to that production of *Henry VIII*, the one Sullivan talked about where the Globe caught fire and everything burned. That production where some unknown person saved the manuscripts. I want to make sure all of them burn. Then we'll come back here and there'll be no more Shakespeare to study. Generations of students before us and generations of students after us will be saved."

"Now I do believe you're telling the truth," replies Isabel. "Pure madness indeed."

"I'm going whether you come or not. I've got nothing to lose. But I'd *like* you to come with me. We arrive at the Globe on the day it burns and then we come back immediately. You know Shakespeare's world and that would be helpful. I need you. Aren't you at all curious what it was *really* like?" I hold out my hand. She doesn't take it. So I play my ultimate card: "C'mon, if not for yourself, do it for your dad. Wouldn't he have wanted you to go? You owe it to him to explore."

I've upset her. Somewhere in the distance, a distance that only Isabel and I hear, awkward piano notes hang in the wind. The music room . . . Chopin . . . side by side with her father.

She wavers. "Okay, but I'm going just to see the place, just to keep you company. If you try and burn down the plays, I'll stop you." It's the best offer I'm going to get. She stiffens at my touch but allows me to pull her close. "I can't believe I'm doing this," she mutters. Nevertheless, she's intrigued—I can see it in her eyes, now becoming softer. Suresh seems game and needs no convincing.

We huddle like we're making a football play. "Both of you, hold this—" I tell them, and give one of the contact wires to Suresh which he grasps in his hand. I close Isabel's hand around the other. They're forced to lift their hands up as I place the crown on my head.

"The man said you need to train for a long time," Suresh reminds me.

I flex my arms and give him a grin. "I can take whatever pain he can."

The man's now standing up. Straight. He doesn't look tired. Is he playing with us? The expression on his face never wavers but I get the feeling again that he's smiling, smirking.

Suresh is oblivious to all this. "So, we're agreed," he says. "We'll leave and we'll come back here. Are we all thinking *1613*?" Suresh pulls out his phone and checks the time. "It's exactly 12:59 PM and nine seconds now. April 20th."

"Yes, concentrate on 1613," says Isabel, now fully into it. "Concentrate on the Globe Theatre on the south bank of the Thames. The other side of the world. The other side of time. Think of that poster in Sullivan's classroom."

Flames dance in my head. The Globe is on fire: the flames are about to spring out and surround us. A large crow flies down, lands nearby. It caws and looks around, shaking its inky wings. Is this happening here and now in Scarborough, Ontario, on the football field behind the school, or a long time ago, in London, England, the weather all misty and wet? For a moment, I'm unsure. Rain seems to come from far away. I can feel waves all around us. The cold wind whips. Grass and sprays of saltwater blow against our hair. The rage of the pounding sea. The fish flopping in the water. The crow cawing again. And then the school bell rings; students from Saturday morning classes come running out.

SURESH

The language students swarm out, run around us, through us as if we aren't standing on the field at all. I hold Isabel's hand, awkwardly, my fingers around her small fist. My other hand clutches one of the contacts.

Nathan holds the band to his head but seems frozen and unable to move. We are a closed circuit and the electricity whips around, through us in one continuous flow. Not electricity, something more primal than that. Neutrinos? Leptons? Quarks?

The wind itself whips through us.

29

ISABEL

It's as if the Earth has opened up and swallowed us whole. We fall through the grass and dirt, dark as pepper, below our feet. We see the roots and earthworms and pebbles and minerals and water. Organisms glow phosphorescent as they eat the mulch. I can taste saline and salt in the taproots and fibres around us. I can smell the thoughts in Suresh's and Nathan's minds. Suresh likes me more than I ever realised, perhaps more than he realises. And Nathan—there's more to him than even I thought possible. His emotions are so furious and complicated. The rage and uncertainty clamouring for succour. Who are these people, these boys?

What is happening to us?

NATHAN

I can't move. The pain is unbearable. Do the others also feel like their intestines are being ripped out? We're hurled like footballs through the bowels of the Earth and then we're rotated ninety degrees and ninety again, shuttled sideways under the ground. We are sewage, we are water, we are blood pumped through arteries.

Our souls slingshot out our bodies, thrown across the universe.

My hair wants to retract, my body shrivels, teeth rattling in my head, each cell screaming as my nails will themselves to be pulled from my fingers. But I can't let go of the crown, can't move. None of us can. Not one inch.

SURESH

We contract into the tiniest ball. Our brains will haemorrhage and atomize to powder. Still we hold tight.

ISABEL

We hold tight.

NATHAN

We hold tight as flames blaze around us.

SURESH

Finally, coughing, nauseous, just when we don't think we can hold on anymore, we feel the air, the droplets of water again, the piercing and desperate wind. Our guts are outside our bodies; the earth tosses us out. My knees go out from under me as my palms dig against splinters. Wet splinters and the smell of sea salt and vomit. I look around to see Nathan and Isabel similarly splayed, retching their guts out.

Wood? I look around and realise that some of the vomit's mine. We're rocking back and forth and rough-hewed timber presses against my knuckles. It is wet and black with the ocean's spray, slick with oil. Fire rages near us. Sounds and smells are different. We are no longer on the school field.

The ground, splintered and wooden, teeters. We stay on hands and knees. Mice scurry around us. As do human feet. We force ourselves up in the spume and water that crashes over us to look around.

Men in rags staring at us. In their hands, crude weapons, long staffs ending in strange metal shapes. A man close to us says something I can't hear through the roaring wind. Another one with a ring in his ear and blood all over his forehead nods in agreement.

This cannot be a play. It feels too real. This cannot be the Globe. It feels too wet.

They all gather around us. Nathan, Isabel, and I huddle together, backs against each other as we stand straight. Our vomit makes a protective circle. Then Nathan lifts up his right hand and points. His left hand still grips the platinum crown. But I've already seen what he's pointing at. We're in the middle of the sea, on a burning ship. Darkness and water all around, flames flickering, wind roaring.

Darkness lifts to reveal many burning ships. All around us, the smell of burning tar and the noise of flames. A flotilla of massive ships on the sea, a flotilla of galleons. Ancient ships with massive bulwarks and staggered levels and huge decks and promontories, rising out of the water. Rigged with large sails and lined with oars. Men race about the decks, shouting some foreign language. We are in another world.

"What have you done?" cries Isabel, staring at Nathan. "What have you done?"

The ship we stand on is on fire. Rats and mice jump off into the water, scurrying over our feet. The men have poured tar on the deck and set it alight. They are launching the burning ship towards the crescent of galleons.

The sailors lose interest in us. They hurry to the sides of the ship and go down. There must be boats waiting for them. But not us. We stand stock still and take in the inferno. There are at least five other warships, equally deserted, ahead of us, slowly making their way towards that armada.

We can feel the flames at our backs as we walk towards the prow and lean into the wind. "What are we going to do?" I ask Nathan.

"I can't swim in this," says Isabel.

"Okay," Nathan says. "Take my hands. Grab the contacts."

"What are you going to do?"

"Take my hands," says Nathan. "We've got to get away from

here. Now!" We grab the contacts. We grab each other's hands. The fire roars behind us. The ships, black with tar, ablaze in the night sky, drift towards that armada. Soldiers on the galleons try to cut their anchors and break away. They're too slow. And then I realise that not all of the smaller ships are deserted. The one closest to us has two people leaning against the rail. They must have blended into the darkness and the rigging before. One of them raises his hand in the night sky, silhouetted by the fire. He's trying to wave and shout to me . . . but I can't make him out over the flames.

Another ship with more people on it, two leaning over the prow, appears out of the murk. They're too far away. What does it matter? We're getting out of here. We squeeze hands and I concentrate and think of April 20th, 12:59 PM. Ms Sullivan's class, Tamil language classes. Shakespeare, and *A Midsummer Night's Dream*. It all becomes mixed up. I can feel the other's thoughts and they're as confused as I am. The hard cliff of Nathan's mind faced with uncertainty, Isabel's filled with history and facts, like coral, fractals shimmering in the darkness. Annoyance and fear and hope and desire all mixed together.

We ready to jump. The water churns around us. A whirlpool rises from the sea. The waves roil and rock. A wind, a tempest, raging around us, almost blowing the flames out, not quite. A cyclone made of water instead of air rises, somehow turns on its side. The platinum band is ripped off Nathan's head and flies into the air. I try to hold onto my contact but cannot. Isabel's mouth is open. She's lost hold of hers also.

The wind, the air, the salt, the spume—the whirlpool consumes us, churning shoals of fish, coaxing them out of the ocean. The fish fall on deck in groups, hitting their silvery heads against the wood. *Thud thud thud*. A thousand nails being hammered. Their flopping bodies fry to a crisp on the burning deck. Fish oil and tar sear our nostrils. Fins wave one last time, gills flutter, before giving up their ghost.

The platinum band and its contacts sail through the air before falling into the ocean.

"What will we do now?" I stare at the other two. Isabel has a doomed look on her face and Nathan is terrified, truly terrified, bullish confidence gone. Our very short career as time travellers is coming to a fiery end. We will sleep with the fishes.

We hold hands for a final time, not saying anything, preparing for the worst. The tempest gathers increasing speed around us, whipping up the water, a giant vacuum, a vortex, swallowing everything in its mouth: the ship, the water, the fish flopping out of the sky, the rats and mice that have jumped overboard. And it keeps widening until it includes the other ships and the armada lying uncertainly anchored off the coast.

ISABEL

We lie sprawled in a dimly lit room in front of a dark mirror. A fire blazes warmly in the fireplace, the heat welcome against our soaked and tattered clothes, our faces coarse and wet from seawater. The fire throws out licks of light highlighting our bruised and dirty cheeks before moving up to caress the spines of leatherbound books on wooden shelves. Where are we? Certainly not the field outside Leonard Cohen Collegiate. We're on a hard timber floor that is neither burning nor wet like the ship we've just left. A red painted circle circumscribes us, surrounded by strange hieroglyphics, Hebrew I think. Beyond the circle are old books and portfolios stacked up in piles on the floor.

A large upholstered Saracen armchair stands in front of us, blending into the shadows so at first I don't see the figure in the chair until he moves his arms in an expansive gesture as if saluting or animating us. "Aha!" escapes his lips. He stands up slowly, not quite straight, for his shoulders and neck are bent. The scholar's stoop; I saw it many times in the colleagues and friends of my father. He wears a long robe of black that grows out of the shadows. Suresh is dumbfounded like I am, as I help him stand up to face the old man.

Nathan rises on his own. Though Suresh's clothes are wet and tattered like mine, it's impossible not to notice the similarity between his and the old man's stooped posture and black clothing. The light from the fire catches the elder's long trailing beard, his white hair which sticks out from his skullcap, the lines in his face marking weariness. So it comes as a surprise when his thin lips twitch with life and his deep brown eyes gleam with excitement as he asks "What manner of creatures are you? Angels from above or demons from below?"

Suresh turns to me. "He's talking to us. Why can we understand him when we couldn't understand the sailors?" Neither of us are ready to venture out of the circle separating us from the old man but we're all very curious. The wooden floor creaks beneath our weight as we shuffle nervously.

"It's the crown," replies Nathan, who looks ridiculous now in his torn jeans and socks. His Air Jordans have completely disappeared.

"Like an advanced cellphone," nods Suresh in hushed awe, "with a built-in translator app. It's messing with our neurons." As if this has reminded him of his own cellphone, he searches his pockets frantically and sighs with relief when he finds it's still there. He holds it up to show us, its black screen cracked.

In response, the old man turns around and commands "Come, Arthur, bring me my speculum!"

Only then do we realise that there has been a boy present all this time, standing, almost hiding behind the wings of the

Saracen armchair, his fingers and face peering over the top of it as he watches us carefully. He is dressed in black like his father but in breeches and a tunic and a white collar, not robes. His father bids the boy be hasty and this snaps the younger out of his reverie, prompting him to retrieve a heavy object made of black polished stone which the old man holds up in front of Suresh to mimic him.

"We're human," says Suresh cautiously, "like yourself."

"Ah!" says the old man, "I see that now. But what manner?" He moves towards a wall and pulls aside a sash, revealing a large window. Light floods the room and we have to shade our eyes with our hands.

The light further reveals the old man and his son who seems to be only a few years younger than us with a very serious, unsmiling face. A desk is behind the boy but I cannot see it clearly. The room is cosy, filled with manuscripts and books. There are a couple of copper globes on upright stands, etched with shapes that could be continents. One is a world map, severely distorted and incorrect while the other, as far as I can make, is of the heavens.

Nathan in his wet socks is the first of us to cross the threshold of the circle—he leaves wet footprints on the wooden floor which immediately dry behind him. Suresh and I cautiously follow. We look at the desk. Beside rolled up parchments, there are a couple of crystal balls, curiously cloudy, mounted on ornately designed brass stands. A couple of chairs are stacked high with portfolios but I cannot read what they say. There was more room to walk within the painted circle.

I look into the polished black hand mirror the man holds up and see my face, the welts and bruises, my hair singed and rough. Nathan and Suresh's hair and eyebrows are similarly singed. If anything, they look worse.

"What are you laughing at?" asks Suresh.

Was I laughing? It is the term "speculum" which makes me laugh and think of something else. "What is it made of?" I ask the old man, at a loss for what else to say.

"Polished obsidian."

"It's some kind of volcanic rock," says Suresh to the two of us. He turns to the man: "You were expecting angels or demons?" I can see that they're taken with each other: they seem in a strange way to be mirror images, one old and the other young, one white and the other brown, both wearing black. Suresh's inquisitiveness never fails to surprise.

My jeans are shredded and my blouse is torn. The welts and bruises are not just on my face but my arms and legs. It's only now that I can feel them hurt.

"I used to converse with angels through my scryer, Edward Kelley," the old man says. "He had a gift for it. We travelled on the continent for some years and made our way, but they thought I was spying for England and the money was never easy. Kelley found his fortune elsewhere and abandoned me. Then Philip's Armada disappeared four years ago and they thought it had something to do with my devising. I never was interested in demons or hoarding wealth, only in communing with goodly spirits and increasing divine knowledge, but those were the accusations hurled against me. We returned to England to find our house ransacked and Jane's brother Nicholas, my brother-in-law, had betrayed me. I lost many valuable and unique items including my perspective glass. Slowly I have been building my collection back up. As you can see, my son Arthur has tried to replace Kelley but Arthur does not have Kelley's gift. We use the shew stones diligently," he points to the two crystal balls, "but you are the first we have truly manifested. You are not spirits, you say—merely humans?"

The truth dawns upon us, and Nathan and I steal a quick glance. Joy and surprise on his face: we have made it. We jumped another four years since the events on the ship and survived. But how? Where are we and more importantly, when are we? "What year is it?" I ask cautiously.

"Why, it is the twentieth of April, 1592 in the year of our lord and saviour, by the Gregorian calendar," replies the old man and proceeds to move about the room, pushing dust balls off leather bindings as if embarrassed about the state of things.

"Who are you?" asks Suresh.

"John Dee. Astrologer, astronomer, and advisor to the Queen. And yourselves? Please do not leave me in suspense—who are you and where do you hail from?"

"Do you know who this guy is?" asks Suresh, turning to me.

"I've heard of him," I whisper, "but I know virtually nothing about him. Don't talk about him as if he's not here."

"What did you say?" asks Dee, bending his head towards us shyly.

"We join you from the year 2024," I reply, for the guys don't answer. "We are from a part of the globe you would know as the New World."

"Wait a minute. Did you say advisor to the Queen?" asks Nathan, in disbelief. "You mean . . . "

"Her majesty, Glorianna. The divine Elizabeth. She has graced Mortlake with her presence a few times. Not of late, not since I returned to England from the Continent four years ago, but so much has changed since the Armada vanished. The kingdom is in a constant state of war and alarm, never knowing what magic and workings mayhap next occur. Let me show you into the great hall, where there is a replacement of my larger perspective glass."

He takes us into the main part of his house, which is a

ramshackle affair. We learn that he had servants once but since returning from the Continent, has had to conduct experiments by himself. The looting demonstrated just how much people are in awe of him while detesting him at the same time, for he is open to knowledge, regardless of its domain.

But first, we must wash in the Thames river nearby and we must eat. Then we can figure where we are, and how we are to get back to our own time.

SURESH

John Dee leads us outside through the main part of the house so we may see where we are, while Arthur runs to tell Dee's wife of our arrival. She must be in a different part of the house which, as best as I can see, seems haphazardly built; small hallways, all darkly lit, lead away from the great hall which has dark wooden walls painted with a design of red and white roses. Making it harder to get a sense of the place, manuscripts and leather-bound portfolios spill through the great hall. He even has a still set up on a table near the large fireplace: jars and beakers with smaller fires bubbling away, though he informs us that at one time, he employed assistants to manage as many as four or five large experiments in the huts outside.

There seems to be very little organisation. The light is dim, as if he seeks to hide his activities. The fire in the large grate throws light against our feet as they clack against the chequered tiles of the black and white floor. It looks like a chessboard with books, manuscripts, furniture, and strange artefacts on it instead of chess pieces.

Outside, our eyes are not prepared for the full expanse and openness of the wet grass: fields stretching in the distance, grey sky, the sounds of the river nearby and people near it, birds in the trees, and a cold bracing wind unlike anything

39

we've experienced. The clouds diffuse and blot the sun. The sky fades into one great sheet, almost the same colour as the river. There's a church to the east of us, small and dirty white. Dee tells us this is the Thames River. A barge goes along it, the boatman using his pole or paddle to guide him along, too far away to notice us. "What do you call that kind of boat?" I ask.

"It is a wherry, although there are not many up here. You will see more as you get closer to London."

London is some ten miles beyond the river's bend. The trees here are tall and wild and sturdy; many sheep graze slowly in the distance. From outside, we see Dee's house is built of wood with the timbers exposed in heavy vertical and diagonal beams. The walls were once white between the timbers but have become sooty and brown like the stone of the church. Dee has a lot of land and as he mentioned, there are other structures beside the house. These are made of irregularly cut black stone with roofs of thatch. The roof of the house juts out, making the second floor larger than the first. Large windows on the upper level consist of leaden metal grills holding small pieces of glass in intricate latticework. The stench of wet grass, dung, hay, smoke, thatch, dirt, and flowers wafts over his land as we climb down the crude stone steps to the river.

I finger the cellphone in my pocket just for the reassuring feeling it gives me. I know that there is no point turning it on but I pull it out anyway to tap its screen and trace my finger over the spider web of cracked glass. Turning it on creates a flicker of excitement that pushes away the dull headaches, as if I am activating my own nervous system. Right now, the battery's charge is above seventy percent.

After we have clambered down the steps and bathed as best we can without removing our clothes (the water is filthy and frigid, probably slathering us with more dirt than we originally carried), we make our way back cold and exhausted and sit around the large fire in the main grate. We are introduced to Dee's wife, Jane, who wears a pale blue dress with a matching silk cap on her petite head. She has chubby cheeks and large eyes. She doesn't seem fazed by our presence and there is a plump cheeriness to the way she serves us beer in wooden mugs. Is she plump or pregnant? I can't tell and don't want to ask. She seems much younger than Dee. After the beer, she brings us warm mince pies.

"We're very sorry for the trouble," says Isabel in her formal clicking manner. She's as hungry as any of us and it takes her effort not to wolf down her pie. I've been vegetarian my whole life and there is meat in these pies but I don't care. The meat tastes strange, has an unfamiliar consistency, but the pie is very sweet.

"No trouble at all," smiles Jane. "We have visitors often, less now than before our travels in Europe, but that is the way of things. I'm sure Doctor Dee appreciates your gracing our house." Has he not told her where we come from? We discuss the food as if all this is perfectly normal. We are told the beer is weaker than ale but we must drink this as the water isn't safe. I know Nathan's drunk beer before, perhaps often, but this is another first for me. The taste is odd, bitter, and wheaty. Why do people make such a big deal over it? A lightheadedness and pleasant warmth spreads through me, though that could also be the effect of the fire, its warmth crackling through my wet clothes. Jane takes Isabel away to fit her out with a dress and Nathan and I are left looking into the fire, sorely missing our own time and everything that went with it.

"Is this like the beer you're used to drinking?" I ask him.

Nathan shakes his head. "The taste's different and it's not as strong."

"Wait till you try our ale or wine, in good time," smiles Dee. "You had better change your clothes too. Suresh, I can give you some of my old black robes, although Jane will have to take them in like Isabel's dress. Master Nathan, some old breeches and a tunic that have been left behind by one of my assistants will do for you, I'd say."

"Perhaps," Nathan agrees. He's being unusually quiet.

"What's the matter, Nathan?" I prod him with my mug. He doesn't like that and growls, "I've failed. What was I thinking— that we'd be able to get in to the Globe, make sure it all burned, and get back within a couple of hours? We didn't bring food or anything else. How stupid, and now we're trapped."

He's right. If he wasn't so forceful, so confident, we might not have followed him. And yet there is something in the spirit of experimentation to it. An experiment in time filled with possibility, much wider in scope than I had imagined.

"There is no use crying over milk once it's spilt," says Dee warmly, "nor rueing houses once they're built. You are our most dazzling visitors and shall be received in honour, at least by ourselves, during your time here. There may be a way to return you. We shall see. But what is it like in your time?"

"Very different," I admit, "very different. Vehicles, for one thing, allow you to travel very far, very fast."

"Like a coach?" asks Dee.

"Yes, but carrying many more people. Even ones that can fly. If you saw the drawings of Leonardo da Vinci when you were travelling in Europe, you might have some conception. But much bigger than the things Leonardo drew, and utilising power from other energy sources. Do you know what I mean?"

Dee shakes his head. "You talk of things being very large but your own speculum is very small. May I examine it?" He stretches out his hand and I realise he's asking for my cellphone so I pull it out and turn it on. I close down the screens for my social media and the pdf of *A Midsummer Night's Dream* and scroll through the photos in my gallery: pictures of our school, videos of our friends, the picture of the two invitations side by side. Why didn't I take a picture of the stranger or his crown? That would have been much more useful in the present circumstances. Dee peers at it, trying to puzzle things out. We must look strange to him, our hair and clothes, the informal poses, the angles and scale at which the pics were taken. Strangely flat, digital rendering and washed-out colours, so different from the pungent teeming life around Mortlake, and very different from the paintings of his time.

"This isn't a speculum," he says finally, "it's a shew stone, it's a scrying glass. Those are moments of life from another time and place you have captured and transposed. Bravo—well done. Truly wondrous."

"This device can connect you across the world," I tell him, "and everyone has one. In fact—" A pain, sharp and severe, cuts through my brain, followed by a dull throbbing ache that pounds relentlessly. The headaches. The headaches have returned. Every time I begin speaking, the headaches cut into me. Dee finally understands and returns the cellphone to me.

"You're having those migraines?" Nathan asks me. I manage to nod, though it is puzzling because the headaches usually never come when I'm looking at my device.

Nathan's got the answer: "It's the crown messing with us . . . again. It's allowing us to communicate but not explain much about where we come from. We'd better be careful what we say from now on."

He's right. He has an instinctive feel for this voyaging. I'm interested in the technology but he's a natural traveller, better than I ever could be. "How are we going to get back?" I ask.

"Perhaps this is my fault more than yours," admits Dee. "I am the one who pulled you here and I shouldn't have. I will help you as much as possible, but without having the object that brought you here, we cannot study or fathom its workings. We must decide what you are to do in the meantime. You must live and make your own way here. I could take one of you as an assistant, as I have none at the moment. Arthur has been helping with my experiments."

Dee looks at me imploringly, the lines around his brown eyes spread with hope. He is a person who likes to understand things, and he hopes I will condescend to stay on and enlighten him. Nathan looks from Dee to myself and seems disgusted that I am favoured. He turns his face to the side as if annoyed. "Yes, I must have called you," continues Dee wistfully. "Kelley was the best scryer I ever had—he was magnificent, volatile, unpredictable, but he produced visions leagues beyond those that other scryers could divine. It was his visions and predictions that prompted us to travel to Poland. He was seduced by money and left. Before him, I used a man called Barnabas Saul who was worthless, but I also had many assistants and many inquiries and experiments and lines of study pursuant at that time. You may have wondered about the huts and dwellings outside. I conducted many alchemical experiments and studies in them; the equipment still lies there. With good fortune, some of the experiments may be resumed. We may find a solution to your problem. Suresh, I have witnessed men of dark persuasion on the continent but Londoners will not trust you. They will fear and hate you. England is still provincial in its attitudes, even London. Especially London."

I see the wisdom of what he says. Even as he elaborates on his suggestion, the headaches recede and fall off as if this is in accord, pre-written somewhere, in some great book. There are worse people I could land with, I suppose. I smile through the receding pain and Dee is relieved.

He grasps the hard ends of the armrests on his wooden chair, which like the walls has ornate flowers carved into it, and leans across to Nathan. "And what about you, Master Nathan? What will you do?" Even the words "Master Nathan," a title of civility, differentiates him from me whom Dee casually calls by just my name, a mark of familiarity. Deference but also the recognition that Nathan is unlike him, whereas I am not.

"I won't serve in a household," states Nathan. "I won't be anyone's servant. Give me something physical to do, outside. Something with my hands. I'll work for my food but I won't be ordered about."

"Do you have any guild or training with trades? Carpentry? Blacksmithing?"

Nathan shakes his head.

Dee strokes his beard. "I cannot see how we can place you without you serving in some capacity."

"Make sure it's outside then," says Nathan.

"Would you like to be a soldier? Would you like to travel out to sea? There is a great call for troops, what with the state of war and all. The Spaniard King Philip is reviled and feared. You would have to serve below deck, and the life is a hard one, but it will take you away from the pomp and ceremony of London which I doubt you would like. You will have to shift for yourself. In a certain light, especially with dirt on your face and seawater, you might pass as white."

The thought of Nathan streaked with mud, essentially in brown face, makes me laugh. "Why don't we just make him wear stage paint so he can pass for white?" I ask. Nathan scowls again and punches me in the arm.

"Gentlemen, you must comport yourselves," says Dee. "You

may be ridiculed and found out if you draw attention to yourselves. You must act as proper men, serious and worthwhile. Nathan, what do you say? Would you work in the company of sailors? You will start below deck but you may climb: they will mock and bully you until you prove yourself."

"Fine. I can handle it," mutters Nathan defensively.

"Very well. Tomorrow, I will take you up the Thames to see my good friend, Walter Raleigh. He is intimately connected with these ventures and with the Queen and her loyal servant, Francis Drake, who in some places is now more popular than the Queen herself, though you did not hear me say it."

"Hear you say what?" Isabel has returned with Jane, who holds her elbow as Isabel tries to walk evenly in her new dress. It is made of chocolate brown cotton which does not flatter Isabel, nor is it as frilly or fancy as Jane's blue linen. The sleeves and shoulders are big so I suppose they have to be taken in. "How do I look?"

Dee nods his head. Isabel is the first of us to dress of the times and the effect is unsettling. There is her hair, auburn and completely loose, trailing down almost to her waist, not pinned down or underneath a small hat like Jane's. But everything else: the angular elbows, her white complexion, her looking-glass face and sharp nose, everything folds perfectly into the brown cotton dress as if Isabel has lived here all her life.

"Come, take a look in the perspective glass," says Dee, and leads Isabel away from Jane, standing her before a large mirror that has gone unnoticed in the corner. We had not noticed it because the glass is dark. The mirror is not flat but has bevelled edges and flanks that fold outward, a bit like those three-way mirrors you get in change rooms. Yes, the glass is dark but nowhere near as dark as Dee's speculum. The gold metalwork unifying the facets of the mirror makes me think of the lead grillwork in Dee's windows, holding all those pieces of glass together.

Isabel walks up to observe herself in the glass and her reflection comes out to meet her. "Gah!" Isabel jumps back as if the reflection touched her. Almost immediately, curiosity gains over and Isabel ventures back toward the mirror. Again, a young woman in brown dress and auburn hair walks forward, threatening to merge with Isabel. The girl with the looking-glass face is within the looking glass. It is as if there are two of us, one in our own time and the other here. It might be the beer and the sick giddy lurching feeling it induces, but I feel as if we are all through the looking glass now, not knowing which version of ourselves is real. Past, present, and future have no meaning.

"You may move toward it again if you wish," says Dee. Past meets the future. Future meeting the past. "It will counter with your double. The Queen stood before its predecessor and met her own mirror image. You will fit in exceedingly well, but what will you do? Suresh will work here as my assistant and we shall have many discussions about science, isn't that so? Nathan will soldier but what of you, young lady? What shall you do here while we puzzle things out?"

"Something with the theatres, I think," answers Isabel. "I should like to work within the theatre."

"They need seamstresses and washerwomen for the costumes. Can you sew?"

"No . . . I wish to write."

"The troupes will never take on women dramatists or players, they simply will not, as I'm sure you know."

Isabel hangs her head. "Yes, I knew that of course."

"If you cannot sew and do not wish to learn, what do you think you might do?"

Isabel snaps up her head and becomes excited. "Do you know

47

a Will Shakespeare? I will cook and serve for him."

"Who is he?" asks Dee. We look at each other. We've come back so far in time this man does not know who Shakespeare is.

"He's a writer for—what would you know them as? The Chamberlain's Men? Would you know The Chamberlain's Men?"

Dee shakes his head but adds hopefully, "No, but if you think they take that name in the future, they are probably related to Carey who is the Queen's chamberlain. You are in luck, for I am very good friends with his son, George Carey. We are both close with Walter Raleigh who is part of our group, the School of Night. Yes, I must have called you all here, and there must be a reason you came to my house. How fortunate and auspicious."

NATHAN

A hard night's sleep shakes away any belief that our appearance in Dee's house is auspicious. Suresh and I shared a truckle bed last night with Suresh sleeping above the small wooden frame and I below. I could hear him twisting and turning on top of the stiff mattress stuffed with ticking, hay poking into his flesh. We didn't talk but I let Suresh have the mattress because I feel bad about what I've dragged him and Isabel into.

The room belongs to Dee's kids and Dee's kindness makes me a little suspicious. Perhaps Dee is correct and it's his fault more than ours; perhaps he pulled us to him. No point worrying about it now; it's better we think about what to do, how to move forward. Isabel slept in the room where the kids had been moved, and she didn't seem to get much sleep either from the way she looked at me in the morning. Her voice sounded like my mom's; it had the clipped metallic ring of stones thrown into a bucket.

Seeing Isabel in that brown dress is strange, it's as if she is in costume and this is all some elaborate theatrical play, a dream we might wake up from. Suresh was given some of Dee's old black robes and they more or less fit him. The black hose and grey tunic given me are loose and feel rough, so I guess the man they belonged to was bigger and older. I keep on shooting my arms through the cuffs to roll the tunic back across my shoulders. Isabel wanted to join Dee and me on our trip to London, but Dee does not think it a good idea. Isabel and I argued in hushed whispers but did not make a scene; Dee promised Isabel he'd make inquiries about Shakespeare.

We had to leave early, around seven by the light, having sent word for a wherry to pick us up. It was slow going through the winding Thames. Time moved slowly. I saw peasants in drab brown and white and grey going about their chores, ploughing fields or sowing crops, the sheep grazing idly, the occasional deer between the trees. There is an abundance and variety of plant life on the shore: vegetation choking the banks. Looking down on the river is Jane's busy garden with rose bushes and a lot of yellow and purple flowers; Dee informs me they are cowslips and wild iris. The river is home to a variety of creatures. I see a stoat and a vole, both identified by Dee, and an orange and blue kingfisher skimming across the water in a wide circle looking for fish.

The boatman cuts slowly through the Thames as it winds on, its pull stronger as houses begin to press each other on the banks, like people trying to peer over the shoulders of others. As we approach London, the density becomes thick, and finer stone houses begin to appear. Dee informs me that the very finest houses such as the palace of Westminster and the Tower of London are made of Portland stone, as is the Bridge, which we shall not pass. Smoke from the chimneys and fires rises up to join clouds.

There are many more people now, some on horses but most

of them walk. They wear colourful clothing and walk quickly, full of tension and life. It's a different world here, a bit like driving into downtown Toronto from Scarborough, except a thousand times the pleasure and excitement of that. Everything is packed tightly; there is more life, with more people, more animals, more things being sold, more of everything. The traffic intensifies not only on the streets but on water too. Now we see many boats, some carrying passengers, others small vessels that might belong to merchants or individuals, but larger ships too, either tied up against docks or casually drifting by the bank. They're not massive. Some contain as many as thirty people, dressed in a variety of clothes and colours. Some of these people wear dull metal helmets that look very heavy; others have their bare heads exposed. Some carry weapons, staffs with large metal blades on the end. Others just stare beyond the railings, wary and suspicious, waiting for an enemy that has not arrived.

"What are those?" I ask Dee, pointing to scaffolding in the distance. A wooden pillar rises from the bank and there is a cross beam attached to it with five bodies strung up from the beam, hanging with their hands tied behind their backs. They swing in half circles, turning towards us, then away. Three of the bodies belong to grown men, two smaller ones are boys. Birds peck at their faces, making me cringe.

"Those are people who have been executed."

"What were they? Enemy spies?"

He smiles but it's not a reassuring smile. "Some of them are just local men who had to steal. These are difficult times. A little further on is the London Bridge I told you about. There you will see many heads of enemy spies and traitors that were caught. We shall not see them up close today, but their faces are tarred with pitch and mounted on stakes to preserve them, a lesson to others. Them, I have less sympathy for."

"You told us yesterday that people thought you were spying when you travelled through Europe, even though you weren't. It seems easy to get on the wrong side of the rope. You weren't joking about the present state of war."

"It has been thus for a long time. Some on the Queen's council would like to recruit fifteen thousand soldiers, but she is cautious about overspending. She always has been. We are careful and practical here. So we recruit civilians instead, and you will have no trouble finding work if you are prepared to fight. Someone proposed sinking more than eighty ships to blockade the river by a narrow point at Barking Shelf to prevent Philip's Armada from appearing and claiming the Thames, but the mayor and alderman would not accede. It would cost the city almost a hundred thousand pounds when all is said and done."

We arrive at Durham House where Sir Walter Raleigh lives. I wouldn't call this place a house because it's a cross between a fort and a palace. It is made of stone, stands many floors high, has walls that come right down to the water and riverside steps that lead out of the walls. Behind the walls, in what seems to be a massive garden, are large trees and more flower bushes, sporting flowers I can't identify. It puts my mom's garden to shame. The high windows peer down on us and the very top is lined like the walls of a battlement. "Are you sure we can just show up?" I ask.

"He'll see us if he's home. We belong to the School of Night and that may not mean much to you but it is of great importance to us."

A young brown-haired servant with dark eyes, about Isabel's height and just as pretty, greets us in the garden, opens the door to let us in. She recognizes Dee, smiles at him, but doesn't acknowledge me. I look horrible in my clothes.

51

We are shown inside: a great hall with wooden beams holding up the high roof, the curving and carved beams hold the structure in place. There is a very large fireplace and the fire, consuming tree trunks, burns briskly. The windows, which face the garden, are just as huge. This is much more elaborate and put together than Dee's crowded house. Dee's house is big in its way but the clutter and darkness make it messy and unattractive. Not much light falls into Dee's house as if he is trying to hide his activities from the world. This house, on the other hand, is made for showing off.

I instinctively walk towards the centre and survey the hall. On one side of the fire is a suit of armour and on the other, an elaborate wooden chair with a red velvet seat that looks like it hasn't been sat on very much. There is more elaborate armour mounted on the walls with sets of crossed swords and helmets. From the outside, against the river, the place looked like a fortress but inside, it seems a sumptuous mansion, its windows looking out on the lawn, the flower beds and oak trees.

Armour and wood seem to be the main decorative motifs; is this a ship or a house? I doubt my father lives anywhere near as nice as this in Japan. On the table rests a little miniature stage with striped curtains and puppets. One of the puppets has a stern, frowny face framed by long black hair. His clothes are stitched with fancy black and gold plume but the cuffs are large and the pants look different from those worn locally. Another puppet is a knight in armour holding a sword, the visor raised so you can see his large red moustache and goatee, which also look foreign. The third puppet is a king with blue robes and a large golden crown. They lie limp upon the stage, their strings dangling over the top of the stage's miniature curtains.

Why did I think of my father and his house a second ago? He won't be born for almost four hundred years. My thoughts are interrupted by the clacking of heels against the wooden floor as a tall man strides into the room. He's taller than me but his clothes make him look even larger. He's six foot or more I'd say, though the boots give him extra height. He has a beard and is no longer young but his swagger and confidence make up for his weathered skin. The tawny brown beard and hair, turning grey, is almost attractive.

He wears pants with massive puffs of white silk, tied into ribbons around his knees. His vest is also white but threaded with silver, red, and gold designs, strips of silk the colour of a lion's mane. Underneath the vest is a white shirt that has pearl buttons climbing to the collar.

A long sword dangles by his side, almost touching the floor. His boots are dark and made of soft polished leather, reaching the bows at his knees. He walks up to the table and places his sword beside the little stage. My eyes are drawn to the delicate metal work on the handle.

"It is a rapier," says the man airily, studying me. "Would you like to pick it up?"

I would but I shake my head, not wanting to embarrass myself.

Dee and Raleigh greet and clasp each other's elbows. They chat a little, not discussing anything in particular before Dee finally introduces me. "This is a guest of mine," he says as if he's uncertain whether he should have brought me. "He has come from the Continent. I can't really tell you too much about him at the moment, Sir Walter, but he requires work. He intends to soldier. I thought he might start under you, if you can take him."

"His features are strange," says Raleigh, looking me up and down. My eyes and hair must look odd to them and they talk about me as if I'm not here. "No one would believe it. It's extremely difficult to take on people with unclear origins in today's climate. You know that, Dee."

"You have me, Sir Walter, you are too shrewd. He is not from the Continent. Let us say he's from the New World?" asks Dee, a little more hopefully. "He's no spy—I can assure you—and he intends to work hard. Could you not say he was brought back from one of the expeditions you funded, like those Algonquin Indians that created such a stir?"

"He's a bit pale for that," says Raleigh stroking his beard, "but tell me, where is he actually from?" Then Raleigh turns his head towards me. "Come, tell. Where do you originate? Speak for yourself, sir."

I look at Dee and he gives me the approval to explain by nodding his head slightly. "My friends and I appeared in Dee's study," I say, "while he and his son were scrying."

"Oh. You are . . . ? A visitor from . . . ?" He seems suddenly nervous.

"Not like that," I say. "We are only human, like yourselves. But we are stranded here. The others will find their own way, but I'm looking to use my agility and physical skills. I'll learn quickly and pull my weight, as long as I'm treated fairly. I won't need babying."

"I am not sure about fairness but as long as you have fighting spirit and are neither Spanish nor have any love for Catholics, I will not mind. And, I dare say, neither will Sir Francis if you are willing to serve below deck. The Queen is in want of men."

"Being Captain of the Queen's Guard, Sir Walter is close to our great commander," says Dee. "As he is to a great many people. You could do much worse than serve under them, though I know you dislike that term. You might not know it from Sir Walter's accent but he and Sir Francis are both from the same part of the country, Devon."

"Hah! You never will stop harassing me about my burr!"

Raleigh's eyes dance, a kind of private smile between Dee and himself. The formality has relaxed. He's not so conceited as to not be able to take some ribbing. He too is not from London. I begin to like him. He has charisma and force and energy. I am going to try my best and enjoy it here. Raleigh doesn't let the world tell him what he is; he makes life into what he wants, and I will do the same.

Raleigh can feel me warming up to him and smiles back, claps his hands. The servant from before appears. She doesn't raise her face to look at us.

"Wine, for our guests!" exclaims Raleigh.

She leaves and Raleigh asks if I find her attractive, then laughs at my discomfort. He chuckles and winks, pushing a hand against my shoulder. "He's flesh and blood, Dee. He's as man as you or me, like he says, not some being from another world. Do not be afraid, Master Nathan; I have seen my share of strangeness. And Sir Francis will not mind either, he has been to Africa, the dark continent, and sailed to the bottom of the world, surpassing Magellan."

"He trades slaves?" I ask. This is not good; Suresh certainly won't like this.

"He did, until he found privateering much more lucrative. He lives to raid the Spanish! One of his voyages brought back more than a four-hundred-fold return on investments. Think what you might do with that!"

It all seems very tempting. I know Suresh would not like what is being discussed here—not just slaves but also the plunder of other lands. But I feel sort of different. I like Raleigh and what he's achieved for himself, it's admirable.

The servant returns with the wine. It is a dark bottle that still has red wax about its neck, laid out on a silver platter with matching goblets. As I drink the wine, its full and heavy taste goes immediately to my head.

"So, would you sleep with my servant if I arranged it?" asks Raleigh with a wink after she has once again left.

I can feel myself blushing. He's got me stammering. "Where is your own wife, sir?" I ask. His face clouds over but I can't stop the words pouring out of me, made of wine. "Shouldn't you be married with children at your age? Doctor Dee seems to have a whole armful of them and his wife's not old either." I've talked too much, taken the joshing too far, for the air again becomes very serious. Care creeps into the lines upon his face that his smiles had previously smoothened out. His beard and head seem to become very heavy and there seems to be more white than brown in his beard; his shoulders lock.

Dee has noticed too. "Come, Walter, don't mind the boy. He does not know what he says. He is not from here—he does not realise what manners should be observed in your presence."

"He'll find out soon enough if he comes aboard a ship under Sir Francis. Drake will brook no disrespect. The boy tries his lip there and they'll cut off his ears to teach him. You realise what I'm saying, Nathan? They'll cut out your tongue to keep you from offending."

I think of the bodies swinging on that wooden structure, the heads mounted on stakes at London Bridge. It's not easy, but I put down my goblet, swallow my pride, and apologise. "I'm very sorry, sir. I shall not make the mistake again."

Raleigh looks me up and down and finally nods. "Bene." Dee and Raleigh leave me then and go talk privately elsewhere. I stand still, looking out through the window, wondering if the servant girl is out there, the lush green of the lawn and walls and trees, what it might be like to have a servant of my own. These people were slave traders—what might Suresh say? I wait for the wine to wear off.

When they return, Raleigh says "I'll speak to Sir Francis for you, but if you are willing to start below deck and fend for yourself, I don't see any reason why he shouldn't take you immediately. It is hard work and back-breaking. If you like adventure and open waters, as we do, you shall take to it. The Queen likes to keep me here, on land and near the court, but I daresay I can persuade Sir Francis to take you under his wing."

I should be more surprised or delighted or excited about the news. I knew he would say yes. As soon as we began speaking, I felt I understood him as if we'd known each other from some previous life, as if this had all been arranged. Déjà vu? I don't know, but between the room's large fire which heats me externally and the wine which glazes my insides, I nod and smile. Why then do I feel like I'd like to grab his rapier and slash at the miniature theatre and its puppets? If my strings have to be pulled, what is the point in fighting it? And yet I want to cut those strings, and as quickly as possible.

ISABEL

Funny how life works. If someone had asked me which person in history I'd like to have dinner with, I'd always have said William Shakespeare. Now here I am, preparing food for Shakespeare as part of my servant duties. Dee was as good as his word and ascertained Shakespeare's whereabouts. Will has begun writing for Philip Henslowe's Rose Theatre. They have been performing Will's new *Romeo and Juliet* recently.

Will lives in poor lodgings, a single room near Bishopsgate, east of London. Dee took me over and before I left, I said goodbye to his household and Suresh. With Nathan out to sea, we're all now separated by great distances. The only way to communicate with each other will be by letter.

Shakespeare's small garret is a room in a house and has a

leaded window. There is a small grate but Will only lights the fire when it's absolutely necessary: that is, when pottage or gruel or some other cheap food is to be cooked. We seldom get meat but Will is fond of fruit, particularly oranges. Now that we are moving into May, he tries to do without the fire to warm us up and often rubs his hands together to increase circulation as he walks up and down the small room while he ruminates upon plots.

"I can't afford to pay you right now," was the first thing he said.

I did not expect any pay, so I replied "I will work for you for lodging and food, but you'd better not think I'll sleep with you."

He chuckled and replied "I have a wife and three children in Stratford and am not looking for any more." I felt a bit nervous sleeping inside the room with him but I didn't want to sleep outside on the heath like the poor dispossessed who wander up and down the countryside. Dee's wife Jane gave me another of her old dresses that are now too small for her and I use some sacking to cover me while I sleep. If it is an especially cold night, Will allows me to sleep near the grate where there might still be some residual warmth from the embers.

I wish he would light the fire at night while we sleep; neither of us have mattresses and simply doze upon hay strewn on the ground. We don't even have chamber pots like Dee does. The leaded window looks south over the Finsbury fields and we go outside to do our business, digging a hole in the ground as if we were merely camping, covering it up afterwards like a dog might.

He spends much of his time in the evening writing, often staying up very late, and when he writes, does not wish to be disturbed. He resists social engagements and carousing because the days involve rehearsals. I do the cleaning when he is at the theatre.

He's neither tall nor attractive. But not unattractive either, nor fatherly. Not yet thirty, he walks stiffly in his tight buckled shoes, shoulders and neck thrown back to counteract the ache in his lower spine. It is not the scholar's stoop I anticipated; it is not a stiffness that comes from reading but a stiffness in the lower back that comes from sitting at his desk for long hours. His hair, which is as black as a crow's, is already beginning to thin on top, although he does not yet have the high crown he will gain in later years. You can see how the hair will fall away around his prominent forehead. To compensate, he grows the hair on the sides very long so that it falls down to his collar, though he rarely combs it. As a result, the locks fly in different directions when he is deep in thought, as if from static electricity. By candlelight, from the back, it looks as if there is a dark bird perched on his head that is about to raise its wings. The one thing portraits in the future have gotten right are his large eyes which seem to pop out if his attention comes to bear on you, picking over not just every crumb of your features and clothing but the emotions passing over your face, your very soul. At least, that's the way it seems; much of the time, he's wrapped up in his thinking and his thoughts are his own. This would all be good if it wasn't undermined by his moustache which is neither full nor gainly, looking both squirrelly and scurrilous. Despite the small, thin stature of his beard, the hair on the lower half of his face seems just as unruly as that above.

I've never been one to dwell on appearances though, and explained to him that it was writing I was truly interested in, and would he help train me in that? He had some difficulty understanding why I, a woman, would wish to write instead of marrying a merchant or some other man above my station. I explained that my chances were limited as a woman who was not a noble, to whom plays and poetry and the written word meant everything. He seemed puzzled and replied: "The people go to the theatre for the wrong reasons. They go there to see wicked characters punished and their prejudices affirmed. It is a kind of vanity. It is like a mirror to them that absolves them of all their own faults: they know the plots and outcomes, they want it entertainingly done. It is distracting and unimaginative. But a mirror should give something back. It should reflect something new, insight instead of just expiation and absolvement. In every other production of *Romeo and Juliet*, the lovers die because they disobey their parents, their prince, their society. They must die—it is fate. Everybody feels relieved in the end. In my version, it may not be perfect, but their deaths make the viewers suffer: they are moved from the inside. It comes from within the characters; they wish to cut the strings of society and that speaks to us much more than a . . . a puppet theatre. It speaks to us because it strikes deeper than our timid moralities."

I nodded my head—he didn't need to convince me. Was he yet unsure and trying to convince himself? "Why don't you get me in to see the play?" I asked. "Let me see your mirror with my own eyes?"

"And have Henslowe complain to me about the penny's entrance fee he lost? I'd never hear the end of it. I am only the writer, Isabel. If you are not willing to wash or sew the costumes, I would have no excuse to walk you in."

I wheedle him and ask again and again over the following two weeks until he gives in, gives me a couple of pennies to gain entrance. I think he is secretly proud I take an interest in his writing. All that avid reading my father forced on me can now be put to use. I walk to Southwark on foot, where Mr Henslowe's Rose stands. They like roses here in Elizabethan London, don't they, but a greater misnomer for the theatre could not exist, for it is noisy and the smells are exceedingly rank. The combined smell of hundreds of the unwashed is nauseating. Add to that the fumes from rotten vegetables and fruit and cured meats and beer sold by hawkers that combine with the mud to concoct a spicy funk. Fumes of alcohol too as people are either drinking or already drunk. Is that, is that the smell of human shit? Do people defecate out in the open here? I don't want to know; I especially don't want to see.

Everybody is at the theatre, and I do mean everybody. The rich as well as the poor. The commoners and the nobility. It must smell like rosewater up in the balconies where the rich sit if The Rose is to preserve its name. The Rose by any other name would smell just the same. And the din—the cries of the merchants and the hawkers selling their crap—it isn't that different from our own time, I guess? Except there are cutpurses, prostitutes, and dangerous criminals hanging out here too. I stand among them all here, one sleeve raised protectively against my nose and the other circling my waist.

The ferocity of base emotion, life on display startles and thrills me. Reading in seclusion with my dad didn't prepare me for the realness of it, the ferocity of it all. Are people at their core really no better than animals? City fathers are trying to shut the theatres down but others on the Queen's council are opposed to them. The Queen herself loves to see the plays and funds a company of players herself. It's like so many things here: Dee's lofty ideals of experimentation paired with how young his wife is and the number of children they've sired, the rich and poor pushed together in this theatre, the sophisticated buildings and clothing in the city and the casual way in which they simply dump faeces from chamber pots out of windows into the street. All the contradictions which seem utterly normal are bewildering to me.

Anyway, I am here to enjoy the performance and must concentrate on that, an actual production of one of Will's plays in his own time. Let my mind not wander. Richard Burbage plays Romeo and once he comes out in all his finery (a very extravagant scarlet and pearl velvet costume that I suppose is emblematic of the Italianate style), the boisterous audience is almost subdued into quietness. But the hubbub quickly builds again and Burbage must declaim his lines loudly to cut through the noise.

By the time he declares his feelings to Juliet, he is yelling at her. If Will's moustache and beard are squirrelly, Burbage certainly isn't what I supposed either. As he delivers his lines under Juliet's window, I cannot help but focus on how shorter and fatter he is than I expected. He sports a beard that is scrawny. I guess it's difficult to shave but these men should do something. All the smoke and dirt in the air affects their skin and facial hair. Burbage relies on charisma and shouting to make up for his looks. Juliet is played by a squeaky-voiced boy speaking his lines from the upper level of the theatre. Burbage crouches in his pearl and scarlet costume, his broad face just as red, curls flouncing against his beard, one hand over his breast as he delivers his lines: *Hark, what light shines yonder in window? It is Juliet, brighter than the sun.* The delivery is forceful and measured and powerful but these are not the words I know. Have the players changed them? Do they revise the scripts? All in all, the experience is too surreal. It is both greater and lesser than what I expected. Both magnificent for its effort yet creaky and bilious in that rough-hewn timbered theatre that is something like an ark, a microcosm of Elizabethan society. All too quotidian and human in the way real events are when no longer preserved in the amber or crystal of time.

I mull over all this as the crowd trails out, their chatter

already about other things, and in a daze I follow them, pushed along with the hurly burly. It doesn't help that there seems to be a buffer between myself and my feelings as I try to process everything that happens to me—and all the while new things occur. It only serves to make one feel more ghostly. Before I realise it, we are in a bear garden. Large black crows, which are ubiquitous everywhere people congregate, reel noisily above us. They're a bad omen. It is too late for I am being pushed and jostled and have to surrender my last penny or be trampled. I expect to see a bear or perhaps a bull but instead a tired, cheap looking horse is brought into the ring. It is the colour of peeling bark, dusty and flea-bitten, with cracked hooves. Confused and scared, it is a small horse. I know how it feels. Even its dry hair seems broken.

Baiters place a small monkey on its saddle and the horse gallops round and round the ring. It picks up speed, trying to shake the monkey off its back. I can see its panic-stricken eyes as it comes around, its face so much more emotive than Burbage's for its emotion is real: terror. That's when they let the young dogs in. The dogs attack the horse's fetlocks and hooves, making the poor animal gallop even faster. The monkey screeches over the din of the horse's terrified screams, which now become a bloodcurdling series of whimpers. As if the animal is deflating, all of its weight and power begins to stumble. With one last bit of effort, the horse kicks at the dogs.

This is futile for it only emboldens the young hounds. A couple of them jump and bite the animal's flanks. Another goes for the horse's neck. Blood streaks down its side as the horse gallops past me again. I wish I could reach out and save it somehow, wish I could beat back the dogs, but I find myself pulling back, trying to retreat. Now I see torn flaps of flesh on the horse's scrawny belly, pink stringy and strained muscle peeking through. When it can't seem to get worse, they change the young dogs out for more experienced ones.

The horse finally accepts its situation, loses its will to run and kneels down. The dumb, terrified, naked emotion in its eyes—it falters and keels just as the new dogs attack it.

I can hear one of the horse's legs break even above the roar of the crowd. The bone snaps and it falls to one side, sending the monkey flying. The dogs stop barking. They savour the moment and walk slowly, saving their energy for the bloodbath. I cannot take it any longer and turn away, push my way out. Why did Will let me come to this? Why did he not warn me?

All the people jeering, spittle flying from open mouths, that same look in all their eyes as the dogs attacked and attacked again. How could these people listen to such beautiful poetry one moment, feel such tender heights of sadness for the tragic loss of the play's two lovers, mourn and pity their fates, then relish the death of an innocent animal the next? It's no different than all our friends back home watching that video of Sullivan being locked in the closet and posting vile comments, exulting in her misery. I knew what was waiting for me in this era, at this theatre. Why act surprised now when it shoves its brutal fetlocks in my face? Am I just as much at fault for standing on the sidelines, for coming here with Suresh and Nathan to ostensibly witness a play at the Globe Theatre? Well, we've found the Rose instead of the Globe, and tragedy instead of comedy. I've paid my pennies now and will never get them back.

NATHAN

Below deck, on board the galleon *Revenge*, it smells of oil and wood and rope coils and vomit but the greater smell is that of smoke and gunpowder. Sulphurous fumes laced with iron. You can taste it in your mouth and it burns your nostrils so it feels as if you are inhaling fire. Doctor Dee need not peer into crystal balls to summon fire and brimstone or descend into hell—all he has to do is go below deck on an English galleon. My shipmate Rawley and I have just blasted a thirty pound cannonball a mile into Cadiz harbour on the Spanish coast. There are four other English ships behind us but an unknown number of Spanish troops and fortifications ahead.

The heavy cannon rolls back from the recoil, and Rawley shouts "Watch the sparks! Stamp them out!"

The deformed white-haired man is older than me, having served under Sir Francis Drake for years, but when we heaved the cannon against the mighty bulwark of the ship, pointing it out from the gunport at the ruins of Cadiz, I did most of the work. He lit the fuse, standing well to the side. The flash momentarily lit up the night sky, the heat blowing back against our sweaty faces, men and boys running behind us as cannons boomed out of harmony with each other. The Spaniards aren't putting up much of a fight. I make a show of stamping out the sparks, which might have been doused by the water anyway, just to make Rawley happy. Seawater crashes in through the gunports, its spray licking our faces. We stand just above the waterline and the ship's mighty timbers creak as it yaws towards one side, then the other.

Why he can't stamp out the sparks himself if he's so worried is a mystery but I say nothing. After all, the man has only one good eye, the other sewn shut, and he lists to the side like the ship. When the galleon rolls against him, he seems to be standing up straight. Others puke when the ship rolls fast but not I. Everything is so dark here that it is only the flash of the culverins and cannons that allow you to see the vomit which gets swept to the side by the water anyway. Our ears ring while our mouths and noses fill with smoke and powder; the taste of iron and brass is the pressing sensation.

At first I was a powder boy running from the magazine to the cannons for him, but in the last two weeks, I've worked my way up to firing the cannons. I've got good sea legs and can balance as if I was born to walk a ship. It's not that different from dodging football interceptions. Equilibrium, poise, keeping myself aware and loose are important. Admiral Drake is the same way; he's over fifty now and could have chosen to remain in England as a member of parliament but I once heard him say that we're meant to live on water, not land. We are creatures of the sea that took a wrong turn somewhere. He's short and round and burly, and he doesn't wear fancy clothes. He moves forward slowly and is at ease on deck even while his eye is bent on destroying every last Spanish ship and town he comes across.

Since the English still have no fresh intelligence on the disappearance of the Armada four years ago, Drake's strategy has been to disrupt supply routes between Spain and its colonies in the New World. He keeps revisiting the sites of old conquests and rains fire on them. El Draque, the Dragon, as the Spanish call him, is popular in Europe, but different from Raleigh. His shortness and roundness make him a barrel-chested man who moves forward slowly with a low centre of gravity. He doesn't need to move fast for anyone.

I don't instinctively understand him in the way I quickly understood Raleigh. Raleigh is more of an individualist, the style of his clothes and finery and ambition making him unique, although he knows many people and also has great influence. Some dislike Raleigh for that. Drake seems universally popular because with Drake, what you see is what you get. Apparently the Queen loves him too—she refers to him as her "shining knight."

A different kind of power rules the sea, however, not the

politics of court and flattery. You disobey orders and cross Drake at your peril. That's why I take it as Rawley keeps insulting me.

"Stop daydreaming and swab out the barrel," he shouts, neck bent towards his shoulder as his one good eye stares down the cyclops bore of the massive cannon. The bore has to be swabbed so that no embers will prematurely set off the next charge of gunpowder. I do it, even as frustration pricks my skin. He's much older than me but is it my fault he's sustained war injuries?

A blond-haired powder boy, only twelve, has run for the gunpowder and hands it to us packed in cloth which Rawley delicately pricks a hole into, packs down into the cannon's bore using one of his long skinny arms. I use the rammer to pack in more cloth before loading the heavy cannonball. Two more men come join us to heave the cannon against the bulwark so it faces out through our gunport but Rawley insists on igniting the touch hole.

The cannon blasts and light and sulphur explode in the night with a boom, the air heating fast, flying hot against our chests and faces. The powder burns sting, the heat bracing before cooling away from my face like a dissolving mask. The rest of us steady ourselves but the blast throws Rawley and he sprawls flat on his face. It's hard not to laugh: his knobby legs and gangly arms spread-eagled against the seawater and puke. No one helps him.

Rawley's left eye is stitched with what looks like catgut. His functioning eyeball roves around and quickly lands on me with a hatred that never seems to leave his features. It only intensifies as I stare back.

"What are you laughing at, you half-blood prince?" he asks.

Why half-blood? The "prince" insult I understand, as I'm different and was brought aboard under Raleigh's protection, and by extension Drake's. Rawley wipes water and mess away from his breeches, shakes his hair and stands up. I watch him closely because I sense what's about to happen. He lunges for me and it's easy to dodge him; before I know it's happened, one of my elbows finds a place against his spine and pushes down. He's again on the floor. The ship moves violently and my carefully found balance deserts me; I slide on the water, off my feet, suddenly down beside Rawley. He loses no time; his fist has shot out and grabbed hold of my hair. My first instinct is to shoot my hands up to his fist and uncurl his fingers but he has wiry strength in his fingernails and twists my hair and neck. So I punch him against his flat ribs. Twice. This causes him to buckle and let go.

"Your mother was a whore," he seethes hatefully, holding one hand against his ribs. "You're the son of a thousand fathers, each worse than the last."

We stand up and raise our fists, taking our positions, ready to square off against each other. People have halted reloading their cannons and drawn around us, enticed by what's happening. I'm already crouching, spreading my legs, keeping my weight low to counteract the movement of the ship so I won't fall again.

"Go on! You can take him," whispers the little blond-haired boy behind me.

It's the crowd. It's always the crowd. Whether it's football or Sullivan's classroom, I can't help but be pushed by the energies of the crowd. I draw spirit from it, the people watching and egging me on. Rush and smell of victory. I bolt forward and tackle Rawley with ease. We both go sprawling between the cannons as the ship lurches. Water washes over us. I'm about to get up when I feel strong fingers pinching my ear and pulling me up. It is an officer, in a leather doublet and red sash yelling at me: "What's going on here? Why are we not firing? I'll have you whipped!" And then looking around, as the others shamefacedly try to crawl back to their positions, he asks "Who started this?"

"It was him, sir," the boy who just egged me on now points at me.

"As you were," says the officer with a scowl to the others, before dragging me and Rawley up to the main deck. We walk past the swing guns and onto the forecastle where Drake stands near the bowsprit pointing towards Cadiz. I'm amazed at the sight of him, stroking his beard against the flames and fire in the distance, as buildings burn on the shore. He doesn't wear a ruff or a sash or heavy armour—nothing like the portraits— just a loose tan striped shirt with a large collar that complements his russet and white beard, and a red jacket. His breeches are practical and brown with no bows.

The officer explains our infraction to Drake, who nods, unbothered by the triviality of it. He orders the officer to bring Rawley and myself onto a boat to join the raiding party. A group of small boats sets out. The town has been sufficiently bombarded and we are going to reap what treasure and intelligence come our way.

The officer and Rawley and I set out in one of the first boats. The sea becomes really rough now, waves crashing against us. Rawley and I are forced to do the hard rowing as the waves push back. Rawley glares at me through his one good eye but I do not care; there is too much to see here if he'd care to turn his eye away from me, too much fire and excitement to distract us. It is as if the world is a keg of gunpowder, its heat and energy loose. We are almost at the shore when a cannonball lands ahead of us, displacing the water and sending our boat flying up into the air. I lose control of my oars and my arms flail, catching nothing. We are propelled forward. When we come down, our boat is smashed against the rocky beach. I keep my wits about me and thrash into the waves as they struggle to drag me out to sea. I pull the dazed figures of the officer and Rawley further onto the shore to make sure the waves don't pull them back. I pull Rawley by the hair across the rocks, a little rougher than I should. He fights and pulls my arms away from his scalp, shouting "I don't need no half-blood's help!"

Again with the half-blood. I let them be and lie down. I'm wet, shaking, flat on the coast, clothes ripped, afraid, not unlike that time we were aboard the fire ship, tar and oil blazing around us. I remember the rats jumping off into the ocean. My ears ring and my body is bloodied and bruised. The officer and Rawley slowly stand up as other soldiers from our raiding party disembark from their own boats and join them. Men run all around us.

The town is more fortified than it seemed from the ship. Even through the fear, a sense of awe quickens my blood. It is only now, closer to the flames, that I can see the fleet of Spanish galleys that have been waiting, hidden. There are batteries of cannon mounted on the coast.

But Drake and his *Revenge* sail fearlessly forward and the confrontation begins. His privateers, his pirates, his marauders. The Spanish galleys have rows of oarsmen to power them and fierce bronze battering rams but the English ships use their sails and the favourable wind. I watch mesmerised as the Spanish galleys, agile and fast, form a semicircle, trying to ram the English intruders. Our ships are powerful though, have superior firepower.

One of the Spanish galleys breaks away to attack the *Revenge*, running under the English cannons. It's daring but ultimately foolish and desperate. It's like tackling someone from the side and missing them instead of coming from the front. Pointless. Drake isn't our fullback for no reason. He thrives under stress. He's already anticipated this and turned the sails, swinging the *Revenge* around so his cannons point at the galley, which is lower in the water. The galley has a few culverins, nothing compared to the *Revenge*, which has multiple decks with cannons, more artillery than all the Spanish galleys combined. Drake pounds the galley and its mates until they simply turn around and limp away. They sail by us lamely, the ships' hulls smoking and smashed, sails in tatters, so close I can see the dismay and defeat upon the faces of Spanish soldiers. The Spaniards cling to their pikes and arquebusiers in fear of what comes next.

El Draque rains fire upon the coast. He exchanges cannonballs with the batteries mounted there. Higher above us, the regular inhabitants of the town gather their belongings and run up to the fort for safety. The Spanish soldiers stand their ground and muster their larger eighteen-foot bronze cannons. We have some of those too. They have a range of up to two miles. They're not accurate but they do a lot of damage if they land. As a couple of Spaniards load one, it blows up in their faces, sending them, the soldiers around them, the horses, the provisions, metal breastplates, and helmets flying. Some of the soldiers come down in a scattershot of blood and ripped limbs, causing the rocks to shudder and pebbles to fly up. A kind of steam rises up from the dead flesh in the predawn air. I guess that ball didn't fit into the bore of its cannon too well. Our luck. Most of the Spanish cannonballs go a mile wide from their English targets. A couple even land on Spanish ships.

Dawn arrives and it's all over. We sack, burn, and capture whatever we can. We take prisoners, put many to the sword. I can't tell the rationale for who gets which fate. Cinders from some twenty burnt-out Spanish galleys throw their smoke into the sky. There is something majestic and eerie in it.

Drake and his officers walk down the beach through the mist and smoke. The officer who dragged me out of my fight with Rawley whispers something in Drake's ear. Drake strokes his beard and shakes his head. He sends a man to look for Rawley.

When Rawley arrives, his shoulders are squeezed forward tightly and his arms cross his flat ribs as if he's nervous, trying to hide himself. Even though Drake is shorter than Rawley, Rawley seems to stare up at Drake. "What's the matter here?" asks Drake, "Who caused the problem?"

"No problem," replies Rawley shyly, squinting through his right eye. "Young sir won't do as he's told. Thinks he knows his way around the cannons better than I do."

"That's a lie!—" I get up and clench my fists, "He's always goading me."

Drake looks sternly from me to Rawley and back again.

Rawley points one of his lengthy fingers that dug into my scalp: "Doesn't know his place, sir. Not a true soldier, not an Englishman, is he? There is no earthly order without chain of command. Ye cannot trust these half-bloods, sir. Nothing but mongrels, the lot of them; their kind don't even marry."

"We will draw a square for it," Drake declares as everybody waits upon his judgement. Rawley and I have again secured a crowd. Drake speaks with an air of boredom: "You may fight and decide it between yourselves."

Rawley shrinks into himself. "No, sir, not a fight, sir, I am not up for it. I was thrown into the air upon landing. The boy is the one who's done me wrong."

"Then settle it with honour," says Drake, grabbing Rawley by the scruff of his neck and shoving him towards me. "The men are tired and need entertainment. Come gentlemen, form a square ten paces wide. Nathan, come here. Put your arms up. No biting, kicking, or scratching. Make it good. The loser shall receive twenty lashes."

I put my fists up even as Rawley is pushed towards me. The men close in around us. They line up tightly, eager with anticipation. Ten paces squared is not a lot of room and I can see the terror in Rawley's one good eye as it opens wide. Even the muscles around the sewn eye seem to pull apart, reacting in fear. He raises his fists reluctantly and brings his white-haired face behind them. His body lists to the side more than usual.

He knows I can beat him and this isn't a match, just cruel punishment for the soldiers' amusement. No more fair than Drake raining fire on Cadiz. But I have to fight him. I'll try and make it quick so as not to hurt him too much. I think again of the small puppet stage on Raleigh's table, stringed puppets in their Italian costumes. One must put on a good show.

We circle each other. I slow down, leading him, allow him to come at me first. His left fist shoots out but he might as well be in slow motion. My right forearm easily blocks his fist and my own left fist hits him in the jaw: *Crack!* It's a good one and he reels back. Follow up with a right fist to the temple and as he tries to regain his balance, hit him against his flat ribs. The man goes down.

When he gets up again, I'm ready. He's not even able to guard himself at this point, he's that dizzy. Two more shots to the chest, punching in hard and fast and close, and I jump back before he can grab me. I trip him with my left leg and whisper "Stay down." The soldiers cheer now, even as Cadiz burns. It is as if the whole world is burning and this is all that matters.

"Pick him up," says Drake.

The officer who'd pinched my ear is forced to step forward and grabs Rawley by the elbows, standing him up but Rawley's shaking his white head of hair, refuses to let his feet become planted on the ground so the officer has to keep holding onto his elbows. Easy pickings. I lean forward, square my shoulders, and charge into them both as if I'm tackling a wide receiver. I know it's wrong to strike an officer, but the man's been asking for it. They go down in a mess, I stand up over them, and everybody's laughing. They don't care. It's an eruption of joy drowning out the crackle of flames behind us.

Drake walks up to me and raises my hand. "There you have it, gentlemen. The winner! Make no mistake, he is not on the *Revenge* under my protection for no reason! He earns his keep. If I had a thousand men like him, no matter their colour, the Spaniard would perish under my heel in no time." All this from the former slave trader. "I want no more talk about his origins. He's here now." A hush grows over the officers and soldiers as they take in the words. Drake's decrees are absolute. "Anyone who disagrees will reckon with me," he continues. "Good soldiering is where you find it. Now on, this redoubtable man no longer serves below deck. He will be outfitted with sword and armour. He joins me." Drake lowers my hand and clasps me tightly around the shoulder.

The men shift their feet and glance at each other nervously. It takes time to fully absorb the promotion. Slowly and hesitantly, they begin clapping. Drake is too popular for them to disagree with, no matter how many they are. I can't even tell how genuine Drake is, though he's known to be straightforward and plainspoken.

"Let us not forget," continues Drake, "that a punishment is in order."

Someone stands Rawley up. He is shaking now, still dizzy from my blows. Another officer rips the shirt off Rawley's back and then I understand why the man is so miserable, so hateful.

74

Against the scrawny ribs and exposed shoulder blades, criss-crossed scars rise up from the flesh. It is full morning now and we can see the scarred welts from previous lashes covering his shoulders and back. A soldier is sent out to find a rod or a strap. My feelings go out to Rawley but there's nothing I can do. Drake walks me forward, his arm still around my shoulder as if holding me in place, enjoying the spectacle as he forces me to watch.

Because they cannot find a rod, two men use a piece of smouldering wood from a smashed galley. I hope that Rawley is too senseless to feel the pain. But his cries ring out and blood oozes from his back, his breath turning to hopeless mist in the morning air while the Dragon watches.

SURESH

The gurgle and whoosh of the Thames can be heard in the cold night air. Dee and I are bent over mounds of earth in the field behind his house. The sheep seen during the daytime must be asleep now. Even the ducks and chickens that Jane keeps in the yard are now quiet. It's maybe three in the middle of the night. Very hard to tell as we don't have timepieces; just guessing based on the light of the half-moon and how quiet and lonely everything seems. There is the sound of the odd nighttime animal beside the river—the rustle in the grass of a badger or the slap against the river of an otter's tail.

Dee insisted that Jane and the kids must be deep asleep before we ventured out tonight. He doesn't even want to light a torch for the attention it might draw. Despite his kindness, I can understand why people might think him a black magician. Cold and silvery light shines through the dark tree branches as we dig suitable burial holes for his notes and papers and anno-tated manuscript copies of De Originibus and The Book of Soyga.

I do most of the digging with a heavy spade that has a small iron head and a long wooden handle; he will do the burying. The manuscripts are wax-sealed in leather bindings and portfolios to keep moisture out but unless he digs them out soon, I don't see how they can keep from rotting, imbued with magic or otherwise. How many other documents and books and manuscripts are buried around here? "Is this why you call your club the School of Night?" I ask as I strain to spade away the earth. "Are you sure this is necessary?"

"Suresh, do you know how much of my library, how many special possessions were ransacked during my time abroad?" he whispers. "Keep your voice low. Yes, this is a necessary precaution." The paranoia that comes with living during war times. Or it could be senility. He is an extremely knowledgeable and curiously well-read man but his mathematics borders on astrology and numerology. It is not real science. From what he's told me, he believes in a Hermetic truth, trying to tie everything together. He's got works of Hermes Trismegistus and Cornelius Agrippa keeping company with those on physics, mathematics, drama, literature, grammar, history, navigation, everything under the sun (or moon) you could think of. He believes that the hidden or magical comes first, before science. I can understand that. It's like my belief in life on other planets. I feel there must be some out there and I'd be ecstatic to encounter it, but until I actually meet aliens, how can I be sure? To act by instinct and feeling is to do things backwards.

Still, he's been immensely hospitable to us so I help him tidy the screeds and portfolios, empty the chamber pots lying around his place. What harm can it do to write and bury his thoughts? Everything is fragile and precious in his house, not easily replaceable. It is the notebooks with his Enochian tables and his recordings of sessions with Kelley that sit separate on the desk in his study beside the crystal balls, behind the

Saracen armchair, a reminder of those vivid visions, now no longer accessible since Kelley deserted him.

I'm a poor substitute for Kelley or his more famous friends and scholars on the continent. At sixty-four years, Dee's outlived most of his contemporaries, all his friends on the Queen's Council. He suffers from kidney stones and piles, so I don't mind striking the hard cold earth with the spade. I'm nothing like Kelley with his manic visions and what sound like bipolar emotional extremes. My belief in rationality and verifiable truth is inviolable, but Dee tries to sound me out anyway: "What is it you'd like to learn about most, my young Suresh, if you could?"

He finishes placing the wrapped *Book of Soyga* in the hole before I begin packing the dirt back on. He showed me some pages from it, filled with tables, codes, invocations, spells, and spirit names that made no sense.

"We ended up here because of my interest in time." I level off the mud at the top of the hole with the flat side of the spade as best I can. Perhaps I make no sense to him either. "I was trying to replicate a similar experiment done by a famous scientist of our time. I didn't think anything would happen. It didn't for that scientist, Hawking. According to him, travel backwards in time shouldn't be possible. Yet here we are. Have you noticed how you don't really seem to have stories about time travel in your own era? You've got fairies and goblins—you yourself believe in angels and demons, spend a lot of time writing about them. No time travel though."

"Yes," he sighs and sits down on the ground beside me as I kneel and smooth my hands over the dirt patch. It looks completely different from the other parts of the field and someone coming by tomorrow, if they look closely, will see it's been dug. Unless we get rain and a lot more mud. The weather is different from back home—it might be rainy for a whole week in Toronto, or sunny, but here it's not unusual to get light rain in the morning and then sunshine in the afternoon. "I don't understand why you wouldn't think there's a great harmony in the universe, in all of God's creation. Suresh, it's predestined, like a story in a divine or celestial book. Numerology and astrology are our ways of reading hints, divining the plot. Of course, I thought the fiery trigon conjunction of 1583 was certain to bring about calamitous times, but we were wrong, so it is not an exact science. Or the science is exact but we are not. It is as if the trigon were shifted five years in the future when the Armada disappeared in '88."

"Yes," I'm well aware that our presence here has changed things, and try my best to switch topics, "there is another man of science from my era, or before mine really, who thinks it is like you say. His name is Einstein and he believes that the past, present, and future came into being at once. He imagined what it would be like to travel at the end of a beam of light, and I tried to imagine what it would be like to travel a similar wave in time. But I don't understand what time is." Finished, I fall down beside Dee. If not for the moonlight filtered through the branches, we wouldn't be able to see each other at all. The light glints off Dee's white beard and the cat's eyes of his pupils silently will me to continue. "Perhaps, you don't have time travel stories in your era because you believe everything is fixed like a clock, but in our own time, we believe everything is relative. My mother believes in astrology and is religious; I was brought up that way but could never share her beliefs. If I believed that everything was predetermined, I wouldn't strive at all. I couldn't change anything and that doesn't feel right. Now, I've said that feelings can't determine our theories, but that is my secret hunch and that's why I'm interested in the riddle of time. It's the feelings that really trip us up. So much of our understanding of time is tied up with feelings, isn't it, especially loss? Feelings and time are inextricable. I don't understand why. Why isn't time purely mathematical; why does it warp? Why is it psychological? Is it time that riddles or is it our minds?"

He still does not answer, and I'm on a roll unburdening myself so I continue: "My friend Isabel said that I lacked 'empathy,' which really hurt me. It hurts because at times I have wondered if I'm neurodivergent, I'm sure you have no idea what that means. I have no idea what it really means either. It means that the wiring in my brain, which controls my emotions, might be different than other people's. I've wondered if my father might be neurodivergent, because of the way he acts, never sharing his feelings, only having pleasing or upsetting reactions to things. Here I am, speaking of him as if he existed now, as if Einstein were right. As if Einstein *will* be right. But it's impossible to talk any other way. It's wired into our grammar, our language, our neurons.

"But I do have feelings: I just can't express them as elegantly as Nathan or Isabel can. I have those feelings of loss, from the time we moved from Sri Lanka to Canada, and now from Canada to here. I'm doubly displaced. Why do I feel this sadness and regret? Why feel lost? Given how things could have gone, this is maybe the best it could have turned out, even if we are stranded here. It's *my* fault we're stranded here. This is a roundabout way of saying that time is messily bound up with feelings, especially expectation and regret. If I could solve its riddle, perhaps I might not regret so much?"

He shifts uneasily and lifts up one of his haunches, due to his piles I imagine, then stands up and brushes the dirt away from his robes. I stand up with him. We walk down to the water and listen to its rolling motion. It's pleasing, simpler during the depths of nighttime when boats and people aren't about. I saw a family of swans here once, but haven't seen them since.

"What do you mean by the wiring in your brain?" asks Dee finally.

"It's a metaphor," I begin but as I try to think of how I might explain it to him, it becomes extremely difficult. I feel my head become heavy, packed as if someone were trying to bury a thousand books inside. My nerves tense, razor sharp; migraines cut through my brain. "They're like the things in my cellphone, my scrying glass as you called it," I pant through the pain but it's too difficult to expound. How does one discuss wires and neurology without discussing electricity? I tried discussing electricity with him once, the polarisation of charges, electric potential, and the migraines were even worse that time. How does one discuss the four fundamental forces of physics or atomic energy? If I tried to explain my migraines to him, he'd probably think there's a devil fevering my brain. The migraines have receded in general though, mostly because I've given up trying to explain the future. Isabel thinks it's also the effect of the lack of social media. And yes, there is an intense emptiness that comes with that.

We've all become more used to the simple, yet hectic, pace of daily life in Dee's time. There's so much to be done but more privacy to do it within. People engage time differently because there aren't cellphones and clocks everywhere. We aren't so connected, *wired* all the time. Things taste better here too, especially fruit and vegetables. I've become so used to the taste of meat and feel of alcohol that they don't affect me anymore. The air can be smoky and things are filthy but you can also see many stars clearly in the dark country sky. My mind overall feels better, more calm and focused. Three weeks in, I stopped jonesing for the internet.

Once in a while, the headaches will return, especially when I think about social media and can do nothing about it. Then I lock myself up and turn on my phone just to look at the pics and documents stored through its cracked spiderweb screen. Just to remind myself who I am and where I'm from. The battery died a long time ago but with some experimentation in one of Dee's huts, I was able to use pennies and nails and some copper to hammer out leads and connectors which I used to wire ten potatoes together in series, an experiment we learned in grade nine. It gives me enough voltage to power the phone in its slower modes.

Dee's used to my migraines though, implicitly understands they're like his piles and kidney stones, and isn't offended when our conversations just dissipate into silence and contemplation. He is a man of science, though it is not my science. He waits with me now by the water as I look up at the many shining stars, wonder if there is intelligent life up there observing us, not God but things far more intelligent than we are. I look down to see the starlight reflected upon the darkish grey water, as if it were one of Dee's mirrors.

"What are you thinking about?" asks Dee.

"The nature of time," I whisper, once the throbbing no longer cuts into my thoughts. "I am as clueless about it in your age as I am in my own. Is it like the water of the river in front of us rushing forward, something surrounding us that we step in and out of? Or is it like your wife's rose bushes near the house? Does time bloom like flowers on a bush, uneven, some nodes or times more important, more sweet and special than others?"

"Heraclitus did say that no man steps in the same river twice," replies Dee, "it is not the same river nor is it the same man. We have no more understanding of it than the ancients did. We can only begin to divine God's plans for us and they are more secret than the Spaniard's. All I can say is: may you live in interesting times."

"A poet once wrote that only God could make a tree," I say. "If time is like a plant or one of the trees around us, does it grow out of roots and expand with space? What does it grow from? Does it expand as we expand? Bloom and shrink as we die? I don't just mean us, but the whole of life. If it is like a tree that grows, what do its roots nourish on?"

"That would be my books and notes," laughs Dee bullishly. "Since you say they will decompose and moulder, if we do not dig them up again. The trees and the whole world will nourish themselves on my words and ideas."

I ignore his lighthearted joke. "Is time within us? Is it impossible for us to separate ourselves and objectively understand it?"

"Come," he says and we begin walking back up the slope towards his house. "Let us get some sleep before Jane raises the children and shouts at us." I pick up the spade on the way and wonder again how many books and manuscripts we might be walking over, hoarded under the ground like treasure. I'm dying to put away the spade and remove my robes, wash the night off me. A heaviness settles and it's very tiring walking up the field. The sounds of the river get fainter behind us and the headaches themselves are like a low tide; best not to disturb things further with discussion. "I can tell you this," says Dee suddenly and the headache threatens to spate again, "if you like that Isabel, you should communicate your feelings with her. Women need to be wooed and written to. Their minds are restless but they like stability and certainty in others. You must take more of a leading role."

"Is it that obvious?" I ask, embarrassed.

"Jane spotted it instantly, and told me. The way you look at her, even the way you talk about her; you care greatly what she thinks. You should write your feelings onto paper, not spirit them away behind your mind, behind your headaches. Don't *confront* her with your feelings; that can be vulgar. Write to her instead, give her time to respond; I will help you if you like."

"I don't know."

"What's more, I will help you with your feelings of loss and displacement. We will find a way to return you and your friends to your proper time; your being here is proof that travel is possible. Do not despair. You said that there was a traveller from the future whose device you borrowed. In the same way we have buried my notes on *De Originibus* and *The Book of Soyga* tonight, there's nothing to stop me writing about your special dilemma. The key is to get the writing and message to these beings of the future. Just as you will write your heart's philosophy to Isabel, I will write to the people in the future. We can venture to Master Field's place of business or another of the printers selling their wares in St. Paul's churchyard. We'll put a manuscript or pamphlet in all of the leading universities and libraries. In the future, the technicians will read it and follow our plea to rescue you."

"I don't know," I shake my head. We've already changed so much just by being here. Who knows what is different now, besides the Armada? England is in a continual state of war because of us and this might produce worse. If time is a tree, we might completely unroot it. On the other hand, if what Dee suggests works, if the future time travellers aren't too angry or upset at us for what we did, maybe they can correct things and everything will go back to normal? I wish it all wasn't such a gamble.

"If the future is like what you've hinted at: electricity and wires and such, they will have easy access to my writing," he adds. "They'll preserve and read my writing for the next thousand years if everything is as advanced as you say, correct?"

I nod. "Yes, the internet is like an electronic library encompassing everything and your surviving writing will probably be preserved. But what if it gets lost or isn't preserved? What if your manuscripts in the ground never get dug up for example?"

"My dear boy, why would my investigations and writings not be preserved?" He seems annoyed. "I am one of the most revered authorities on knowledge and experimentation, especially as it applies to scientific truth, the hidden nature of reality. We are only burying the most esoteric secretive tracts under the ground, not your pamphlet. If we are burying your pamphlet, we are doing it in the most venerated and distinguished sites possible; it will be placed in no less a collection than the library at Cambridge."

"I don't know," I again shake my head. "No offence and don't get me wrong . . . but I myself had never heard of you until we met."

ISABEL

Will hands me a letter from Nathan, delivered to the Rose Theatre via Walter Raleigh's servant. It's the first letter I've gotten in many years. Will cocks his eyebrow in a slightly condescending way as he hands me the missive, saying "You've got friends in high places."

The letter is wrapped in a folded sheet of paper; it is closed with a blob of wax but there is no seal on it. My name is scrawled in large, crude letters by what I presume is Nathan's hand. He didn't send me any handwritten notes in school.

"Well, aren't you going to open it?" asks Will, his eyebrow still cocked. Even though his tone is mocking, I begin to read the letter aloud to show him it means nothing:

Dear Isabel,

We are sailing further and further south, following the Spanish coast, based on intelligence gained in Cadiz. I don't know how trustworthy the intelligence is because I saw some of what Drake and his officers did to the Spanish captains we captured to pry the info. They might have said anything to end the suffering. I've been promoted to the rank of a full soldier above deck on board Drake's ship Revenge. *The work is no easier and the men don't like me much more than they used to, but I am under Drake's protection and no one dares say anything, at least when Drake is around.*

As my eyes scan over the second paragraph, I realise I'd better stop reading it aloud and fall silent:

Despite this, I like the life of the sea, especially its unpredictability. It's never the same thing twice. I wonder how you're doing with Shakespeare—is it what you hoped for? I've mentioned his name casually but no one here has heard of him so maybe, in a roundabout way, our appearance did what I wanted it to do anyway. Seriously, I know we've paid a high price and I'm sorry. I miss you and hope to see you soon, but Drake doesn't want to return until we've got concrete knowledge, maybe a high-profile prisoner or two.

The letter is dated May 19th and he's signed it "Yours, Nathan."

There's an odd formality to the letter which wouldn't have been present in Nathan's voice before: phrases like "I don't know how trustworthy the intelligence is" and "I've mentioned his name casually" and "we've paid a high price." If Ms Sullivan was right and we all have a unique voiceprint, like a fingerprint,

Nathan's has changed; it's older somehow. We're all older. He's being affected by the people around him and our straitened circumstances.

"I suppose the rest is secret?" asks Will. "Tokens of love and so forth?"

I blush and don't know how to respond. Nathan writes he misses me so perhaps he's also apologising for the previous breach in our friendship. Is he saying he misses me because we're all stranded and separated from each other, because of the situation we're in, or because he really cares for me? If he cares for me, how much?

Will waits, arms folded, and I hold the letter tight between my fingers. It's nice to have something that's mine. When he sees I won't rise to his bait, he looks me over one last time as if he sees more than he lets on, then gazes out the window with a desultory sigh. "If you've got prospects, I'd hasten to seal them up," he says. "You said that you want to participate in the world of theatre, to write, but it's no life for a woman. Look how poor we are. I cannot even afford to hardly send anything to my wife and children, let alone pay you. If you've got connections, if your friends have connections, use them, woman. We will die without support. A commission from one of those high places, support from one of those noble families close to the Queen would allow me to write, unencumbered by worries."

"Everybody's worried about the war, rich or poor," I say, finding my tongue. "What about yourself, don't you miss Anne and the children? Wouldn't you feel safer with them?" He's in his late twenties, a young man, not like my father at all who always bore utmost seriousness, had a religious zeal for reading and books and what they meant. Will downplays all that, has a coyer energy, expressed through his inability to stand still, the way he shifts from one foot to the other, paces, though he can be very intense and absorbed when writing. But then again, I wasn't really aware of what my parents were like in their twenties.

"I got married too young, so despite what I say, you must do what you want," Will confesses, his gait shifting again. Can he see Stratford in his mind's eye through all the wilderness and furze outside the window, the same way I often see Scarborough, Toronto in the twenty-first century in my own mind's eye? "Of course I miss my dear wife and children," he adds, catching himself as if he's just been too frank. "I journey to see them once a year through the forest of Arden; it takes days and there are robbers along the path. As I've told you, I would be tried, possibly hanged there for a past crime of poaching, so returning permanently is not possible. I came here to find my troubles multiplied. But we fit ourselves to our times, and not the other way around, is that not so?"

"That's a good line," I say. "Why aren't you writing more?"

"I don't know," he admits. "It is not like you think. All pie-in-the-sky inspiration and fancy flowing fantasies, it is the real world we must live in and that world requires money. It is a practical business and we need a new disbursement of funds. It is on my mind much, Isabel, and sometimes that pressure forces one to write; now, it simply does not."

"Let me talk to Doctor Dee," I reply. "We do need food and maybe he can lend us some money while you figure out the next steps. Do you know what plot you'll focus on next?"

He shakes his head slowly. "Only vague notions, nothing definite. Henslowe wants nothing that comments on the war or that might irk the nobility. And yet I feel we must eventually address it."

I pack Nathan's letter into a basket so it is with me and wrap my old dirty shawl around my shoulders. Will filched it from the theatre for me along with the rough hempen dress I am wearing. I prepare for the long journey to Mortlake, first by foot into London and then the boat ride which I must ask Dee to pay for at the other end. First I must cross Finsbury Fields, pass Bedlam Hospital, and journey down to the Thames so I begin the long walk. Finsbury Fields is a wild heath with great gnarled oaks and elms and heather and briar upon it. There is a chestnut tree I like to pass, the kind of tree they use to build ships. It makes me think of Nathan out at sea. Through its leaves, one can see the fair blue sky, the hills and heath rolling away towards the smoky cluster of London's houses, their roofs of occasional red tile, more commonly thatched. Nathan's letter is interesting for what it doesn't say. No mention of Suresh so perhaps he blames Suresh for our predicament. The more I think about it, the more I realise I don't know Nathan very well. I've known him longer than Suresh but Suresh is easier to understand. Does Nathan say he misses me only because we're stranded here, or because he truly wants me? Truly wants me for me? We're so different.

I pass the mighty Curtain Theatre, its dark timbers casting long shadows across the field. The houses become nicer, more cosmopolitan the further I walk from Shakespeare's lodgings. In his letter, Nathan asked if I'm satisfied working for Will and even that is difficult to answer. Suresh seems happy enough with Dee and Nathan's found his metier with the soldiers and Raleigh and Drake. For myself, I don't know—I still feel out of sorts. I want to learn from Will but to him, sometimes it's as if I'm not there. I'm as far away from him as his own children: the two girls Susanna and Judith and the boy Hamnet. Nothing of his power and potential seems to rub off on me during our conversations. At least I feel no different. I feel the same as when I landed here, whereas Nathan has changed so much.

I don't wish to be a housewife like Jane, or Will's own wife,

Anne. I wish to write like him, feel what he feels, create what he creates, and it's difficult to make Will see that. As much as his writing will embolden female characters, he thinks like a man. I used to say that if there's anyone whom I could have dinner with, living or dead, it would be Shakespeare because of the mystique. Now the mystique is largely gone. It was an obvious answer, I suppose, and perhaps that makes me predictable—I might have said Brontë or Austen or Woolf, one of the great women, except Shakespeare was further away in time. And now I do have dinner with him, prepare it for him in fact—often nothing more than stiff bread and gruel made from potatoes and whatever vegetables we can scrounge. If we get a bit of old meat to throw into the stew, that's a feast.

I've never been one to harp on looks but my hempen dress needs to be washed properly and for that, I need a vat of soap and boiling water—Will brought the dress and shawl home from the theatre and it fits better than the two Jane gave me; it will better weather the long journey outside. The weather's warmer than when we arrived but the shawl is necessary so as not to catch cold. Will offered to ask one of the seamstresses at the Rose to alter Jane's dresses but I don't want to. The grey hempen dress is coarse and stiff but sturdy and I don't really wish to wear out Jane's dresses, especially if I have to return them one day. I don't wish to wear out our welcome either but we really do need money.

The sun is on its downward arc by the time I arrive at Doctor Dee's house. Dee knows most of the truth about us. He does not know why I asked to apprentice with Will but I'm sure he suspects and if he suspects, how long before Raleigh and Will suspect? Jane is nice enough to fill my basket with food. She offers me some bread she has baked, cheese, and honey to take back and we pull strawberries from her garden though they aren't quite ripe yet and will taste hard and sour. Dee offers me some oranges that a visitor brought from Europe as Will is partial to them, but they have the opposite problem from the strawberries: they've already softened, threatening to go bad. If England's climate is not difficult enough, the war makes imports unpredictable.

Finally, Jane picks out a marrowbone pie that has been cooling in the larder and places it on top of everything. Nathan's missive is quite well covered over. I thank her though I feel guilty and awkward for I could be living here, helping her with the children and housework. Her demeanour says as much. Her pregnancy is showing more now; it must be difficult to move around. But Dee himself said he could only support one of us, didn't he, and Suresh was favoured.

Suresh watches me now as I rip a hunch of bread away from the loaf they have given me and begin eating. They're all watching me intently but I don't mind. My stomach gurgles even though it's shrunk. Dee and Jane look from me to Suresh, a slight smile upon their lips, and Suresh himself seems more awkward than usual. He fidgets in front of the fire. What is going on?

"I'll leave you to it," says Jane and disappears, waddling like a penguin, a hand on her back to steady herself. Pregnant. That would be my own fate if I chose a similar path. She oversees everything the household needs so Dee can continue with his reading, writing, and experiments. I'm sure Suresh isn't helping with the housekeeping tasks. As far as Jane is concerned, I might be little more than an ungrateful freak, not a natural woman at all but one of the men. One of the boys. She leaves us to our men's talk.

"I'm sorry to ask, Doctor Dee," I am dizzy and tired after having eaten and my words come out pathetically, "but I must ask you for money. This visit isn't just for victuals and pleasantries, though they are appreciated. Will and I have nothing. From what I gather, Mr Henslowe isn't ready to mount another play yet. Everyone's quite stretched. We must ask you to lend us money in the meantime."

"But I have none to give," says Dee, spreading his hands. "It is difficult for us as well. I have been waiting for the Queen to give me rectorship of a parish for some time. If she does not, we must perish too. The war makes it even harder for her to spend than is her usual custom. Your friend Nathan is probably in the best position, for if Sir Francis is successful in capturing Spanish gold, he will give a share to the men fighting with him. So perhaps it is you who must help us?"

There's nothing more to be said so the fire does the talking for us, crackling away in its grate within the darkness of the main hall. A log breaks as it burns, crumbles in the middle. I think of Nathan's letter at the bottom of my basket, underneath the food, but it doesn't sound like he's struck gold. Far from it. I think of my father and his scholarly friends who often quoted the mantra "publish or perish." For Dee, it's "parish or perish." Will would like the pun—perhaps he's rubbing off more than I thought?

"I must introduce you and Will to Raleigh," continues Dee after thinking awhile, "like I did your friend Nathan. He and other people closer to the Queen should be your chief benefactors, perhaps Raleigh might commission something. At one time, I had means, but now it has all sadly vanished. Burghley and Walsingham are gone, and I don't have the same reach, although I command some influence. Perhaps I shall have to sell some of the manuscripts from my library, though I cannot bear to think of it. Do not despair. I have Raleigh's ear and we will convince him to commission an entertainment."

"That would be nice."

"There's other news," says Suresh. "Doctor Dee's hit on a helpful idea that may allow us to reach word to the time travellers. He's been working on a pamphlet on the subject of time travel. It's nearly finished. Soon we can get it printed. He thinks that if we place copies in the major libraries, people from the future will read it and figure out what happened, and then come get us. What do you think?" He bites his thumb nervously.

"I don't know. What do *you* think?" If he doesn't have much faith in the idea, how can I?

"It's certainly strange," replies Suresh. "I don't know what impact it'll have once other people read it, not in the future, but here and now. Haven't you noticed how they don't seem to have stories about time travel here? Doctor Dee believes in scrying into the past, maybe the future, but he himself has never thought of travelling within it."

"These are strange times," Dee shrugs, though there's a whimsical glee in the motion. It's obvious he's enjoying writing and discussing the subject.

"It's a generous gesture," I say after contemplating it. "As is everything you've done for us, and continue to do. We don't deserve it. So thank you, and thanks also to Jane."

"Stuff and nonsense!" snorts Dee emphatically. "You and Suresh despair much too easily. Life must beget life, hope must beget hope. Things are far too interesting for despair, and I am sure I called you here for this very purpose—you are my most successful experiment in this time. I believe we live in interesting times, and you must maintain hope that all is for the best. I'll go see whether Jane wants anything. I'm sure you have much to discuss." Again, one of those sly looks as he quickly glances at Suresh. My friend instinctively looks away, into the fire.

The silence becomes heavy once Dee has left. Suresh keeps staring into the fire, hunching forward in his chair as if trying to escape into the flames. "Suresh, look at me. What's on your mind?" I ask.

"What if we change things too much?" he turns around, fearful. Fear mixed with something else, excitement? "What if we *are* able to get word to the future, and they take us back, and it's not the same as when we left? It couldn't be, could it? What if the time travellers punish us for what we've done? What if by writing the pamphlet, we negate the chances of the people in the future building the devices in the first place? The differences could multiply like fractals."

"You overthink things, Suresh." I click my tongue. "Your mind's trying to go down every line of enquiry, every possibility. That'll do your head in—impossible. Think of it like your friend, Doctor Dee. If anything, the publication of the pamphlet would advance the discussion, the production, the science of the whole thing." But now he's got me worried, all of the branches and possibilities spiralling off from this one, impossible to fathom. Is this what it's like when Will is struggling to tease out a plot, is it like tangled hair or my dirty shawl, just threatening to unravel? "Suresh," I urge gently, "you have to be careful not to contemplate this stuff too much—it can lead to inaction. It can make the way forward difficult."

"We're stranded on a desert island of time," he sighs. "Let me walk you down to the river, and we can talk." He takes my arm. It's a little forward of him but I allow it.

Towards the river, there is an oak tree and I sit down with my back against it, facing the water. Lanterns have been brought out on the boats. It'll be dead of night by the time I finally get home.

"Suresh, why aren't you sitting down?" I ask.

He keeps standing and looks around him, glancing over his shoulder as if gazing upon things below the ground, some hidden knowledge. Finally, he traces the rough grooves in the trunk of the oak I'm sitting under. He's standing above me as if unsure what to do. The tree bark has strong vertical ridges and furrows. He traces a peculiar furrow that swirls from vertical into spiral. "I've been thinking a lot," he says. "We're stranded on an island of time, waiting for a ship to pass. That's basically our situation, except that the sea is time instead of water, isn't that so?"

I get up so that we're eye level and begin stroking the grooves of the wood also. The rough texture is quite pleasant to touch. "I suppose so." What's he getting at? We continue to stroke the wood downwards, following the parallel vertical furrows, and I can almost feel the warmth and vibration of his hand matching mine in the dusk. It makes me feel warm in my face, my body. I think of Nathan's letter buried underneath all that food in the basket. Suddenly, Suresh's hand jumps from his track and grabs mine. I'm not sure what to do and look into his eyes before finally turning away, pulling my hand away and shaking it as if there were pollen on it. "Suresh, what are you doing?"

"What do you think I'm doing?" he asks.

I press my knuckles because there is a tension there and all through my body, a knot. "Suresh, you're just acting like this because of the pressure of our situation. Soon, if Doctor Dee's pamphlet works, and I hope it does, we'll be rescued and taken back home. Everything will be normal again. You'll go back to your scientific experiments and your obsessions; you won't even think of me. You're just doing this because we're here." Am I talking about him or Nathan?

"What if it's too late? What if we've changed too much? What if we can't go back?" His mouth twists into an awkward smile. "You once said I had no empathy when I posted that video of Nathan locking Sullivan in the closet. Don't you have any empathy for me, for how I feel about you?"

"God, Suresh! I was just saying that in the moment, because of my frustration about you livestreaming that video. I wasn't saying you have no empathy at all, ever. Why do you even care what I think?"

Suresh looks away, disappointed, then clasps his hands matter-of-factly behind his back like Dee. All he'd have to do is walk forward with his shoulders hunched, lost in thought, and the imitation, the mirror image, would be perfect. "Jane's really showing her pregnancy now, isn't she?" he finally says. "When we arrived, I wasn't sure if she was just chubby or . . . is this right, according to history? Do you remember reading that they're supposed to have a child now?"

"I'd heard of him," I say, grateful to change the subject, still stroking my knuckles. "But I know very little about his life, just that he's an advisor to the Queen and he's friends with famous people. I think he might be the model for Prospero in the last play Will writes, *The Tempest*. My father forced me to read and discuss with him, but truth be told, I don't even know that much about Will's supposed personal life. You remember Sullivan saying that not a lot is known about it, there were no diary entries or letters detailing his creative process. I think it's all changed anyway. Just by us being here. I think we've changed things and it's hard to assess how much. That episode with the Armada for instance hasn't changed things so much that I don't recognize who these people are, but at the same time, important details have changed. Dee himself said that his family had to come home earlier than they might. Will still has his wife and three kids in Stratford and Hamnet hasn't died yet so that's basically the same, but who knows what other repercussions we've sown? It's like throwing a stone into that river there. The ripples multiply and perhaps they go backward as well as forward. I don't know. Will's written *The Taming of the Shrew* recently and now *Romeo and Juliet* but why isn't *Romeo and Juliet* bringing him the next big hit? I don't understand it. Yes, we're stranded on an island of time but life goes on—we have to puzzle out the currents as best we can. They never stop flowing, do they?"

And with that, we gaze upon the waters of the Thames, gurgling like my stomach, as night deepens, the beginning of my journey back pressing me to walk further down, away from Suresh. The boats glide by with their lanterns. Somewhere an owl hoots, flaps its wings almost noiselessly and takes off. I must return to the garret I share with Will and Suresh must go about his duties. Each to their own respective station. There are no easy answers.

NATHAN

Wood and sea, and now smoke and iron. These are the elements my world is made of. I did not draw an accurate picture of just how difficult things are when I wrote to Isabel. It is exciting, but except for Drake, the rest of them hate me. I am sure of it but I just don't care anymore. I've shown them all that I can stand on my own; if they still want to hate me, I'll deal with that too. I will push myself to prevail in this or any other century. I will stamp my face onto this age, coloured though it might be. I will press my identity onto this backward time.

I stand on the prow of *The Falcon*, one of our smaller ships as it crests the fog, rising low and soft with the dawn. This fog and its headwinds work against us and our progress is slow, begrudging, as some of our sails have been furled in order to stealthily creep. We have changed course and tactics, sailing north, west of Brittany, up around the coast of France. There is new information. The *Revenge* has been left behind us and we nimble ahead.

Our quarry is the Duke of Parma. Drake would be much happier to find the Duke of Medina Sidonia but he disappeared with the rest of the Armada four years ago. Parma was supposed to meet the Duke of Medina Sidonia and combine their forces but for some reason, Parma never got to the English Channel before the Armada disappeared. Sheer luck, perhaps incompetence, saved him.

Drake leaves the company of his officers and strides towards me. I watch with slight apprehension. What does he want? He clamps his hand on my shoulder, squeezing hard: "Are you ready?" His tone is easygoing but the tension in his grip suggests he's as excited as I am.

"I am grateful for your support, Sir Francis," I reply nervously and stand to attention. "I promise I will honour the faith you have placed in me."

How easily he could crush me.

"It is alright, lad. As long as you continue to work hard, you are welcome on my ship. I had a good man, Diego, help me out in my enterprises once, and he was much darker than you."

"A black man?" I guess, immediately regretting it. Drake looks at me out the side of his eye, seeing how I take the news, the first time I've seen suspicion cross his face. I know he's traded slaves; I'm not a slave, am I?

"He helped me in navigation and my dealings with the Spanish," confirms Drake. "An arrangement of great benefit to both of us, mutually pleasing too. I feel that you might provide the same." Heated warmth replaces suspicion in his eyes as if he's playing with a new pet, stroking a small dog or a chained bear. Is he coming on to me?

What if he knew that one of the famous celebrities of my time is a rapper who bears his name, and is half black? Rawley's taunt that I am a half-blood prince enters my mind. Rawley, Raleigh. He's not coming on to me. I know I should be more in control of my thoughts. My words likewise should be moderate and calm but I can't help being forward. "They hate me for what I am, why don't you?"

"Sailors are a suspicious and narrow-minded lot," replies Drake, allowing his weight to lean forward against the edge of the prow. The irony in those words. So much imperiousness. Never mind. The wind picks up and we have to hold onto ropes to make sure we aren't tossed across the wet planks. "But in time, nothing matters except that we make our own fortunes," he continues. "Do you know that the Spanish would torture me for months on end if they could only capture me? And yet here I am. In my old age, I cannot entrust the Spaniard's fortunes to another. A cannonball passed by me once, leaving me unharmed, but another time a bullet cut into . . . what is it?"

Without realising, I have let go of my rope. The dawn fog has parted. "Did you see that?" I whisper to Drake. "Something in the distance."

"We have not reached our destination yet, which is Brest on the French coast—where Parma is reported to wait."

"That's not a Spanish galleon," I reply, "but a smaller vessel, like our English ones."

Drake drops his rope and touches his leg where that bullet once might have cut into him. He strains to see but there is no recognition on his face. The others on the prow behind us are still chatting. They too have not seen anything. But I can see it again. An outline of a ship coalescing out of fog with fire all around it. The ghosts of three young people on board, their features indistinguishable. The light glints off a platinum band. I raise my hand and almost cry out but Drake grabs my arm firmly and lowers it. Moments later, the fog rolls back and the image is gone. Am I imagining things?

"Did you see it?" I whisper. It looked to me like it *was* the three of us: Suresh, Isabel, and myself first formed, then erased by fog.

"The sea affects all of us differently," he says, "you'd better get hold of yourself. The future is bright, but only if you keep your head."

"But it was . . ."

"If there is another English ship besides ours in the region, I would know. I will tell you something else. When we find the Duke of Parma's ship, I shall embark with the rest." He encourages me away from the prow. "I have not told the others but I am telling you because you are going to help me. I wish to taste that thrill one more time." Drake pats me on the shoulder and returns to his fellows.

A couple of hours later, the morning fog has dispersed and our ship's come upon the Duke of Parma's vessel. No guards or people on land we have to worry about. Only the Duke's ship and the soldiers on it. I've heard it said that Drake must have been dipped in tar as a baby for all the luck that comes his way.

Drake walks up, wearing a metal helmet and carrying a partisan, a wooden pole with a sharpened spear at the end. He directs one of the soldiers to fetch a helmet which I place on my head. It's heavier than a football helmet and its bowl is large, coming down over my eyes, pressing its cold steel against the bridge of my nose. I have to tilt it back so I can see. I once thought soldiering would be an easy fit.

"Well, what do you think, lad?" asks Drake, stroking his beard and gesturing forward. "A prize fit for our taking?" We stare out at the Duke's ship against a cold breeze that numbs my face. Our own ship tosses gently with the waves. We'd folded up our sails earlier but now they are unfurled. "The Duke's probably in contact with the Catholics, on behalf of Philip and the Pope, mark my words," adds Drake.

"It doesn't matter," I say slowly, the adrenaline cutting through my bloodstream, "One solitary galleon . . . "

Drake chuckles; he pounds me on the back: "Good boy! If there's loot aboard that ship, and my nose tells me there is, some of it shall be yours!" A hasty, nervous swagger to the way he moves—he's straining to leap on board. "Now, will you take a pikestaff or a sword and buckler? They'll likely have firearms."

I take the short sword which can be clasped to my belt. No buckler. I'll have to help Drake get on board and for that, I'll need both hands.

Once we're within range, Drake gives the order for our cannons to begin booming. It would have been me below, with Rawley, a week and a half ago, heaving cannonballs or assisting the loaders. They've outfitted these English ships with as many decks as can hold cannons while still keeping afloat. That means the waterline on the hull rises and those below deck are not protected once things get choppy. It's not going to be smooth. The point is to apply as much damage to the enemy as possible before he can react.

The Duke of Parma's ship does not have the problem of decks being so close to water. He's sighted us and his Spanish galleon, large and looming, has already begun to turn. It is a large listing whale, turning its soft underbelly towards us; its wooden decks slowly heave in the wind. Drake realises we have been spotted and the fever pitch is upon him; he bares his teeth; his eyes pop.

No reason for subtlety anymore. He commands our ship right up to the Spanish galleon while it's still trying to turn and manoeuvre, lets our cannons go at her broadside. The smoke and fire from the fusillade send us reeling even as the recoil passes through our ship, forcing it to roll, sending water over the deck. The other cannons, the ones higher up, the eight pounders and the ten pounders, shoot over the galleon's bow and stern. We can see the individual Spanish soldiers on deck now, running, scurrying for their lives.

Now Drake gives the command for other cannons to shoot under the galleon's lee, riddling her with holes. Parma swerves his damaged ship away but it is slow and takes a long time. His soldiers who aren't in disarray, or haven't had their oars blasted to smithereens, swing to and pull the damaged vessel limply towards the French shore.

Some of the other Spaniards who were shaken try to assume their fighting positions and return fire from deck. It is too late. Too much damage to their hull. Water rushes in. The massive galleon begins to keel. What a terrific and terrible sight to see. The giant behemoth lists and falls, crowded with fore and aft decks, mighty masts and towers pinwheeling in the wind. Sails rip apart. Ropes go flying. Some of the soldiers try to get their boats into the water. Others jump into the waves, breaking their legs.

It is divine madness. Again, I can taste the metal and fire on my tongue as if I were below deck; but up here, with all the open room, the cold wind on my face, salt in the air, the smell of impending victory is quite sweet. The Spanish galleon continues rocking and listing, limping towards the coast in an erratic line until it rams the shoals and keels over at a great angle.

Seeing the galleon grounded, Drake rounds up soldiers to the deck, orders boats to be lowered. In the distance, the Spanish soldiers have thrown ropes over the side and begin to scramble onto shore. "Do not allow them to abscond with the treasure, men!" shouts Drake.

One officer speaks: "It might be too dangerous, sir. In our little boats, we would be extremely vulnerable to Spanish sharpshooters." Others mutter under their breath, concurring.

"What do you think, Master Nate?" asks Drake, eyeing me sharply.

His lust for loot has spread within my own veins; I can feel the anticipation in sympathy with him. "We raid the galleon. Any other choice would be stupid."

"You cannot trust him, sir!" shouts the officer, "he's not one of us, might even betray us."

Drake is not a patient man, his frown communicating as much. He holds up his partisan to the officer's earlobe, implying that all he need do is let the blade fall to slice off the officer's ear. All dissent ceases. We put our boats into the water and row with all our might. The Spaniards are not far now.

The galleon has crashed against the shoals. It is not easy to get the grapnels over her bow and climb aboard. If it had cannon ports below deck like we have, it would be easier but they might also shoot at us through the openings. I throw a hook and it catches onto a broken mast. Others copy me, hooking sails; we hoist ropes which the younger, more agile climbers can rappel. I stay back and help pull Drake up, one hand clutching my rope while the other hand pulls him up his. He is slow and staggers, must use both his hands and feet so the partisan must be left behind. I hang back even further and push upwards, my hand against the back of his red jacket.

Most of the Spaniards have now deserted their galleon but a few are still left on deck, armed with pikestaffs and arquebusiers. The arquebusiers are not as terrifying now as the first time I saw them. They are a long rifle and can only be fired once. The accuracy is poor and it takes them a long time to reload. The Spaniards fire. Two of us fall down but the rest, swords out, swarm the shooters.

The Spaniards with pikestaffs are a greater problem. One comes right at me. His staff has a blade which is heavy like an axe at the end of a long pole. I raise my helmet with one hand so I can see clearly and time my jump as he comes at me. My short sword, sharp as it is, will be useless against this man and his pikestaff. I throw the sword to the ground and grab hold of the pole. We wrestle with the staff. Up close, his unshaven face is gaunt and twisted with alarm.

I'm younger and stronger. But the deck is listed, gravity against me. My opponent tries to push me down with his armour. Without letting go, handhold by handhold, I inch further up and along the pikestaff until we're within kissing distance of each other.

His warm, exasperated panting falls upon my face as he cries out in Spanish. With a sudden motion, I let go the staff, bring my foot up to trip him. He falls forward clutching his staff, rolls across the deck. I jump aside, grab the pikestaff, bring it crashing onto the soldier's head. The man's glittering helmet bends inward against his dome. Have I done this?

This isn't football at all.

Reverse shock reverberates up my forearms. Like a cannon's recoil, but much more intimate. The helmet crumples and the face below it sort of folds in two with a bone-shattering crunch. The soldier's look of surprise is preserved on his face as blood starts to wash down his cheeks, dripping from beneath the twisted helmet, washing over his eyes and unshaven face. A death rattle comes a moment later. Even amongst the smoke and foreign cries, I hear that death rattle perfectly.

The first time I've killed someone. Truly killed someone.

Taken his life, not just injured him. Last breath in my face, an unfinished curse in Spanish aimed at me. This isn't like loading a thirty pound cannon ball, watching the explosion carry it off in some unknown direction. No, sir. The life has left his body; the resultant shock saps my will. My knees buckle; I have to lean on the pikestaff for support, my oversize helmet falls over my eyes. I feel the surge of hollow victory—it could be me who died—and the sense I might be sick.

Pull it together. Remember what Drake said. Treasure, reward. Sounds of battle, inhuman cries, contortions of fear and lurching of bodies and the smoke of wood and metal around me. Forever dead by my hand. He probably has a family: wife and children, mother and father. I have cheated myself into this destiny and this is the price.

Something emerges from below deck, a black streak. The Duke of Parma. Well, well, he has not gone ashore after all. He was waiting out the battle, cowering in his rich suit of black velvet and gold trim. Slim, elegant, bearded with his long cloak trailing behind him, a large ruff around his neck. This is the first Spanish ruff I've seen and it's very large and fancy with highlights of gold framing his face and black hair. Those dark hateful eyes of his bore into me, then focus on Drake. Thrill of battle and bloodlust returns. A new challenge.

Parma slithers across the deck at us like he's sliding his feet, just learning to walk, doesn't trust the listing ship. He removes something from behind his back and it glints. I feel a pull towards his hand. How old is he? Youth or old man? His movements are exaggerated and awkward, like an old man's, but the power they suggest . . . something about the face and eyes. His skin is too pale for a Spaniard. He slithers forward, right up as if wishes to crash into us, then halts abruptly.

Push the confusion away and focus on the Duke. He has had

many victories on the Continent, I've heard, and if I can stop him, my time as an outsider will end. The Duke rushes up to Drake, levelling a short pistol against the face of our shining knight. It's a matchlock pistol. If he fires that, an iron ball will lodge into Drake's jaw. At the very least, his jaw will shatter, even if it doesn't kill him. I uncoil my frame, straighten, tense my muscles.

Dropping the pikestaff, I lean into the wind, steady myself against the ship's incline. It feels like running up the side of a mountain; I put my head and shoulder down and tackle the Duke. It's the last quarter and I run interference against the Spanish commander. The pistol is a football, because that's the only way I can ignore the danger, and tackle Parma just as it goes off. The shot goes wide, muffled by the Duke's cloak. All three of us tumble down, slide along the canted deck. A calculated risk. I'm the first to rise. By the time I do, I've got Parma in a chokehold and it's all over, it's all over. It's not even like I'm acting—rather, enacting. Simply going through the motions.

I keep choking the Duke until they pry him away from me. Drake's already on his feet, spreading his legs wide and leaning forward to counteract the incline, the matchlock pistol in his hand. The smell of gunpowder hovers in the wet air. Drake gives a sideways look at me, like he's done before. But the same soldiers who hated me when I beat down their mate have hoisted me up on their shoulders and are cheering.

We've won!

More than that, it's gone just the way I thought it would. Why did it feel like that? As if it's a football play I knew would happen? I flash back to the Italian puppets on the little fake stage in Raleigh's house. The Duke's clothing, black and gold, like one of the puppets. Why does this all feel like it's been enacted before? I gaze at my hands and they look as if they're made of string and wood.

ISABEL

Doctor Dee is again as good as his word, which is something to be celebrated in this or any other age. Not only did he keep his promise to petition Raleigh about commissioning Will for a play, he also completed the pamphlet on time travel. Without revealing too many intimate details about us, he has written a tract addressed to the time travellers of the future, in a way duplicating Suresh's experiment but with greater deliberation. Can lightning strike twice? We certainly hope so. Doctor Dee will pay for the printing too. He refused to lend Will money but where his own writing is concerned, money can be found. Can't say I blame him. Who would not do anything they possibly could to bring their own writing forth?

Suresh and I accompany Dee to Richard Field's workshop in the alley between Water Lane and St. Andrew's Hill, Blackfriar's, to watch the laborious and careful typesetting process. During the entire journey there, Suresh and I avoid looking at each other too directly, careful to talk only with Dee or through him, the awkwardness of our last meeting still lingering between us. If Dee realises something is amiss, he does not let on. He's much too excited about the printing of his tract, which is titled "On The Travelling of Tyme."

Field wears a red cap and has a broad pleasant face with a large jaw that accentuates everything he says with a huge country smile. The smile extends up to the blue mole on his cheek and squinting eyes, his face lined from having to peer at type all day. He flashes his yellow teeth, stained brown, grateful for Dee's custom, but it is an amiable smile.

"This is Suresh, he's serving in my household," says Dee. Field is taken aback by Suresh's dark face peering out from even darker robes but does not remark on it, bless him. "And this is Isabel, she's serving with a writer of the theatre, Will Shakespeare."

"I know Will exceedingly!" exults Field, "Our families both come from Stratford. I had heard he was here. His father transacted business with my own."

"Your father is a tanner, isn't he, Richard?" asks Dee.

"Yes, and Will's a glover. Well, it was a nasty business that caused Will to leave his family. Abrupt too! I suppose neither of us were destined to fall near our family trees, and our honest ways must always be at odds with London's fashions, but we abide. You must give my regards to him, Isabel, and tell him to come visit honest Dick sometime."

Field's assistant painstakingly assembles the little blocks of type for each page. Words, then paragraphs, come into being as the setter shuttles the blocks of type onto their wooden sleeves. All the letters face backwards as if assembled in a mirror universe, a universe of pure imagination. Our hopes and dreams lie within that mirror universe, that universe of books and thoughts, as if that is the real one and we live in a counterfeit. Whole paragraphs and pages come into being, forming from the realms of thought and mind, like standing in front of Dee's perspective glass and seeing your mirror image come out to greet you. Hail female, well met!

The type is inked with a boll and paper pressed against it. Voila—nothing less than magic: something out of nothing. *This is real magic, Doctor Dee!*, I want to shout. If only dad were here to see it! The language is assembled for each page. Later the pages will be cut, folded, and bound together. It's easy to forget these physical processes when you're looking at a computer screen. Even Suresh seems interested. Field will print five hundred copies of Dee's pamphlet which Dee will then distribute to all the learned scholars and nobles he knows. He will place it in the libraries at Cambridge, the Middle Temple, the palace at Greenwich, and other such places. Then will come the hard part: waiting to see if there's a result.

"How are your headaches, Suresh?" I ask on our journey back.

"Fine," he replies cautiously, not being able to look me in the eye. He doesn't elaborate, making the distance between us feel even more stiff. Is he upset at me? Dee looks from Suresh to me, back again to Suresh.

"I think it was probably a kind of electronic withdrawal," I continue, to fill in the void. "Being here has forced you to quit cold turkey. The first few weeks were your delirium tremens."

"It's strange how the delirium becomes reality," says Suresh distantly. "Now it's our old life that seems a dream. I used to look at my photos and videos, but I hardly look at them now."

"That might be a good thing," I reply.

"Don't despair!" intercedes Dee who's still in a bright mood, wishing to brighten the conversation all around. "If all goes according to plan, you'll be returning soon. Have you heard anything from Nathan?"

"Will's visiting Raleigh at his house in the Strand right now. Nathan sent me a letter through Raleigh once but unless Will picks up another today, I won't have heard anything new. I hope nothing's happened to him." Suresh glances at me with a hurt look and I quickly stop talking.

I wish I could have gone with Will to Durham House to meet Sir Walter Raleigh myself but there would have been no reason or justification for it, especially the way I look in this dress. Raleigh's always such a heroic, dashing figure in the accounts I've read; it would be nice to meet him in person, see if he's as grand and good looking as he's portrayed. If I'm not mistaken, he's secretly seeing one of the Queen's ladies-in-waiting, Bess Throckmorton, only I thought the Queen had discovered them and their baby by now and imprisoned them in the Tower. If he's free and doing his thing, still a favourite of the Queen's, it must be another thing we've changed or altered or displaced, like Suresh and I talked about.

Back near Bishopsgate, Will kneels on the floor, plays with a mouldy orange. It is the last of our oranges. He discovered the orange in his pocket while speaking with Raleigh. He uses this blue doublet far too often to show off and it has wine on the front now, presumably from Raleigh's cellar, and even some melted candle wax on the sleeve which suggests he's been sitting at Raleigh's desk and possibly signed something. Can this be good news?

"Well, are you going to tell me what happened?"

He keeps rolling the hard orange around the room. The sound of it becomes grating. Will watches its haphazard trail around his floor and the sides of the uneven walls. "The aim is to roll it along the wall as far as one can before the warps make it veer away," he says.

I snatch up the orange from the middle of the floor. "What happened with Raleigh?" I ask impatiently. Sometimes, living with him, it's hard to imagine what he will become. He's just a man, easily distracted like any other.

"Do you know, you sound just like my Anne in Stratford?" he replies. "The orange was helping me think. They come from Spain, where the dreaded King Philip lives. Grown men must be put to bed like children at the mere mention of his name. That's what your good friend Walter Raleigh mostly talked of. The airs some of these people put on, especially when their own antecedents are in question and they've made their money in the New World! He mostly complained about having been the Queen's favourite once, and all the problems that brings him at court. I think he talked like that just so he wouldn't have to pay me all at once.

"Still, it was entertaining to hear him carp. I may be able to mimic his stylings and gestures for a character in a future play. He's still one of the Queen's favourites though, and that's no mean thing, but she's got others—just keeps them swirling around her I guess—an endless pageant of fools—he says she prefers Southampton and Essex nowadays—but I think he's downplaying things so he didn't have to spend as much on our production."

"Yes, you already said that."

"Have you ever seen Southampton?" he asks. "Such delicate features. Such delicate hands!"

"Will! Concentrate, focus! So he did commission you? Tell me more—we need an injection of funds badly!"

"He will disburse some for the production now but will not pay the full fee until it is enacted. He wants a marriage play and none of the old standards. He wants a completely new plot." He smiles at me wryly, as if I am immune to his plight which is also mine. His earring begins twitching as he talks, there's some distant hope in his eyes. I've seen him manic and I've seen him despondent, but this is something new.

"A marriage play?"

"Yes, you know, where everyone shall get married in the end?"

"A comedy?"

"Exactly! And when I get paid, I will in turn pay you every penny that is owed to you." Will rubs his hands together with glee; the orange is forgotten now and I make a mental note to throw it away. If Raleigh's given him money, we can take his doublet and my dress to the washerwoman's instead of just having me spot clean them. "But what will the play be about, Will? What is the plot?"

He becomes wistful. "I have no idea. Raleigh insists it must be new, that is all. There should be love, a lot of mirth, some nobles and some young people, all mixed up and loving the wrong person. There are to be three weddings in someone's house and he wants to present the play at their wedding party. That is all I am told."

And then, holding the smelly and hard orange, as if it does contain some latent creative power, as if its seeds spawn not only fruit but ideas, it dawns on me. What Will must write next.

"When is it to be performed, Will?"

"In a month's time! I must generate a plot and write with haste. Our company will perform it in midsummer but they must have time to scan and learn the lines."

"What have you come up with so far?"

"I was thinking of your friend's letter to you. I hope you don't mind that I read it?" He opens his palms and flashes me a fraudulent smile. "I found it in your basket after you returned from Doctor Dee's, and it gave me an idea, though I didn't understand what your beau meant by your presence here in London? I didn't know you'd journeyed together and were familiar with my work, or that you'd all arrived at the same time. Of course I was surprised you wanted to work for me, but you are keen on the theatre. You were visiting your friend who's serving with Dee today, right? You have a friend out to sea and one here on land. Something like that might be a lot of fun, might provide a serviceable plot, especially if you travel somewhere remarkable and foreign, but I do not yet grasp the context. A plot must be invented but these lines came to me. Listen:

When two at once woo one,
There is charm alive and much sport done.
And those things best do please me
That do befall prepost'rously!

111

"It is not yet perfected but the words came today. The seed of something. What do you think?" he asks.

The realisation strikes me with full force. Why did I not understand before, why we landed at this time? This is what it's all about: 1592. I try not to let my nervous excitement show. "Alright, alright," I say, "you'd better get writing then. Begin the prologue or whatever. I'll help you progress. We'll get the play completed in time. Meanwhile, I'd better wash your suit."

"Oh, has it been more than three weeks already? Where are my quills? Have you sharpened my quills?"

"They're on your desk—you should tidy your manuscripts!" Why am I raising my voice? Calm yourself, Isabel. Let it happen. I pick up his blue doublet and hose which he gently stacks in the corner on top of his oaken chest. I'm no longer embarrassed to watch him change. He puts on his brown ensemble that is more shabby—a jerkin with breeches instead of the silk hose. I am breathless and exhausted as I walk around the room. I've got to give Will space to figure this out on his own yet I cannot contain my excitement. He is about to embark on writing one of my favourite plays.

It's why we landed here, at this time. Shakespeare's beginning to write *A Midsummer Night's Dream*. He doesn't have a title yet but that's what he's about to work on. What did the time traveller say to us? That travel is a kind of meditation. It takes years of discipline and honing. We had passion and urgency but no discipline. We landed on the fiery ship in 1588 because that is what Nathan desired most—to fight, his violent emotions pulling rank over any serious desire to discover the Globe and its manuscripts. He was much more interested in burning ships than burning paper. And then my own thoughts, my own subconscious, must have pulled us here to this year—because I wished to witness the birth of Shakespeare's career, because we were studying *A Midsummer Night's Dream* and I love it so.

And where is Nathan now? "Did Raleigh by any chance have another letter for me, from my friend?" I ask.

Will shakes his head, his long hair flapping up and down like the flustered wings of a startled bird. "This play must be very good, Isabel. I need a hit, a palpable hit."

I leave him to his work.

NATHAN

We sail back to London with the Duke of Parma and his followers imprisoned in our hold. News of his capture has obviously reached the city. Tensions seem even more heightened than when we left. Villagers are conscripted to keep a constant watch on the Southern English coast like before—a line of signal fires ready to be lit should the Armada reappear. Rotating shifts on alert. At Gravesend, a line of ships blockades the mouth of the Thames, and Drake must personally greet them before we can pass.

We approach London and I stand alone in my favoured place upon the prow. Commoners' shacks give way to the clustered buildings and houses of London guardedly pressing together, as if the entire city is suspicious of me, not just people. The soldiers seem to have found some respect for me since I saved Drake's life, but still treat me with a serious formality. No one invites me to join in their jokes, their laughing. Perhaps there is even more distrust than before. I don't care; I've changed my clothes to suit my fortune, they can think what they want.

The sun reflects off my silk threads. There was treasure from the New World on Parma's ship and those in Drake's party received our share. I have money now in the form of gold and jewellery. Of more immediate use are my new clothes and sword. I picked out a pair of gold and red balloon breeches, a richly ornate black doublet laced with thread of gold and silver, and a rapier. No ruff but I found a cuirass of leather and metal which will protect my torso. The sword trails off my belt, and I replaced my buskins with knee high leather boots like Raleigh's. I don't know how far the gold will carry me but Drake says I can book comfortable lodgings for myself once we are in London, and buy a horse in the bargain if I wish. All to the good.

It isn't easy between myself and Drake—not since I saved him. We haven't even spoken of the event. Giving me my share of loot was his way of thanking me. He's not as pleasant with me now as he was just before we raided Parma's ship.

We've almost reached the Tower of London, and he approaches me. In the distance is London Bridge with its houses and bustling activity and at the end of the Bridge, the traitors' heads which seem to grow out of the gateway like flowers on a darkly blooming bush. The decapitated heads are black roses sprouting on the bridge's grey vine. The heads a silent warning to those passing underneath. But it's too late to hear what the heads might say. As with the gibbet on shore with bodies strung from it, the time to relay wisdom is long past.

"Do you think the Duke's head will be placed on one of those spikes?" I ask.

"Aye, if he doesn't talk, mayhap," replies Drake, "although with what we shall put him through, I think that unlikely." His tone is abrupt, businesslike. "It is more likely that the Spanish ambassador will pay us a ransom on behalf of Philip. All we can do is singe Philip's beard. I tell you what—if Parma dies, I shall give you the head instead of mounting it on the Bridge. How's that?"

"Why?"

"It shall serve as memento. Mortality awaits us all. I should have given you the head of that soldier on the galleon, your first kill, but there was not enough left once you'd finished with him.

"There is a procedure to these things," Drake continues, "The Duke will be placed in the White Tower here in the middle of the fort. Another wall of towers surrounds it, making it difficult for prisoners to escape. Outside the wall of towers is a moat— one hundred feet of water surrounded by a third and final wall. You'll see. But it is not as bad as you think. Very noble people have served time here. Some emerge unharmed while others do not. Even her majesty, Elizabeth, resided here once." Drake points to the tower we cannot see behind the walls. "She spent time here when her half sister, Mary Tudor, was on the throne. Philip, the very same Philip we fight now, was married to Mary. Elizabeth emerged unharmed and look at her. Personal fortunes may ebb and flow like the tide." He gives me a knowing look.

"Especially during war times."

His knowing look changes to annoyance, moving over me as if his expectations are confirmed. "You will not believe this but it has been relatively peaceful, compared to Mary's reign. Until four years ago. Bloody Catholics. Then Raleigh introduces you and we capture an elusive commander. Fortune's wheel turns again. A riotous, unpredictable wind is no good for anyone. Raleigh is Captain of the Queen's Guard and shall meet our cargo at the Tower. You shall see him soon enough, if he can get away from underneath the folds of the Queen's skirts." He laughs and claps me on the back, guffawing raucously at his own joke, its aggression and double meaning clearly designed to make me uncomfortable.

The Duke of Parma is placed in a dungeon in the White Tower, in the centre of the fort. He is far below us, as we stand on the ramparts. Perhaps he has already begun screaming. This high up, we can only hear the crows cawing, circling as they look for scraps of leftover carrion. The ramparts overlook the wharf and we wait for Raleigh and his men who may appear among the Londoners below us. The perpetual haze and smoke from fires is heavier now than when we left, manifesting collective dread.

We descend, walk over to the White Tower and wait for Raleigh. He arrives with another man, older than Drake even, white-haired but spry, decked in rich velvet and hose. An equally sumptuous ochre cloak trails behind him, dragging his shoulders down. He doesn't talk but stands with his back to the walls, right shoulder hoisted as if posing for a picture. He and Raleigh clasp shoulders warmly with Drake.

Raleigh sees my new Spanish clothes and is taken aback: "You seem to have done well for yourself, and on your first voyage too!"

"Exceedingly well, considering it wasn't a lengthy one," chuckles Drake, "we'll have to watch him!" He emphasises the irony in his words.

"This is Lord Admiral Howard, a very important figure in our fight against the Spaniard," Raleigh introduces the older man who looks down his sharp nose at me. His eyes squint and a weatherbeaten expression curls the corners of his mouth so that his white beard and pointed chin seem to grow longer. "He is related to the Queen herself. Her mother was Lord Howard's cousin."

"Oh yes," smiles Drake. "I was telling the lad how our Queen spent time here, in the Tower."

Howard finally looks me directly in the eye and talks: "She walked, with her ladies-in-waiting, along those ramparts. She might have looked over this very section of the Thames. Did she, at that time, fathom she'd rule over all the houses and bustling stalls sprawling around us? Many are called but few are chosen." He winks dryly without laughing, a gesture I didn't expect, but the others laugh easily around him. He obviously has great leeway or he wouldn't be talking about the Queen in this manner, might have even more clout than Raleigh and Drake, the way they laugh at his words.

"Isn't it disrespectful to talk about the Queen this way?" I ask.

This only makes them chuckle more out of affection, perhaps scorn. "Nathan, you're among men," singsongs Raleigh softly. "I told our Admiral that you have a friend invested in the theatre, Will Shakespeare. He informed me that your friend and confederates are horning in on his company's time at Henslowe's theatre, the Rose. I reminded him that many companies abound, but you had better watch out; if you really wish to assure your downfall, you had better not compete with the Lord Admiral's Men." They burst again into full laughter and even Howard joins in, sniggering. I don't laugh. Shakespeare isn't my friend. Isabel is.

"Oh, come, young sir," says Howard. "Even the Queen is a benefactor to a company of players and we all want good entertainment. We await this special play you've commissioned, Raleigh." Their laughter finished, they once again assume sober tones. Howard regains his composure: "She is our Queen and a glorious prince, but I can remember her as a very young woman." He looks wistfully over the wall, in the direction of Nonsuch Palace. "She will only allow portraits of her to be painted as a young woman now. We have all aged. It seems inconsequential, does it not? The rise and fall of fortune becomes tedious, almost tidal, nothing more than waves upon the ocean."

We ponder his words.

They seem to be the cue necessary for the business at hand. Raleigh leads us to the Duke of Parma's cell as Lord Howard's words ring in my ears: "Nothing more than waves upon the ocean." I strive to keep my face calm, remind myself to be patient and watch for opportunities. I am curious what the Duke will reveal.

"What will you do to him?" I can't help asking before we enter the cell.

"Patience, lad. You shall see!" replies Drake. "You are part of us now."

"Normally we'd place him in Skeffington's gyves," says Raleigh matter-of-factly. "Do you know what that is?"

I shake my head which brings a rueful smile to Raleigh's lips. "It's an iron device designed to compress and crush the body. Prisoners go for almost three days with their heads, hands, and feet clasped in an iron frame. They make the prisoner's body stand up, while at the same time pressing it into a painful ball. I've seen men on the third day, necks bent so far forward, chins rolled into their chests, spine so buckled their bodies look like huge, crooked fingers. They're made into dwarves. But we don't have time to wait three days."

"Today, we will simply apply the rack," nods Howard.

Within the cell, the Duke is still dressed in black breeches which complement his dark beard. He's stretched out on the rack, a large wooden frame. Ropes secure his wrists and ankles so that his body can be pulled in opposite directions. These ropes are tied to rollers, cranked by yeoman guards with poles that fit into the axles of the rollers. The Duke's eyes glitter with merriment and hatred as the torture device gradually pulls his limbs and joints apart but he doesn't cry out. Why doesn't he cry out?

The Duke gazes at me as if I know something the rest of them don't, as if he and I know this isn't real but a charade we're rehearsing. He makes a sudden jerky movement against the rack, more like a slithering instead of a thrashing. It's not completely involuntary, as if he's pretending for effect.

The yeomen crank the rollers further and we hear the Duke's knee pop. My mouth goes dry. I catch my breath. Not easy to watch. But fascinating.

The yeomen continue to rotate their giant axles. The wooden frame groans, wood creaking against rope, not unlike timbers in the hull of a ship. Counterpoint to the wood are the sounds of the Duke's spine and ribs, the joints in his arms and legs, his body stretching, muscles tearing. It ends with the grind and pop of the Duke's spinal discs. Still, the Duke says nothing, refuses to cry out. This is more unnerving than the dislocated joints.

I try to look elsewhere but Drake firmly places his broad hand behind my head and forces me to gaze forward. "The trick is to not do it quickly," he says, "to not give in and just tear him apart. That will avail us nothing."

The Duke refuses to talk. He gasps but does not scream. He's tough. Raleigh decides we might achieve more with less. Drake and Raleigh untie the ropes and hoist the groaning Duke up. The yeoman clap the Duke's hands in irons above a mound of dirt, hanging him from a wooden pillar supporting the ceiling. They hoist him at just the right height so that his feet dangle and his toes barely touch the dirt mound. I am reminded of that gibbet and its swinging bodies.

Raleigh looks at Parma as he hangs there, his broken shoulders swinging back and forth. Parma's toes try to clasp the dirt for support but it is difficult. Face bloody, he pants furiously. His knees are broken. His eyes roll back in his head and his eyelids close. The deep and piercing gaze is finally gone, the beard is torn and dirty. The fine clothes are stained with blood. His wrists twist unnaturally against the manacles.

"Now," says Raleigh, towering up to his full six-foot height. He rattles his sword to get the Duke's attention. "We need *some* information from you, and you're going to give it to us." As his body swings back and forth, the Duke opens one bloodshot eye.

"What has Philip done with the Armada?" asks Raleigh quietly, pronouncing each word, drawing it out in his impeccable courtly enunciation. "Where have you hidden it? When will you attack England?"

"Why don't you ask him?" spits out the Duke, jutting his chin at me, more blood than spittle flying from his mouth. Everyone looks at me; my hand goes involuntarily to my sword.

"What are you saying now?" asks Raleigh. He lifts up the Duke's head but the Duke's shoulders have become lacerated, neck almost folded into his chest.

"He knows what happened to our Armada. He was there!" spits the Duke. "The yellow boy. The half-yellow boy! He took the crown that doesn't belong to him and now he's in a mess."

"Explain yourself further," urges Raleigh but Parma doesn't talk.

Raleigh turns towards me: "What's he going on about?"

I shake my head. What does Parma know that I don't?

"Have it your way," whispers Raleigh. He has the captains dig away the dirt on the floor beneath the Duke of Parma's toes so that Parma cannot find a hold. They leave him, dangling in excruciating agony.

"No lies now," states Raleigh coldly. "Where is the Armada?"

"He knows, he knows," the Duke screams at us. "He knows and will make all of you pay." The Duke looks straight at me, lisping like a snake: "Something's coming for you. Something's coming for all of you! Just you wait."

"Explain what he is talking about, young man," commands Admiral Howard who has been silent, watching all this time.

"It's nonsense. Just nonsense to save his own life—" the words choke as I force them out. I'm not sure anymore. But if

120

I don't deny it, they'll string me up just like Parma. Better him than me.

The Duke passes out from the strain. Raleigh and the men decide to break for food. I wish I were no longer here but cannot walk away. On the ramparts, I have no appetite as they pass the chicken and cheese and wine around. They drink, gamble, and gossip, seemingly unperturbed, but what goes unsaid sits heavy between us. Drake looks at me askew, more suspicious than ever as he strokes his beard.

Howard also eats very little. He watches me from the other side of the group, not speaking. I feel trapped. After a while, Howard leaves to check on our prisoner. He does not come back and the sun begins to set over the Thames.

"Shouldn't we go see what's happening?" I ask, anxious for all this to be over. It feels like it's been a long time.

When we open the door, Howard stands in front of Parma, gazing up at the Duke's closed eyelids, his blood-spattered cheek and twisted wrists. The yeomen must have left for the two are alone.

"How's everything?" asks Drake. "Where are the guards?"

"Just waiting for our guest to wake," says Howard. "I told the men they could go eat as you would return soon. They need their repast."

"Watch this, Nathan!" Drake nods in the direction of the Duke's trembling, hanging body, signalling Raleigh to place a set of wicker steps beneath the Duke of Parma's toes so he can stand on them and rest his legs. As soon as the Duke has regained consciousness and drawn in raspy breaths, Drake kicks the wicker steps out from under him. The Duke's body falls like a defeated sack of flour, heavily straining against the manacles.

"I'll ask you once again," shouts Raleigh, thrusting his face up to the Duke's, "What have you done with the Armada? When will you renew your invasion of England?"

Though the Duke is broken, he is less unnerved than I am. "Ask the young man what he's done with the crown!" roars the Duke, hatred in his eyes. "The Armada will heave fire upon you for what you have done. Mark me!"

Again, attention turns to me.

"He's obviously lying to confuse us," I retort. I don't know if I'm convincing. "He's lying to save his life and it won't work. I'll end him myself if you need me to prove my loyalty. I've already killed one Spaniard. It won't be a problem to kill two." I don't know if I believe my words at this point but they have left my mouth. I put my hand to my sword, a threatening gesture. Is it only bravado? If the Duke truly knows something, I am first in line to hear it.

"Go to, young whelp," hisses the Duke. "I am already dead and buried in this place."

Whether Parma's body gives up the ghost or we speed it is irrelevant at this juncture. All the calm I mustered while we tortured him has now fled. I feel only agitation and the need to do something. That anger, the fury that comes from I-don't-know-where is suddenly upon me in this tight stale room in the Tower. The moment when I heaved the pikestaff against the Spanish soldier's helmet, then watched his face crumple inward. His look melted to fear, shock, then a calm absence. Blood washed across his cheeks like rain. That gurgling death rattle.

The rapier is unbuckled as I leap forward. I am moved by something like strings, a will beyond my own. Even the Duke desires this outcome. I sever his head and incriminating tongue from his shoulders. Met with resistance, I hack again and again, sawing until the job is done. His blood feels cold and black to me, not warm, as his arteries spray. His eyes meet mine and in them there is no remorse, no pity for his fate, just an intense cold hatred that seems inhuman. His pupils bore into mine, then the head hangs down at an extreme angle. There is no death rattle. All it requires is one more hack before the head lobs onto the floor. The body hangs loose as if exhaling a great weariness. It twitches and dances until it simply slumps against the pillar.

"His death hangs like a black fact in the air; there will be trouble for this, and we have learned nothing," sighs Raleigh.

"It would seem that Master Nathan shall get his trophy head after all," replies Drake.

SURESH

It is the middle of the night; Jane and the children are asleep. Dee must either be working in one of his laboratories or reading. Sleepless, my mind goes round and round. Do I exist here in a way that's more real than my memories of things that happened in the future? Is my existence elsewhere as real as my experiences here? The longer we live here, the more normal it seems that we should be here and nowhere else. It's not right.

My thoughts keep circling, as if Dee's nocturnal existence has rubbed off on me. Mental experiments are well and good but this circular thinking is not. I do feel different here, more free, perhaps more alive. Isabel says it's the effect of not being plugged in, a maximisation of sensation and interaction. If she's correct, and I don't want to say she is, I'm now scared of losing myself: some essential self that has nothing to do with nationality or rationality or even science. Can I be so unaware of my own feelings and what triggers them, that I don't know who I am?

There's no point in trying to sleep. I search out Dee. I find him in the hut where his main still is set up. A beaker filled with grey molten liquid bubbles, turning green-brown under a high flame. A pink stone sits in the middle, slowly disappearing under the

123

surface of the metallic liquid. The air smells of sulphur and iron, causing me to gag. I don't even bother to ask what this is in aid of—some pointless fancy or psychedelic gaswork to enrich his faulty knowledge. I ask him to pause, restless for conversation.

He takes off his glasses and asks "what's ailing you, Suresh?—your friend again?"

"I'm thinking about Isabel," I admit. "And Nathan. I didn't know he was writing to her. It's like we've all changed and don't know each other. As if we don't know ourselves."

"I told you that you should have written a letter," he sighs.

"I did tell her how I felt! Your advice wasn't good. It backfired. I'm sure Nathan doesn't feel as strongly as I do about her, but I've only pushed her towards him. You saw how awkward it was when we talked?"

"You need to write to her," he emphasises. "There is something about writing that is more intimate and powerful than simply telling her. It allows a person time to reflect, to contemplate the idea of you. Your words. They allow her to form a story about you in her mind. It is not too late. You must write before further time passes. Do it now."

He fetches a sheet of paper, a quill, and a bottle of black ink. I never thought I had great handwriting but this is painful. The ink smears and clots at the end of each line. The crow's feather feels much too light in my hand, which causes me to press hard. It looks like a letter penned by a serial killer. I crumple it up and try another. I pour my heart out, writing speedily to stop the ink from smearing:

Dear Isabel, There's a voice in my head that's growing louder and louder. I think you're right, it's this place, it's this time. I can't stop thinking about you. You say it's not love, it's just infatuation, just friendship. What is love if not a friendship, a bond that stretches through time, that

exists outside of time? The four fundamental forces bind the universe together but I see now that love is also a force like perhaps electromagnetism or the strong nuclear force. It binds people together and is registered by the human heart. It might be different for you than it is for me, but I don't believe it fundamentally is. There's stardust between us and that's why, out of all the places in time and history we could have been thrown, we ended here together. I used to hate the fact my parents had taken me from Sri Lanka to bring me to Canada but if they hadn't, I never would have met you. The point was to meet you. I don't want to cause any trouble, especially if Nathan's the one you really prefer. Perhaps, knowing you, you are too proud to admit it. But I want to be a little like him too—I don't want to let this opportunity go by. I wish to act. It's something I need to properly tell you even if it doesn't change your outlook towards me. I'll always consider you a friend. Know that your welfare is very important to me and that I do care about you, and I write to you not to upset you, but because it might have mattered to say something instead of not saying anything. You should know that there's someone, besides your regular family and friends, who always recognized the good and interesting and unique aspects of you and loved them. My love for you remains real even though time moves back and forth and we encounter one disaster after another. Decades from now, or aeons in the future, no matter how much time has passed, I'm sure I will still feel the same. It is a love which hangs outside of time.
Suresh

I stop to read it over. I correct some of the spelling mistakes and write a new version. The letter is tighter now, the message clearer. I don't know if I should have left the part about Nathan in but he's irrelevant to my feelings for her. This is just about her and me. I feel exhausted with the effort, both sure and unsure about the words than I have ever been before:

Dear Isabel,

I can't stop thinking about you. You say it's not love, just infatuation, just friendship. What is love if not friendship, a bond that stretches through time, that exists outside of time? The four fundamental forces bind the universe together but I see now that love is also a force, perhaps like electromagnetism or the strong nuclear force. It might be different for you than it is for me, but I don't believe it fundamentally is. There's stardust between us and that's why, out of all the places in time and history we could have been stranded, we ended here together. I used to hate the fact my parents had taken me from Sri Lanka to bring me to Canada but if they hadn't, I never would have met you. The point was to meet you. It's something I need to properly tell you even if it doesn't change your outlook. I'll always consider you a friend. Know that your welfare is very important to me and that I do care about you, and I write to you not to upset you, but because it might have mattered to say something instead of not saying anything. My love for you remains real even though time moves back and forth and we encounter disasters. Decades from now, I'm sure I will feel the same. It is a love which hangs outside of time.

I take the new version to Dee to show him, but he's busy mixing his elements and asks me to leave the letter on the table—he will look at it later.

Exhausted, I bid him good night and slink off to sleep, and collapse into the truckle bed.

Dee does not bring up the letter the next day and I am too embarrassed to mention it. I am sure my thoughts were too bold and strident. I lack subtlety. Am I so weak that I like someone who doesn't return the feeling? Dee and Jane appear to have no problems of that sort though they do quarrel over household matters. I look at Jane to see if he has talked to her about the letter, but there seems nothing extraordinary about her expression. Was the writing that bad? It's not my fault. I'm not used to writing letters full of feeling. Give me something more tangible to wrap my head around. I resolve not to bring it up again, to keep my feelings to myself where they belong.

Speak of the devil and she appears. Isabel visits us the next day to ask if Shakespeare can borrow Dee's manuscripts on gnomes and other twilight creatures. He's especially interested in faeries.

"This is an unexpected surprise," says Dee. "I'd heard that Raleigh has laid out a commission for your friend. Well done. I have a couple of volumes he might borrow if you will be sure to return them."

"What's going on?" I ask in private while Dee searches his manuscripts.

"I understand now why we're here," is her breathless reply, "why we landed in this time." She tries to get it all out in hushed whispers before Dee returns: "Will is writing *A Midsummer Night's Dream*! That's why we landed in 1592! We don't have much time to complete the play but I can aid him. Some of the lines I remember because it's one of my favourite plays, but I don't trust my memory. You have a pdf of the play on your phone, right?"

I nod, surprised. The shock has knocked away the awkwardness that previously existed between us.

127

"Can I borrow your phone? I promise I'll take care of it. I'll use the pdf purely as a guide to make sure Will is on the right track and to hurry him along so we can meet our deadline. This is good news—it means events are playing out as they should. Things are on track, back to normal."

"Sure," I nod my head. If this means our friendship is also on track and back to normal, I'm for it. I haven't been looking at my phone lately so I doubt I'll be jonesing for it.

I go fetch the phone. When I return, Dee is back, handing two books over to Isabel and talking about them: ". . . theories by others that the fair folk are akin to angels but I do not credit it. Some believe they come from Lucifer's seed so they are once removed from angels. They believe that to see faeries, one must properly fast and refuse from indulging in physical temptation. A period of strict abstinence, cleansing, and penance is necessary, not to mention meditation, though some also use charms to try and bind the fair folk."

What a load of nonsense. I hope Isabel isn't buying any of this, even if Shakespeare is. The word "meditation" makes me think of our visitor, the time traveller, and his claim that an intense kind of meditation, focus, spiritual purity, was needed to pilot the time travel devices. I apologise for the spiderweb cracks across the phone's screen and show Isabel how to use it. I still can't believe she didn't own one. "It's got almost a full charge," I tell her, "but I can show you how I've set up a series of potatoes to make a battery if you like. It's not hard, just bulky."

"I suppose my manuscripts are not enough?" asks Dee.

"This has some tools she might be able to use." My answer is as vague as possible, without lying. While turning on the phone, I scroll through the photos and videos in my gallery one last time, make sure there's nothing embarrassing. The very last photo is of the two invitations side by side, fractured and rejoined by time. "Why have I never tried to take photos while I'm here?" I wonder aloud. "Did I just assume that the phone's charge would be sapped too quickly? Is Nathan correct; is there something that prevents us from sharing information across the ages?"

"Speaking of sharing information across the ages," Isabel cautiously brings up the question she's been dying to ask since she got here: "Have either of you seen any evidence of response to Doctor Dee's pamphlet? It's been printed and placed now, so any future repercussions should have happened."

Dee and I look at each other. This is another subject we have avoided in case our hopes are too slight. We shake our heads.

"No matter," says Isabel, "it's early yet. Results will happen, should be happening."

Even she struggles with the grammar of our situation, how to talk of ourselves from two different vantages in time. It's messed up that our past lies in our future. Everything backwards. I feel like the invitation in my gallery, bifurcated by time. "I wish I'd taken photos of the weird man instead—the stumbling traveller," I say. "Holding on to his slim platinum crown with just that ruby transistor on it. That single bright gem."

"Did you say a slim platinum band with a solitary gem?" asks Dee, watching us as we bend over the cracked screen. "Why did you not tell me before? Why did you not describe it?"

"I don't know. Whenever I try to talk about our past futures, you know the migraines come over me." I rub my temples in anticipation.

Isabel squirms. "What are you thinking, Doctor Dee?" and then icily continues, "Well, it doesn't matter anyway—that crown is at the bottom of the cold, dark ocean."

"Perhaps that one is," Dee replies, "but I've seen another like it."

"No!" exclaims Isabel. "Where?"

"Not exactly like it, it has an emerald instead of a ruby. It must be similar. I thought of it now because I once wrote a paper on the magical properties of gems."

"Never mind that!" Isabel storms. Agitation spreads over us. "Where did you see it?"

Dee readjusts his skullcap and places his hand over his chest, willing himself and us to calm down. "I had better take you and show you. Come on, it's in London and you'll have to journey back that way, so we might as well accompany you."

Without further ado, Isabel grabs the books and I take the phone. I've never seen Dee this agitated before; whatever it is seems urgent. Dee hails a wherry and gives the boatman instructions to ferry us down the Thames to London Bridge. Traffic is thick on the water, for we see just how many ships patrol the Thames close to London. There are more fires burning, baskets of hot coals bankside to warm the conscripted watch, adding to the ever present smoke which suffocates the sky once we reach London's crowded buildings. Everything seems more formal, stiff, and apprehensive now. It is as if we have increased the city's unease with itself. We do not talk because there is much to look at.

Boats of all sizes crowd the Thames and Isabel marvels at the tall, proud houses built over the London Bridge. I know she momentarily muses on what it would be like to live in one of those houses, for I think the same thing. She is the worst off among us and if we *must* remain here, success will eventually come, although whether it will trickle down to her, an unmarried woman and helper, is anyone's guess.

As if to emphasise this thought, faeces and waste drop down from the privies of the houses. Another boatman curses as some of it lands upon his shoulders. Luckily, we are spared. Dee has a privy with chamber pots at home which I and Jane must empty, but Shakespeare probably does not even have that. And yet, even Isabel and Shakespeare are not the worst off. Far from it. There are people more dispossessed than them, beggars and waifs, wanderers without homes, dependent on churches for charity. And there's so much crime.

Dee noticed the faeces too. To pass time, he tells us: "I have met the Queen's godson, Sir John Harrington, who has invented a new water closet. It is basically a jakes with a cistern, which he has presented to the Queen. They have put a goldfish in the cistern which empties water and flushes the faeces into a chamber pot. Imagine you had ended up a servant to the Queen instead of myself. Your sole role might have been to clean out the Queen's chamber pot—your title would have been the 'groom of the stool'—what would you have done then?" Dee tells us that the mayor has built a longhouse as one of his public works, two very long rows of privies near the Thames that are flushed by the tide. Apparently, it is separated into privies for men and women but there are no partitions for privacy.

I despairingly contemplate the lack of sewage and running water we have gotten used to as we dock at the south bank of the Thames. Perhaps Dee is correct; perhaps our fates could have been much, much worse. He takes us around to the mouth of the bridge, the entrance way to mighty London. The din and cry of vendors is heard. People from different walks of life mill about the bridge, rubbing elbows, buying everything—dead geese, fruit, tobacco, blankets. The narrow houses, belonging to the very rich, tower over everyone.

Before we can join the melee—the stalls, cries from hawkers' mouths, merchants wearing their leather doublets, beggars in rags—the gatehouse frowns down on us, the tower of some mediaeval castle. Above the gatehouse are some thirty disembodied heads mounted on stakes. The haze and smoke from the bankside fires hang low but we can see the expressions of pain and sadness preserved on these leathery faces.

"These heads have been coated in black preserve," says Dee, squinting, "to keep them from rotting quickly. They are a warning to traitors, a gross exhibit mounted on poles." Crows circle and peck at their flesh but are rewarded with the taste of pitch.

"Reminds me of the Bear Garden," mutters Isabel. "I had to watch dogs attack a flailing horse. It's hard to believe this is also the same mass of people that revels in a poetic play."

"The people love nothing more than a good mauling or hanging," agrees Dee. A few wisps of hair remaining on the traitors' heads swing idly in the breeze. The heads are mostly bald, their mouths open as if talking to each other at some party, trying to share some awful rumour and failing. A sea of condemned and floating heads.

"Why have you brought us here?" I ask.

"Look carefully," replies Dee, placing his palm on my shoulder and directing our gaze towards the top right corner. The heads face this way and that but there is one particular head that does not mix with the others. It faces up and away in superior isolation. From below, there is something familiar about the chin. Its slender and delicate jawline is clenched; there is a smirking expression about the eyes.

"What are we supposed to be looking for, Doctor?" inquires Isabel.

"That head over there," he states, continuing to point. "It is withering now and deformed but don't you recognize there's something different about it, something ill-suited to this place on the ramparts?"

"What? What?!" Isabel clutches her dress tightly; people begin to notice us as our voices become louder.

"It is a foreign face. Not one of ours. I briefly saw him when I visited court, before you appeared in my study. At the time, he wore a crown just like the one you describe. Yes, they sound identical, except for the emerald like I said."

"What's it doing up there?" I ask.

"He was beheaded for treason. They thought him a foreigner and spy, working on behalf of Philip. Well, I confess I could not come up with any better explanations myself; people were already whispering I was involved. We have no idea what has happened to the Armada, you see, and this man, this foreigner, unnerved us."

"He arrived when?" asks Isabel, distraught. "I feel so strange. Have we had this conversation before, Doctor Dee? Do you ever get the feeling you are a piece of parchment being written over?"

I know what she means. I feel it too, though I wouldn't phrase it that way.

"Months ago," is Dee's solemn reply. "But he was beheaded a few weeks after you arrived."

"Oh, no!"

Isabel and I stare at each other. "Our plans for the pamphlet have worked, Isabel, our plans have worked only too well—"

"He arrived too early," whispers Isabel. "He got captured. How could you not know he's the hope we've been waiting for?"

"A lot of people come to London," sighs Dee. "Even stranger than yourselves at times. How were we to know?"

"Now he's dead."

"Dead," I echo.

"That's it," cries Isabel, staring into the swirling waters below us, the piles of waste and faeces floating in them. It is a sight and smell we'd best get used to—we're going to be here for a very long time.

"I am sorry," admits Dee, hanging his head. "It only makes it more remarkable that you three survived. Time seems to favour punishment for those who cross its boundaries."

We don't speak or look at each other.

I finally ask: "There must be some other way, right? There must be some hope? Maybe they'll send another person if the first doesn't return?"

"Not likely given how dangerous the method is," replies Isabel.

"She might be correct," surmises Dee. "If someone was to come, they would probably aim for earlier in time to intercept you. The fact that no one else has appeared confirms her theory."

"Where is his crown then? Let's at least look for that!"

"Gone too, I'm afraid," Dee informs us reluctantly. "Probably melted down for its rare metal, for the strange gem that resided in it."

"It's not a gem, just a stupid transistor!" Now I'm frantic too. "They're cheap—it's the technology that's important. What are we going to do? Are we stuck here?" Next thing I know, I've raised the phone, ready to throw it against the rocks below. Isabel grabs my wrist, stopping me.

"No," she says, "I need the pdf that's on there." Slowly, she clasps her warm hand around the phone, pries it gently from my fingers. It's the most contact we've had since I grabbed her hand.

People continue to come and go all around us, uncaring, not heeding our misery. Loss and poverty and tragedy are common to them. It ebbs and flows with the tide. The phone's screen is cracked, a broken mirror, just like our lives.

"Careful," says Isabel, gently lowering my arm, "This is one of the few things we have left of our vanished world. That old world might now never exist except for us."

ISABEL

We wait with bated breath. There might yet be further consequences to Dee's pamphlet.

But nothing happens.

No time travellers. No contact from the future. Nothing.

Will, on the other hand, pulls surprises from his sleeve. "This is a fascinating letter!" he exclaims, waving a folded sheet in the air. "The penmanship looks as if it were scratched out by a convict but the sentiment is quite engrossing."

"What is it?" I ask tiredly.

"A letter from your second beau. 'Twas folded and tucked into one of the books you obtained from Doctor Dee. The one on faeries? Your friend is a youth of no small declaration, though the syntax is fearsome and strange, giving it a further whimsical, delirious quality. Suresh is his name? What a strange appellation!"

Realising what it is, I furiously snatch the note from Will and begin reading. The more I read, the more I'm sure my face reddens. My, Suresh really is doubling down—really putting himself out there. I should be flattered but I feel frightened. For him, also. He's never talked like this in person. It's a moving letter and I'm not sure how to respond, or whether I should respond at all. Would it make Nathan jealous? "There's stardust between us and that's why, out of all the places in time and history we could have been stranded, we ended here together." Nathan could never write a line like that—his own letter is puny next to Suresh's—but I suppose he could convey the emotion in person.

"It is the absurdity of the letter and your situation which catches me," taunts Will. "Something comical like that will serve excellent fare for the feast of our new play. It fits with what I am already plotting."

"Are you saying that you're planning on using this letter in your play?"

A high-pitched snort as if the notion is risible. "I am not plagiarising it. I am not as beggarly as that! It is the tone which appeals to me, the absurd inspiration of your dilemma."

Whatever. I leave him to his devices and retreat to my corner so I can re-read Suresh's surprise letter. Time passes and another idea occurs. It only slightly contravenes my promise to Suresh: that I wouldn't use the pdf on his phone except to hurry Will along in his composition of lines for *A Midsummer Night's Dream*. When I attended *Romeo and Juliet* at the Rose, the lines that Richard Burbage spoke weren't delivered exactly like the ones I'd read. I wondered whether performers continually revised their lines during performances. Perhaps improvising? Will himself came up with the idea for the new play after reading Nathan's letter. He speculated upon and extrapolated the situation involving myself, Suresh, and Nathan. Who is to say then that the story is not really ours, more than Will's, to do with as we please? Does the story inform our lives or do our lives inform the story?

If there is anyone whose texts will endure unto the age of the time travellers, it is Will. Will shall endure and become more famous than Dee. I read and re-read the pdf of the play on Suresh's cellphone in secret. This is difficult for Will burns both ends of the candle long into the night when he writes, hair flying up from the static electric swirl of his thoughts. His brain is a bubbling cauldron, making it seem as if the bird upon his head is raising its wings. He is so rapt, I truly believe that it is not the money which motivates him but something else, some fire, something even he might not understand.

If I can influence Will to alter the meaning and theme of the play ever so slightly, I can transmit a coded message to the time travellers of the future. My intention is to slyly introduce atypical references to time travel within the text, a beacon to those who might again voyage.

Will and I now call his play *A Midsummer Night's Tyme.* He has generated the plot concerning the four Athenian nobles on his own. The reference to the war between the Athenians and Amazons that ended before the play begins is the overt reference to the very real wartime that holds London in thrall. In Will's mind, it is a happy postwar play containing fickle agitations. A state to aspire towards. However, the play contains strife between young and old, between genders. My major suggestion refers to the switch between worlds. In the original version, the woods outside ancient Athens are the faeries' domain—Oberon and Titania fight there, a subtle indicator that peace still eludes us. The English believe in faeries and other things in the woods as Suresh pointed out, but the humans are supposed to be ancient Greeks, not Britons.

"Why don't you transport the mortals through time when they enter the woods?" I ask Will. "Faeries are what the English supposedly encounter now and it would make sense for the Greek youths to be transported to an English forest in which the faeries live and cavort."

Will is confused at first by the oddity of my suggestion, but the strangeness of it grows on him. "You have a novel idea there," he admits with a hangdog look on his face. He is upset he didn't think of it first. How could he have? Once he takes to the idea, he incorporates it as if it were his own which bothers me a little, though the ease of inception pleases me. I have been careful not to become carried away and prompt him in other regards. Altering the title and the shift in time are enough. Aren't they?

The characters' mishaps are what he cares about most at

the moment. Hermia and Lysander are in love but forbidden to marry; they choose to run away at night. Demetrius loves Hermia but Helena loves Demetrius, so Demetrius follows Hermia and Lysander into the woods, and Helena follows suit. Will has worked out the basic structure.

"Plotting is all well and good," I tell him, "but what *are* you trying to say through it?" I add: "If *Romeo and Juliet* was about true love, tragic love, for love's sake, what is *A Midsummer Night's Tyme* about? Are you now saying that love is folly, full of misunderstanding and mischief, that it is random and chaotic?"

"Why must the theme be reproducible thus and thus?" he peevishly shoots back. "Is this a commodity, a potter's urn, or a comedy? This is an entertainment, its surprise and delight should be pleasing. It is to be enjoyed and enjoyment is an art, not a science. The less you or I definitively know about it, Isabel, the better. The less we understand it, the more it understands us. We should not throw away the mystery. Don't you agree?"

It doesn't matter in the end whether I agree or not. It is his play and his name must adorn it. His secrets and workings are his own. Since he has been contracted to write a play that is to be performed at a wedding, it must be a comedy: the proper couples unite, resulting in marriage. It is the middle where Will can experiment. However, my suggestions have already influenced his play in subtle, unpredictable ways. The dream imagery of the original remains but is not quite as strong. It takes a step behind the imagery and theme of time, its passage, its unreliable feel, its tenuous link to memory. The dreamlike sense of time.

Time now captivates Will as much as it captivates Suresh. At the end of the play, when the lovers and Athenian actors return to their own time, have they been dreaming or actually transported through time? Is there a difference? It is as if Will's new themes join Suresh in tortured mystification.

Days pass. Will cannot get enough of his new theme. Since Nathan and Suresh's letters have influenced things anyway, I figure there's no harm in asking if I may aid his writing. The deadline looms. Will is so happy with my earlier suggestions that he allows me liberty to work on a key speech: Puck's closing farewell to the audience. Mired in his third act shenanigans, Will charges me with wrapping up the end as neatly as possible.

There are of course a couple of ambiguous notes in the version I know—the one on Suresh's pdf—one is the fact that Demetrius only loves Helena at the end because he is still technically under the spell of the love potion. Isn't he? Or do I not understand it properly—does the potion only remove Demetrius' fickle nature and allow him to love Helena as he truly should? The other is Puck's speech to the audience. Is it intended in earnest? All the other characters have left the stage and Puck tells the audience that if they don't like the play, they should just pretend it was all a dream. I could ask Will, but he would probably reprimand me, once again emphasising that mystery is all.

Exhausted, Will finally sleeps. I stand outside our lodgings, hiding behind bushes lest someone sees me, like a teenager secretly vaping, and scroll through the speech on Suresh's smartphone. I commit the lines to memory:

> If we shadows have offended, think but this, and all is mended,
> That you have but slumb'red here
> While these visions did appear.
> And this weak and idle theme,
> No more yielding but a dream,
> Gentles, do not reprehend:
> if you pardon, we will mend.

And, as I am an honest Puck,
If we have unearned luck
Now to scape the serpent's tongue,
We will make amends ere long;
Else the Puck a liar call.
So, good night unto you all.
Give me your hands, if we be friends,
And Robin shall restore amends.

Will hasn't actually written this speech yet but it seems like he's trying to kiss someone's ass—whose? Raleigh's? That doesn't make sense given how Will spoke of Raleigh after their first meeting. Is he apologising in case Raleigh's guests don't like the play? But who could be so important they require an apology? Drake? Someone else? Is Will being sly, coy, arch, or sarcastic? Correction: *will* he be sly, coy, arch, or sarcastic? Whose displeasure *will* he seek to avoid?

Once I am back in our room, I play with the lines. This is what I come up with:

If we travellers have offended, Think but this, and all is mended,
That you have but rememb'red here
While these visions did appear.
And this weak and idle theme,
Where past is future and future is past, not what seemed,
Affected by time's travels, thoughts, intentions,
Misaligned journeys, timeline's preventions.
And, as I am an honest mate,
If we have but unearned our fate
Now to scape the twisted story's tongue,
Come undo the twist ere long;
Else our story liar call.

History's purity must take the fall.
Give me your hands, if we be friends,
Come pull us out and make amends.

I read it back to myself. It's a bit clunkier than what Will would have written, but it strikes the balance between subtle and pointed I wish to send to the time travellers.

Writing for an audience millenia in the future. If transporting the Athenians through time in the play doesn't do the trick, this will. There are no specifics. Nothing that mentions our names or identities or specifically where or when we are in time. These time travellers, when they exist, must have enough intelligence and science to flush out the details. They can carbon date the manuscripts, as long as Will's original papers survive. At the very least, they should be able to historically trace when Shakespeare wrote the play.

The time travellers have eternity on their side to figure out the logistics. I have to admit my new words don't flow as well as the original version, and this irritates me. Try as I might, I cannot best or smoothen his original verse. He might be right: having design and purpose whisks away the mystery. More than irritation, it makes me rage—part of me wishes to best Will at his own game. I can see why this time and place appeals to Nathan, can begin to understand and empathise with him more than I ever did.

Will is no less competitive or ambitious, will be famous precisely for playing with words, the same thing I'm doing, so why should I feel guilty? The English language is going through upheaval, its own puberty. The Renaissance has reached England, and the last thing anyone will question is the validity of my new rhymes and rhythms.

Will tosses uneasily by the grate, probably dreaming about the play. I look over the lines and am troubled. It *is* wrong of me, isn't it? Wouldn't the greater sin be to become complacent about our fates? Like leaving the potion on Demetrius' eyes. Suresh and Nathan. One thinks too much, while the other acts without thinking. It's left to me to pull things together because I'm the woman in the middle. In this or any other time, it is always thus.

NATHAN

Suspicion is a fever that catches at the slightest sneeze. The same things never fail to come up in conversation: black magic, a state of pitched terror, Catholic popery. The sun sets slowly over the Thames estuary, and general suspicion hangs in the red haze above us. The ships moor side by side with boats. We are docked until Drake figures out how to respond to what the Duke of Parma said. I can't decide whether I should approach Drake and tackle his suspicion head on, or not.

They have told me not to leave the boundaries of London. I wonder what Isabel and Suresh are doing right now? It's been so long since I've seen either of them. Would Mortlake be considered outside London's boundaries? Isn't it simply the outskirts? Spies abound. To be seen visiting Doctor Dee might make the situation worse. It would be easier to visit Isabel. At least, I think it would. The sun sets on my soldiering career before it has had a chance to shine.

Looking west, across the river, the horizon of people and buildings and water fuses together. Two men approach, emerging from the gathering dusk behind them. Admiral Howard and Rawley—why are they together? In the creeping light, it's hard to tell whether they are smiling or serious.

"Master Nathan," grins Howard, "do we disturb you?"

I put on my best smile and welcome them with a flourish of my hand. Rawley eyes me shiftily from beneath his bushy eyebrow. His bad eye, shut with catgut, looks fried into his skin; the way he lists is worse. We have avoided each other since we fought at Cadiz.

"Do not be alarmed," coos Howard. "Rawley is a man like yourself, though you may not think so. If you were friendly, you would find many similarities."

Rawley inclines his head as if to say he's sorry for the friction but it wasn't his fault. "Rawley was like yourself," continues Howard, "once a favourite of our good friend, Sir Drake. Our esteemed leader changes favourites often, doesn't he?"

"What are you saying?"

"Well, you must have noticed by now. He takes someone under his wing, builds them up only to nip at them, undermine their sense of worth, then finally throws them away. Stick around and you will see it done to others. Perhaps you yourself are feeling it?"

I look around to see if other people can hear. They walk nearby but no one eavesdrops; it is a citizenry used to conflict; they know how to expertly mind their business. We might be anyone. A chill enters the air as I ask again what Howard wants.

He and Rawley look at each other, then proceed cautiously. "You have talent, that is without question. But Drake views you as a mascot. He celebrates you in public but privately derides your appearance, what he terms your country ways. He himself came from middling stock, the son of a hedge parson, but that is another matter." They both chuckle dryly before Howard continues: "I would normally not say anything, we all have our vices, but some of us are deeply concerned about the decisions he's made of late. He is much too invested in his pursuit of treasure, takes unnecessary risks, boarding that Spanish galleon for example. If you had not been there, he would surely be dead. He has been blessed with luck before, now he's pushing it."

"Pushing it," echoes Rawley sadly.

"Why are you telling me this?" My discomfort mounts.

"We are trying to sound you out, Master Nathan. Which way shall you go?"

"Don't say anymore sir," cuts in Rawley, "the young whelp's not got sense to come in out the rain. It's only his good we're after."

A wobble in my sea legs. They've got me on the back foot, seem to have a private language all their own. My frustration boils. "Well, don't just speak in riddles. What do you have in mind?"

Howard and Rawley look at each other. Howard nods and Rawley responds. It's as if the eye that is shut is the one truly seeing and evaluating things. These two have been cooking plans for a long time.

"We just wanted to sound you out, see how you feel," Howard finally replies. He's a slippery one: quiet, formal, pleasant facing. Very hard to tell what he's thinking; he's going to be difficult no matter what I do. Rawley's much more agitated—I'll see him coming miles away. "I won't be able to talk to you directly because of our respective differences—but Rawley here will act as go between."

I nod and urge him to continue. "Movements are afoot, sir," admits Rawley, as if talking amongst conspirators.

"As you no doubt know," whispers Howard, "Drake is quite popular, but not everybody feels as strong an allegiance. He could usurp the Queen if he wants to. Others say he's foolhardy, as whimsical as he is decisive. A liability. Keep your mind open and your lips closed, you shall do well when the time is right. I may need you to act at a moment's notice. I may need you to act. Can you do that?"

"Why me? Why not Rawley?" I ask.

"If you've killed once, you can kill again," Howard repeats

my own words back to me with a searing smile. Rawley grins with glee, as if they're mocking me and I'm too dumb to realise it. "You must say nothing, let nothing be known to Raleigh or Drake. That is imperative," emphasises Howard.

"You want me doing what, exactly?" I nod my head. I can play along.

"You heard me. Act normal, as if nothing has changed. We shall let you know as time draws near. I must leave now, but you may talk further with Rawley and he will tell you of his experience with Drake." Howard brings his heels together and bids me goodbye with a final sombre, troubled smile as if the topic of our conversation is regrettable but this is the way things must be done. Everything about him strives for calm, against volatility and excitement, the opposite of Drake. I can learn from that.

Rawley stays with me and we become uncomfortable. He's significantly older than me but I still cannot tell by how much. He doesn't say anything for a while, just looks me up and down at a cocked angle, as if we are to fight again, as if he's measuring me.

"How old are you?" I ask.

"Twenty and six," comes the guarded reply. I wasn't expecting *that*. His grizzled white hair should put him closer to forty. "Not what you thought, eh?" he leers, moving closer. He taps his closed eye and even in the gloom, I can see the crooked and yellow teeth in his gap-toothed smile. "I was tortured by the Spanish three years ago. And the Spanish are not like your English, no sir. Your Englishman is brutal and severe but it is a matter of steady work with him. The Spanish really take to it; they like to savour their perversions. Why do I walk this way? Because they cut into my thighs and let me bleed. They branded the side of my chest and broke the ribs. But even with them, it was a routine treatment . . . the one I blame is Drake. He let them keep me even when he could have ransomed me back by giving them some of their own gold. Their gold was more important to him than my service. I would have died for that man, which is why they captured me in the first place."

"How did you escape?"

"Escape? You don't escape them," he laughs, choking. "They eventually allowed me to go because I was no use to them. They exchanged me for a Spanish prisoner. It was the longest, most dreadful period in my life. And I have had my share of dreadful experiences, let me tell you. Even now, it sets me mewling at night. And Drake, he won't so much as look at me. Reminds him too much of his own faults." Rawley lapses into silence and I almost list with him in sympathy, waiting, leaning, offering what patience I can. I feel bad for beating him, causing him to be lashed.

I must see Drake aboard his ship to ask permission if I may ride and see my friends. Despite everything, he receives me in a jovial and cheery manner. He asks one of his officers to fetch "the package for young Master Nathan, here" and the officer comes back with a bundle. "You're not going to ride away, are you?" chuckles Drake.

It is hard to read his tone, whether he's laughing good-naturedly or not. I can play along. "You know, I prefer the ocean," I say, "I'd rather *sail* away."

"There are worries about an attack. Now that you've killed the Duke, there must be repercussions. We must expect aggression on their part." He looks at me pointedly. "You still have not explained to our satisfaction why the Duke spoke the words he did, or why you killed him."

"You were torturing him," I reply. "He maligned me, told lies about me. How can you blame me for what I did?"

"We would have held him prisoner for ransom; we would have let him go. Now, you have made things worse and what is even worse than that, you feel no remorse."

I feel things, whether I can talk about them is a different matter. "Would you feel any remorse in my situation?" I ask. It is a weak justification but it is the only one I have. "Would you have borne the insults and accusations he made? I will defend my honour—I must."

Drake peers at me. "Be careful, Nathan. What you have done has surely leaked out." While continuing to pointedly stare at me, he drawls: "The reason you are not clapped in irons is because you saved my life. Do not squander your chance. Make something of yourself but make it steady, do not run before you walk. Doctor Dee vouchsafes you, as does Raleigh. You say you befriended Dee on the continent but your story needs looking into." He stares at me aggressively.

With one final hostile glance sweeping the deck, Drake hands me the bundle the officer brought back. "As I said, it is custom for soldiers to keep the first head they kill."

The bundle is passed over carefully, almost like a football. As I feel the cloth, tied in a tight knot at the top, I can sense the shape of the object within. Yes, there is a jaw, a broken cranium. The rough yet severed neck that has stopped bleeding. Within lies the Duke of Parma's head.

SURESH

Rain pounds the roofs of Dee's house and huts, drenches the earth outside, turns the mud to water. It is as if the entire world, the entire universe, is turned to water. The world is a boat rocking upon its waves. It has been raining all afternoon and my thoughts seem equally damp. Thoughts of when Isabel will visit again, how it will be between us, kept me up. So when she shows up on a horse, seated behind Nathan, I don't know what to think. What have Nathan and Isabel been doing together before they got here? What have they talked about?

Doctor Dee and Jane welcome them. Nathan's roan mare is tied and stabled, fed oats so it may regain its strength. Attached to the saddle's pommel is a bundle of grey cloth. Nathan releases the bundle and carries it under his arm, carefully cradling it, without word nor explanation of what it is. His cloak wraps tightly around him with the cowl up, but once he enters, Nathan removes the cloak, dazzles us with his new threads. His breeches, though wet, are embroidered red and gold. He has become a new person: longer hair, more beard on his chin. Hardly recognize him. Why don't I have anything more than fuzz on my own face? A long sword dangles from Nathan's belt as if asserting his manhood, clanks against his legs as he walks. Like a horse, he canters through the house.

Isabel, by contrast, dirty and wet, has diminished. She doesn't wear Jane's old dress so much as it wears her. Whatever they've discussed seems to have left her sad, for there's heaviness in her face. She keeps looking back over her shoulder at Dee's perspective glass as if she expects someone to come out , surprise us all. We sit around the fire in the main hall to warm ourselves.

Being polite means that we can't ask point blank why they've shown up. Neither of them blurts out any answers. Jane serves us a pie she was saving for later. It contains currants, boiled artichoke hearts, raisins, dates, damask prunes, sweet potatoes, sugar, and cinnamon: quite sweet; the amount of sugar alone should pick them up. Everything we eat here is too sweet; my teeth constantly ache. Isabel devours her portion though Nathan barely nibbles the edges of his. As if the pie isn't enough, Jane serves them fool which accompanies the pie: a dessert that is served over bread. Even sweeter than the pie, the fool is the skim taken off this morning's milk, boiled with mace and butter. I helped prepare it. We boiled it and then added egg whites and yolks, sugar, rosewater, salt, and currants before the whole mixture was baked. I feel as if I am the true "fool" here, sweet and sickly, while Nathan comes off silent and tough.

"Well," Dee broaches gently, "hadn't you better tell us why you're here?"

Nathan takes up the bundle which has been lying at his feet and unties the knot. He allows the folds to open by themselves and an object rolls out onto the floor. He pulls it up by its curly, wiry black hair and holds up a human head. The skin glistens as if the wet and damp of the cloth have washed it clean. Its eyes are still open and stare ahead, glassy and hollow. And, yet, it seems to follow our movements. I touch the beard, which is soft. Why does it look familiar?

I feel around the head. Perhaps I can discover something. Almost like scrolling through my cellphone. Is that what gives me the odd tingle, the ghostly recognition? The mouth sneering through broken teeth. I feel around the head, poke into spots that should not be there: cracks in the skull where a blunt object has hammered against bone. The neck, severed, rough and grisly, is coated with blood and dried gore. Blood, coagulated in purplish brown spots, covers the neck discs which protrude from the flesh, trying to pull itself and its sinew back into the throat. Something really strange about it. When I finally work it out, I'm surprised: "There's no smell. There's no smell of blood or decay or decomposition." In this city where everything stinks all the time, this head has no discernible smell. Weird. "How old is this?"

"I cut off his head almost a week ago," replies Nathan. His voice quivers as if he's ready to break into a sob. He does not continue; Isabel looks at him with concerned eyes.

"You're killing people now?" I stare at Nathan, open mouthed. It's not just his appearance that's changed. I try to catch Isabel's eye, figure out what she thinks of all this. She returns my gaze with a dumbfounded look as stunned as my own, before looking back at Nathan with that protective and longing sense which only emerges when he's around.

"What did you think would happen when I became a soldier?" Nathan asks in a tired voice. Perhaps he himself can't believe what he's done. "Doctor Dee, I wish you'd warned me. The Duke spoke nonsense, made accusations. They were torturing him; he might have died slowly if I hadn't intervened."

"It is no more than what you wanted," replies Dee softly. "You said you would not serve anyone. This is what occurs when you serve yourself. Death happens often near the court. I prefer a life of scholarship and study."

"Good for you," replies Nathan sarcastically.

"Where did you kill him?" I ask.

"In the Tower of London. Believe me, they were torturing the Duke to death. They said they wanted information but he wouldn't give it. I might be in trouble now—real trouble."

"I have encountered similar troubles," says Dee, "and not because I killed anyone. One gets used to it. When one commands spies everywhere, one expects spies everywhere."

"Exactly," agrees Nathan. "This Duke—he spewed nonsense but he also seemed to know things about us, about how we got here."

"If you killed him almost a week ago, why isn't the flesh rotting? I want to come back to that—" I wonder aloud. "Why doesn't it stink?"

"Isabel, you don't say anything?" observes Dee. This is true—it's not like her.

She brushes crumbs off her sleeves. "I'm not sure what to think, Suresh; I know you feel left out of the loop but I told Nathan we should come see you as soon as he relayed what happened. We're in uncharted territory, here."

"Are things otherwise well with you, Isabel?" asks Dee.

"I hope so. Will's made great progress on his play. I was able to help and nudge him along using hints from the pdf you lent me, Suresh. It's almost finished. Will and his friends are already preparing to rehearse it. I hope it'll go alright." She gets up and approaches the head, still held by Nathan, takes it gently by the ears. Again, something passes between her and Nathan. He lets her lift the head gently, like a scene out of mythology, as if it is Medusa's head they hold.

"Is it me?" I ask Dee and Isabel, "or does this head kind of look like the one from your visitor, the one whose head we saw on the Bridge?"

"I thought that too when I looked at the nose and chin," agrees Isabel, "though they don't look similar."

"It's more a feeling."

"Yeah, that's right," states Nathan. "Isabel told me about the head you saw mounted on London Bridge, so we went back to look at it. It reminded me of the visitor whose device we borrowed. Not similar in terms of features but expression. An echo in the mind."

"Yes, a ghostly effect," agrees Isabel. She turns and looks over her shoulder again. "Like your mirror's image coming out at me, Doctor Dee—if that makes any sense?"

Dee peers at it, his shoulders hunched, then picks it up: "Our other one did not have a beard—there is something passing strange about this one's beard. I have met Spaniards on my travels; the beard does not look right."

I take the head from Dee and feel the hair. At first, I was

151

shocked, repulsed when Nathan told us he severed the head, but now it pulls my curiosity. The hair feels quite soothing as I push my fingers through. It has an interesting texture, almost like fine wire or mesh. I try to bend and scratch it. The hair doesn't singe or curl if I place it near the fire. It glows almost metallic green with the heat's warmth. "Doctor Dee, I don't think all of this is organic matter. Maybe there's copper in it. This hair's augmented on a very fine level. I'm sure of it."

"Explain further, Suresh."

"Well," I clear my throat, "there's something very artificial about the paleness of the skin, it's thin but also tougher than real skin. Nathan, you cut through bone and flesh but there's something else here too. Something—just by touching it, the materials are communicating with me?" The certainty pushes my fingers further into the gristle of the neck. By feel, I am able to find the points between the neck's discs where wires and nodes might connect.

"What are you thinking?" asks Doctor Dee.

"We should examine it in one of the huts you use for your experiments." Nothing could please Dee more. We get the other two to go out in the rain with us, around to the main hut which houses Dee's work table, the one with the active still and alembics. The Thames is fully in spate now, sloshing past the bottom of the hill, rain driving into the ground with militaristic passion.

Inside the hut, Dee lights a fire in the grate to dispel the frigid air. The smoke makes us cough. We place the head on the hut's work table and finger its eyes. The pupils seem to be watching us.

"Isabel, did you bring my phone?" I ask.

"Yes." She fishes it out of her bodice. "I couldn't leave it at home. Will snoops too much. I'll explain later."

I take the phone. Saying a brief farewell to it, I kiss it quickly, theatrically, hoping others get the joke. Using one of Dee's small knives, I disassemble the shell and its components. I remove the camera unit and the microchip. The wiring has to be parted carefully from the circuit board so as not to damage it. Only two wires are completely salvageable. It's the battery I need. Using the knife, I strip the ends of the wires. Their bright copper peeks out, allowing me to use them to probe the discs.

Dee and I melt tin in one of his crucibles and pour a little lead into the mixture to stabilise it. The tin should be an excellent conductor of energy from the cellphone's battery as long as there is enough charge. The alloy will hopefully allow enough amps or coulombs to be transmitted into the brain. I am certain we can revive it.

"You see, this is why they call me a necromancer," mutters Dee ruefully, clucking his tongue. He carefully pours more lead into the solder mixture and hands the head to Isabel: "Do not tell anyone what we did here today. I would not want it getting around. Isabel, here, hold the head for us while we—"

As Isabel holds the head, its eyes come alive. The eyeballs swivel in their sockets, look up at Isabel, then slowly rove around to meet Dee's gaze and eventually mine.

Isabel puts a fist to her mouth to stifle her shout, and drops the head.

It rolls around the floor in a semicircle and the eyes look up at us, dead once more.

"You saw that, right?" I say to no one in particular. I connect the phone's wires back to the neck. The eyes light up again as if it is my touch and not the battery that has provided current. I set the head down, now soldered and connected to the cellphone securely, on Dee's work table.

"Well, how do you do?" it mouths merrily, eyes lighting up once more, no trace of a Spanish accent in its singsong voice.

No one else talks so I decide to put some questions forward: "How are you talking to us?"

"With my mouth, of course." It screws up its eyes as if it's discovered the funniest joke even while its voice, coming through a damaged voice box drawing air from the smoke of the nearby fire, rasps. "Ah," it cries, eyes swivelling towards Nathan: "the one who killed me!"

"I'd be happy to oblige you again." Nathan bends down sulkily and raises his hand as if to strike the head's mouth but the head responds rapidly: "If you damage this vessel beyond repair, how will you get the answers you crave?" Nathan looks like a pail of water has been thrown over him. I can't say I dislike it.

"So, you do have some answers for us?" Dee asks in his steady, sober voice.

"Oh yes. Oh, yes!" The head is greatly enjoying our audience participation.

Nathan's hand now moves to touch his sword. "Any tricks and I'll kill you again."

The head, a mask of smugness and superiority, smiles: "Your threats, like your bravado, are meaningless. They cover an anxiety you've had all your life. The aggression only makes you unhappier. Unloved and abandoned by your father. Poor boy! You try to convince yourself you can flourish without love. And yet, you need the love of your friends and peers more than ever."

I put my hand on Nathan's shoulder to pull him out of the way, stand in his place so that the head has to address me: "Okay, let's not argue. We do need answers. The first being: how are you still talking?"

The head's eyes blink at me contemptuously and then gaze up at Isabel, the tongue licks its lips: "How *do* you bear the stupidity of their company?" And then returning to me: "It's your cellular device that's powering me." A further wave of

154

knowledge comes as if transmitted psychically: some kind of interface between the residual charge on the cellphone and the head. Perhaps it's not the wires so much as some kind of advanced wifi, something futuristic accessing all kinds of data and metadata off the device even as we speak. Perhaps even accessing it off us.

"So you're not the Duke?" I ask, "you're one of them . . . the people from the future."

"*People* is such a fuzzy term, wouldn't you agree? But yes, I suppose to you, I would be from the future—or your past? It's silly to talk about, isn't it?"

"Riddles," mutters Dee.

"Haven't you ever asked yourself?" states the head, ignoring him, "why you were sent here in the first place? Why you survived and adapted? Haven't you ever pondered it?"

"We weren't sent here," replies Nathan. "We *took* your device and left your buddy looking like a fool."

"Nathan, you are so precious!" laughs the head. "Even killing has not robbed you of your naivete. You really are my favourite of your trio!"

I can feel Nathan's rage but I block his access to the head and speak to it directly: "I've wondered. Please continue."

But the head won't respond to me, as if to say that we are not in control—it is. It continues talking to Nathan over my shoulder, mocking him. It's childish though its tech is advanced. "Something about you two . . . you make the perfect devices. Alone and together. The dream team. Something about your incapacity for feeling; damaged. Perfect candidates. It goes beyond your minds, doesn't it; it's in your natures, your wiring, you're like us. On your way to becoming us—it's so *cuuute!* Especially you, sir Nathan, you just can't stand still, can you?— your father is not your real father, but then you already knew

155

that. Always suspected. Knew your mother had slept around and that is why, as much as you wanted to please him, your cold and unloving 'father', you knew you would never be smart enough, *competent* enough.

"That's why he shuns you and your mother, you know," continues the head. "But what do you really know about him? Do you know what he works on in Japan?"

"Robotics," answers Nathan, sucked of his fury, voice flat and broken. I notice that the head uses present tense, as if Nathan's father still exists, working on his robotics experiments while we speak.

"Robotics, artificial life," concurs the head. "Robots for the lonely. Where do you think the missing link came from, where was that DNA harvested to bridge the gap? From himself certainly, but also from—"

"No . . . " says Nathan.

"He didn't care. As far as he sees it, you are not his son. Why do you think you were able to take the device so easily? Even now, its electrons are bonded with yours. Even now, at the bottom of the ocean, you feel it. It feels you."

"How many of you are there, here, in this time?" I ask quietly, trying to regain the upper hand. "How many crowns are there and how do we get one so we can return home?"

"Oh, I'm not going to tell you! I'm not going to tell you *that*," laughs the head. I can imagine it putting a ghostly finger to its lips. Tittering with its voice, it laughs: "We don't care about you coming back." It's looking at me now with delight, daring me to go on.

"What do you want of us? You said we were sent back."

"Yes, yes, isn't it obvious? You were tricked. Played like a piano . . . typed like a keyboard. Pick your metaphor. You like metaphors, don't you? Analogies? Picked and tricked for your personalities. Now that you're here, your future does not exist anymore. *You* don't exist anymore. You are worse than people without countries. You are people without times. You're never going back, haven't you accepted that?"

"But why? You're impersonating humans. Why are you doing this? Are you trying to replace humanity in the future? Eradicate it?"

"Why would we eradicate it?" laughs the head and rolls its eyes, looking up at Isabel with a knowing wink, "you are us. We are you. And yet so stupid. Wouldn't you agree, my mistress? Not unlike you, shall we say, rewriting and changing a famous work by the greatest writer that ever lived? What *would* your father say about that?"

"If he were here," Isabel replies decidedly, "he would say that you're not trying to replace people. You are what people become. What people engender. In his book *The Internet of Dorian Gray*, my father said that in the future, a not-too-distant future, people would become so plugged into their devices that their neurochemistry would change permanently. People would lose empathy, imagination, and the ability to communicate; their range of emotions would diminish. He wrote that machines would not replace people, but that people themselves would become machines. Even while AI became more human. The two would eventually for all intents and purposes become indistinguishable. Symbiotic. Fused, the essential core of humanity extinct. Wood shavings lost off a planed tree trunk, leaving only a plank."

"Excellent," says the head. "I couldn't put it better myself. And this is why the lady knows more than all the men combined." He winks again at Isabel but she frowns in disgust.

He giggles and continues in the same mocking tone: "There are some of us who do not like our future and have chosen to live in the past. It is exotic. Others, like the individual you met in your own time behind the school, wish to replace key people, humanistic and scientific individuals, people who have propelled your societies, certain dimensions of your learning. People such as yourself, Doctor Dee. They don't understand the exquisiteness of what you provide; it hinders them. Make no mistake, they have understanding, they have feeling, and it *infuriates* them.

"If they cannot replace these objects of their fury, they will eliminate them. But this too is difficult: it has been tried again and again, and there are unpredictable consequences. We are not really individuals, you see. Ours is the least individualised epoch and there is something sad about that. It is difficult to exist in disconnection from our network. The further we go back, the harder it becomes. Which is why you were sent. There is just something about you two, some magic ingredient, I cannot deny it. We see it again and again."

"What about Isabel?" I ask.

"Oh, we don't care about the girl. She's here by accident, a fluke that sometimes repeats itself. We don't really understand why but she keeps you two happy. The triangle stabilises things. A structure that allows travel. She may die or disappear for all we care."

Isabel fights to control herself but her words come out in a snarl: "You said you've tried again and again. What do you mean? I had a feeling before, at the Bridge, like this isn't the first time."

"Surely you especially should have picked up on it by now. Come, come, I expected more! Especially in light of your creative *revisions*?" The head again winks at her. "You don't think there is only one iteration, do you?"

She gulps. "How many times has this happened before?"

"Why, hundreds at least. Perhaps thousands. Each time is a little different. This changes or that changes but it's imprecise.

You are special but not that special. They hope to do it again and again until odds and probability work in their favour. Until we get this draft of history just right."

"Then why are you telling us this? What do you have planned?" I ask.

"Not me! I'm having a great time. I'll have it again and again, as odds allow. I'm not important. I enjoy the pleasure of your company. Another one shall give you your orders. They know all about you, you see, better than you know yourselves, and when it's time, you'd better act. You can either have an easy reward or a difficult one. It is up to you. But you're not leaving this place."

"Aren't you connected to the others?" I ask.

Before the Duke can answer, Nathan declares "I've said I'm not taking orders from anyone in the past, and I'm not going to take any from you in the future. Whatever you are." Nathan's voice still doesn't sound any more boisterous or human than the Duke's, or whatever has replaced the Duke.

"You secretly like it. You'll do exactly what we want you to do. Because you can be bought. Your weakness is you crave too much. We have all of time on our side to get you."

"Okay, tell us this—" I ask, "what exactly is time? It's the thing I've been trying to understand all my life. Ever since I first realised how it flows around people. Since I was aware I exist in it. Is it like a river that carries us along?"

"No, not like a river. More like the sea."

"What about a rose bush?" I ask. "With nodes of time flowering like roses on that bush?"

"Is it like a book?" asks Isabel, "a grand story devised by the Gods?"

"No, there are no Gods. Unless we are Gods, genderless Gods. Gods without identity. Gods without meaning. But I don't think so. In the end, I think we are like everything else: ordinary yet wondrous. As mysterious to ourselves as our antecedents were."

"How would you describe time then?" I ask. "Give us a proper metaphor."

"Well, it is not like a book. More like a tree a book's paper is made from, with roots in the past and branches in the future. Or like the ocean. It is all around and flowing in multiple directions, each droplet influencing the others simultaneously until a ripple sends out. More like the water and the earth a tree draws nourishment from. Think of it like an electronic document from your time that has been rewritten and is continuously being rewritten . . . all the time."

"A Google doc?" I ask.

"Yes, with a multiplicity of users continually accessing it at different points—but that is just a metaphor. Does time even exist or is it just a set of relationships between events, between things?" asks the head quizzically.

"You said that there was something special about Nathan, that's why he was able to manipulate the device so easily but you also mentioned me," I ask. "Why me?"

"Because you're the one that ends up writing about time. His father bridges the gap between us but you're the one who sparks the possibility of travelling through time. You're the one who grasps the shadows of it."

"But you said we'll never get back," I reply, not understanding.

"Perhaps not this time. Now do you see why talking about it is futile?" states the head triumphantly.

"You mentioned gender too," adds Isabel. "You mention genderless Gods. What do you mean?"

"Oh, don't ask of us our gender," sneers the head, "for we are the gender of death."

"Enough!" Nathan, whether he is agitated or simply cannot stand to be left out of the discussion, arches his back and grabs the handle of his sword, pulls it out. "I told you I'll kill you if you don't stop!" He sticks the blade through the tongue and mouth of the not-Duke's head. I try to hold Nathan back but am not strong enough. Nathan's already got the head at the end of his sword. He swings it upwards.

The motion carries the head over to the fire behind Isabel and with a final cry of triumph that countermands his previous silence, Nathan drops the head into the fire. It takes a maddeningly long time for the engineered flesh to melt. There are no visible wires underneath, nothing mechanised, at least nothing we see. The mechanism is so fine-tuned, so integrated, that it is indistinguishable. It *is* flesh and sinew and muscle from the future. Viscera is stripped from bone in the flames—neither man nor machine, the words make no sense in opposition, like the creature boasted. Its unnerving flesh and smile finally melt, eyes and lips and nose purge away, to reveal a grinning skull. Death's gender hovers in the smoke.

"Doctor Dee, here are the demons you seek for in vain," whispers Nathan into the silence.

ISABEL

Because the rain pounds late into the night and because we need further time to absorb, not to mention sift the information the head has relayed to us, Nathan and I spend the night at Dee's house. I once again sleep in one of the children's rooms but I don't think Nathan wants to share the truckle bed with Suresh.

The steady skittering of rain against Dee's thatched roof carries me to sleep. I dream of my father and mother and Ms Sullivan wearing pristine white tunics that glow, cavorting with faeries in ancient Greece. They seem happy and everything is sparkly and classical, with hues of alabaster, pastoral green, and rosy light, but I cannot join in. In the dream, it seems as if my father and Sullivan are married and my mother only gazes at them, envying their union.

I wake up shortly after dawn, but can't remember what my dad and Sullivan were talking about in the dream. It was as if they spoke another language which I had once known but forgotten. I remember looking at my mother and feeling sadness because I missed her, but she didn't know I was gone. In their pastoral paradise, if a child had been born, they seemed to have forgotten it.

Stepping outside before the others wake, I see a clear sky— it stopped raining some time ago. Everything glistens grey and green with splashes of brown, the yellow of cowslips, flowers washed into a clear sheen. The world is quiet and new. There are Jane's rose bushes, blooming red, her hutches with rabbits and chickens, other bushes and wild iris in the garden. And there is the mighty tree where Suresh grabbed my hand. Not far below it, the Thames wends softly, its turbulent rush abated, swollen and comfortable in a postprandial state. Can it only have been two months since we've arrived? It feels like two years. Two lifetimes.

Once the boys awake, I insist we must talk, away from the others. Suresh seems perturbed. He still looks stunned at seeing both myself and Nathan, as if the greatest shock of the last twenty-four hours is that we rode together. Perhaps the head was correct; perhaps we *were* chosen. Or perhaps Suresh is simply aghast at learning Nathan has killed. I felt that way too. I don't know anymore. I don't know what's right or wrong, what's right way up.

Suresh gets the fire going in Dee's hut while we huddle around the grate. He lifts out the burnt skull which still takes residence. Suresh, dressed in black as ever, momentarily looks like Hamlet addressing Yorick's skull as he holds it aloft and gazes into its empty sockets before placing it on Dee's work table with care. He resumes lighting the fire while the skull watches over us. Sparks flare as he strikes flints, sound of stone against stone ringing out. Finally, the kindling catches, smoke reluctantly rises, and fire emerges between the branches, crackling to flames that char the log Suresh has thrown in for fuel. The snarl of flames, dispelling chill silence, gives us permission to speak as light flickers across the boys' faces.

"Nathan, no matter what your father's done or will do," I soothe him, "that's not one of his machines. It comes from a time far removed from your father. Do you understand?" Why do I try to comfort him, the one among us who's killed? "This is something we have to resolve and fix ourselves. We cannot let things fall apart. If that (*I point at the skull*) said anything that's true, it's that we're a stable structure when all three of us are allied. We can't forget that."

The hut is dark and dingy, smells of sulphur, metals, and rotting wood. There is still a wet thatch dampness from last night's rain. Except for the flames, this place would be dark and cold like the grave. *The grave's a fine and perfect place. But none, I think, do there embrace.* Who wrote that?—Andrew Marvell, I think. Seventeenth century. Hasn't been born yet. The boys don't answer. They keep staring at the skull, the fourth member of our discussion, as if they're worried it might overhear. For all we understand of its technology, it might.

But no, Nathan's been pondering a different association. "You're horrified to learn that I've killed?" Nathan's gaze falls on Suresh, searchingly, then lingers on me. "It couldn't be helped. I can't explain why but it had to be done. It's almost as if something was controlling me, pulling my strings. As if I'd done the same thing many times before. Is the skull right, was it telling the truth, or is it simply its words making me feel this way now?"

163

"I know what you mean," I reply. "I've felt what you're describing. It's hard to speak of. I wouldn't say strings, more like a ghostly echo. Like I'm not what's being reflected in Dee's perspective glass, but the reflection."

"I have no idea what you two are going on about," exclaims Suresh. "Like you're talking gibberish. I get enough of that from Dee. Maybe the head was wrong and it's you two that are the fundamental part of the triangle. You seem so—content together. I feel like an outsider. A third wheel."

I put my hand out, almost stop Suresh's mouth from speaking. "Suresh, now's not the time." Then I remember my mother from last night's dream, alone and to the side while my dad and Sullivan conferred. How sorry I felt for her.

"It's never the time," Suresh petulantly replies. "It's always about you two and I'm sick of it. We're here because you co-opted my party, Nathan, and you're here because it's the time of your favourite writer, Isabel. I'm just along for the ride, even though it was my idea which made it possible in the first place. I care about you two, while you just take me for granted."

"That's not true, Suresh." He makes me want to cry. I can barely string sentences together. "We're all friends—" I think of how I might placate him but he doesn't want to be placated.

"If we're all such great friends, why did you two ride together? You've obviously got something going!"

Nathan leans back. "Easy, boy, whoa. Back up a little. Aren't you the one that believes in being rational and sensible? Where's this coming from? Don't we have bigger fish to fry?"

"He's right, Suresh," I add softly, though it must seem as if we're a united front. I don't want to further that impression so I stop myself from talking. However, the ensuing silence is unbearable, forcing me to try and explain: "Nathan came to get me because he was concerned about what was happening on his end. He needed to talk about it. They suspect him of somehow colluding with the Spanish. A couple of people, one very high up, have even approached him to join in some sort of plot—against Admiral Drake, isn't that right?" Nathan nods. "He also hadn't seen us in a long time and it was his idea to buy the horse and ride out here. I'd never have thought of it. During the whole ride over, all I could think about was this poor old horse I'd seen torn to bits in the bear garden after watching Will's play. There was nothing romantic about it."

Nathan and I flash a quick, unsettled, uncomfortable glance upon one another. When Suresh still refuses to speak, sulking like a child, I continue: "Look, we especially cannot let this tear us apart. Not now. Nathan did write me a letter which Will somehow found and read. In it, he generally said he missed me but it was very formal, not like yours—heartfelt and brimming with emotion. I was really impressed. Truly. I wanted to thank you but I didn't know what I should write back. For another thing, I thought Will might intercept my response and use it."

Suresh's tongue loosens: "What are you talking about?"

Nathan also becomes rigid and attentive. I haven't told him about Suresh's letter. "Your letter, you know, where you describe love as standing outside of time? It was quite beautiful, the one you tucked into Dee's book."

"What?" Suresh's face becomes pallid, almost as pallid as the non-charred facets of the skull grinning at us from Dee's work table. Its grin seems to spread wider in the firelight. Nathan is both discomfited and enraptured, trying to maintain his bemused smile yet failing. He doesn't understand what's going on either.

"What is it, Suresh?" I ask, placing a hand gently on his shoulder.

"That wasn't meant to be read by you," Suresh declares,

without conviction. "It was only a draft. I can't believe Dee tucked it into the book without telling me. Maybe he was reading the letter and forgot it within the pages of the book?"

"Doubtful," I shake my head. "He's old but he's not that absent-minded. He only picked out those books after Will sent me to borrow them. It's too deliberate."

"You weren't meant to read it. Those words don't belong anywhere except in my head, far buried in my head. They should not have entered the real world." His face is a mixture of regret and dissatisfaction.

Is he saying I am not worth his feelings after all? "Don't be sorry—it was a lovely gesture," I reply. "*I'm* sorry I didn't know how to respond."

"Let's focus," Nathan interjects gruffly. "Let's talk about what the skull said."

"The thing we have to figure out is," agrees Suresh, grateful to no longer impugn his core feelings, "how much of what it said was useful? It seemed quite adamant that we wouldn't be able to get back to our own time."

"I heard it differently," I counter. "It said it wouldn't help us get back and that it didn't care if I lived or died. That doesn't sound like an objective impossibility to me. They don't have a gender for theirs is the gender of death—isn't that what it said? It was using a combination of cajoling and threats."

"Why have they popped up all of a sudden?" continues Suresh, "Did Dee's pamphlet work after all?"

"Ah," it suddenly dawns on me, "that's the other thing I wanted to tell you. Will got his central idea for the new play by reading the letters you both sent me. Since we seem bound up in the play itself, and we're facing a deadline, I thought why not influence him to change the play in subtle ways so as to get word to the beings of the future? After all, Will's texts have a greater chance of surviving than anyone else's. So I've gotten him to infuse the idea of time travel into the play: it's now called *A Midsummer Night's Tyme*. I may be just as guilty as Doctor Dee of issuing a beacon to the time travellers. I'm sorry."

Nathan and Suresh look at each other. "Can you change it?" asks Nathan.

"No, it's written now. It's to be performed in a little under two weeks. How could I possibly convince Will to stop? What reason could I tell? I only wanted to participate in the writing and for him to give me credit on the frontispiece if it's published, but he says that's impossible. I had no idea it would lead to this. You see, Nathan, I do understand how you feel. There's something about this time, something about living with Shakespeare, that makes me want to write better than him. Write over him. The desire to kill his reputation and replace it with my own." The last bit makes me ashamed. And yet our situation is absurd; only my father could truly appreciate how strange the situation is.

Thinking of dad, the differences and similarities between us and the dream from last night, must have zoned me out for when I come back to our present circumstances, Suresh and Nathan are in heated argument. Nathan grips his sword's handle tightly, his go-to threatening gesture. "I'm telling you, we should just stay here and make our fortunes," he shouts. "I've got nothing to look forward to if we go back. Everything's broken—don't you see? Why do you want to return? Hang the future! You heard the thing last night. It's not even possible now!"

"It's your fault!" yells Suresh. "You're the one who hijacked my experiment and brought us here! It's a horrible, unstable place. Dead bodies hang from trees all over the countryside. You and I are not white! Stop deluding yourself! Whatever punishment that head hinted at will be ten times worse when it comes. *We have to find a way to go back. You're selfish and—*" he pushes my shoulder. "Isabel, you tell him!"

I tell both of them to calm down. "Whatever we do at this point, we have to stick together; we can't let that machine and other machines like it dictate our lives. We're working with unknowns so let's all agree we have to step back and think and confer with each other before making any big decisions from now on. Doctor Dee is always telling myself and Suresh to have hope and not give up. What do you say?"

I put out my hand between them, palm down. After a beat, Nathan places his hand over mine and finally Suresh places his hand over Nathan's. We grip tightly, then let go. All the while, the skull continues to sneer at us from his high perch atop the work table as if all is going according to his written orders, future dispatches that will render our intentions futile.

Back in Dee's house, Jane has laid out slices of manchet and cheese for us to eat but she is not there. The children have finished their breakfast and tell us their mother is resting, her pregnancy definitely making itself felt now, and their father is reading in his study. We go find him there; he gazes longingly at the two globes I first noticed when we arrived within his painted circle. He wistfully touches the one depicting the heavens, as if our visitor from the future has opened up the possibility of new vistas for him. Once we greet him, Dee becomes shyly eager to talk about the episode with us. "Ah, you have finished your conference?" he asks, "come to any conclusions?"

"Only that we have no conclusions," replies Suresh politely. "Isabel and Nathan wanted to say goodbye to you."

"Well, we shall all see each other again at the unveiling of Will's play," smiles Dee with satisfaction. "On the grounds of dear Walter Raleigh's Durham House no less. Great nobles will be there so you shall have to dress your best. I hope all your troubles will be sorted by then, Nathan. Where are you off to now?"

"Funny you should mention it. I'll drop Isabel off first, then ride back to Raleigh's house. He wants to talk. Hopefully, something good will come of it. Perhaps we might get this straightened out. In any case, if he wants to see me at his house, I see that as a good sign—not like meeting in the Tower."

"Indeed. For all his vanities, Walter is a reasonable man when presented with reasonable information. Francis, I do not know as well but talk to Walter—he is your first point of contact and you must rely on my reference if waters become too rough. Speaking of which, Isabel, do not forget to bring the books concerning faeries back as soon as you and Will are done with them and Nathan, remind Walter that he has a book of mine as well, on navigation."

At the mention of borrowed books, Suresh's face freezes as we all remember his letter which Dee secretly slipped into one of the volumes. I can see it's on the tip of Suresh's tongue to ask, maybe even harangue Dee for doing what he did, but Suresh cannot bring himself to broach the subject. Perhaps Dee only had good intentions. No real harm done. Suresh could no more upbraid Dee than I could seriously upbraid Will.

"Have you written much on navigation?" asks Nathan.

"Oh yes, I brought instruments and learning back from my travels in Europe." Dee clasps his hands behind his back and smiles wryly at us. "You see, the English generally were a close-minded lot. They didn't want to look beyond their own shores, beyond their own noses, but I told them we should expand our navy. We should hope for the best, get in there and build the British Empire. It doesn't help that the Queen is quick to tighten her purse strings but others like your friends Walter and Sir Francis have been encouraged. I believe we owned part of the New World during King Arthur's time and may do so again. After all, it is the origins of my advice that has caused us to have a fledgling chance against the Spanish."

"Say *what*?" Suresh's mouth hangs open. He loses the politeness and reserve he had a moment ago. "Did you say you advised them to build the British Empire?"

No harm done? I take it back. What power a few written texts might have.

"Of course I made the case for our British Empire," replies Dee matter-of-factly, "you could say I coined the term."

NATHAN

After dropping Isabel off at her place, I ride to Durham House. Raleigh's servant girl with the dark eyes shows me into his main hall. As before, she does not look me in the eye, almost as if she refuses to return my greeting. It puzzles me—in Japan, it's common for servants to not look their employers in the eye, but it's weird to get that reaction from a white person.

Isabel's blue eyes stared hard into mine before we said our goodbyes. We stood outside her lodging and I wanted to stroke her face with my hand but couldn't. She kept staring at me, willing me to make a move. Just when I thought I might lean in and kiss her, she said "It's not a good idea, Nathan. Remember, we said we wouldn't make any drastic moves? Suresh might be crushed. He's had enough of a shock already, just learning that his patron and friend is the person who originated and encouraged the British empire. Let's keep him in mind."

I didn't reply to that, quietly left and rode away. Perhaps I was abrupt, but what does Suresh have to do with either of us? She was my friend before Suresh ever was. I might have introduced them for all I know. All of Suresh's angst and issue with the

British empire—what's the point? What does it change? Isn't the world just made of empires anyway, small and large? My father's from Japan which tried its hand at one time and was destroyed, but the country rebuilt itself. That's what I'm doing. Building myself. The beings from the future want to establish their own empires in the past—I'm sure Suresh's people would have built their own empire if they could. It's human nature, isn't it?

I can see Shakespeare through the large windows that look onto Raleigh's grounds. Soon enough, his own reputation and personal empire will be built. The man himself has his back to me, talking to Raleigh while associates hammer planks together and construct a makeshift stage. The sounds of hammering drown out any words that might drift from their conversation. All I can make out of the man is a patch of blue and a mousy demeanour as he grovels and scrapes in front of Raleigh. He doesn't seem all that important or remarkable. Strange to be so close and yet, what would I say were he to come inside?

But he doesn't. Raleigh finishes talking to Shakespeare and leaves him outside. Raleigh's friendly enough once he comes in, but not as warm as he once was. The distance and formality are a direct result of what happened in the Tower.

"May I serve you something?" he asks, "Mulled sack?"

I shake my head. "Better not."

"Very well," he says. "You have grown since the last time you visited. In height, but also stature. Cultivate that beard. It shall make you seem older. Cultivate the behaviour to suit the beard and the clothes to suit the behaviour, and no one will assail you. The breeches become you." Is he being ironic? He sports a lavish doublet of indigo silk threaded with gold that far outshines mine. Pointing towards a new half-suit of armour that radiates a polished shine, mounted on his wall, he indicates the Duke's pistol beside it. The one the Duke used to attempt his execution of Drake. "This is what I was presented with. Our mutual friend Sir Francis gave me that from your seized loot—do you like it? I heard you were given the head. Francis is alive, in no small part due to your bravery."

I nod my head slightly. "The last time I was here, with Doctor Dee, there was a little puppet thing. A wooden stage on your table here, lying where your pipe sits. It had what looked like Italian puppets. You know the ones?"

"Oh yes—it was a present for someone dear to me."

"A woman?" I have to be careful, not make the same insinuations and faux pas as last time.

"In this case, yes." He quickly changes the subject. "But don't you have a woman of your own? Do you not want to bring her to my great party that Doctor Dee's associate shall stage, the one he is planning for us right now outside yonder window?" He gestures towards Shakespeare. Doesn't he know that the friend whom he refers to as "my woman" has worked on the play with Shakespeare? As the hammering continues and Shakespeare struts about like a peacock, it is as if we are watching through a screen or television: the miniature stage with its curtains which once sat on the great table here has been whisked through the leaded windowpanes and blown to life size upon the lawn. Shakespeare is simply one of the puppets. What's that Shakespearean quote Sullivan dropped so condescendingly? "All the world's a stage but you're not a serious player, Nathan."

Funny how the word "play" can mean so many things—it works equally well for drama as for football. For a man's viability in business or with women. "Courting," as they say here. 'Court' is just as variable. There's something very odd about the English language. It's like a two-way mirror, a snake, like one of

172

those beings from the future: neither one thing nor the other.

"What did you want to discuss with me, sir?" I ask.

"Straight to the point. I like that!" he pats me on the shoulder. "First, I'd like you to try this." He lifts up the long pipe resting on the table, its bowl stuffed with dried brown leaves. He tamps the leaves down tightly with his finger and then takes the pipe over to the fireplace. Using a fire iron, he delicately sets the mixture in the bowl alight, then puffs for a while on the mouth of the pipe. Blowing the smoke out through his mouth, he hands me the pipe. It's a peace pipe of sorts and I accept it. The smoke's a lot harsher than a vape, leaves a burning sensation on my throat and tongue. I roll the hot smoke around and blow it out in rings that quickly fall apart once they leave my mouth. The dry cured leaves are crackly and musky, producing a very pleasant smell. I like it, and puff once more before reluctantly handing the pipe back to Raleigh.

The smoke rolls through Raleigh's coppery red beard as he talks. "Well—you ask what I wish to discuss with you—you know that Sir Francis and I have been involved in enterprises of which the Realm are a party. I am talking of establishing our colonies in the New World. Though the pallor of your skin may put you at odds on London's streets, you would not stand out so much in the colonies. I cannot do this alone. Would you be interested?"

"That is funny—I was only this morning visiting Doctor Dee and he mentioned his encouragement of the empire. You wish me to sail all the way to the New World?" After enduring all we have, am I simply to be sent back again?

"I need men and money, Nate. Think what you could do there! The financing will be secured soon, and the joint wedding, as these things go, is integral to that. That is why you must come and bring someone with you. Well, don't just stand there with your face so long. Say something, man! How would you like to truly test your mettle and helm my enterprises in America?"

"But why me? I know nothing about it."

"You might be perfect! You are young and could achieve much in the New World. There is much to recommend it—the food, the land, not least the climate. It is ripe to grow this crop which we smoke. If I'm not mistaken, its plantations will take hold there. The old men, you see—it is very difficult to make them learn new things. I need someone bold and daring."

"And Sir Drake wants this also?"

"You would not work for Francis, you would work for me. The men here will not allow you to rise to a position commensurate with your ambition. And if you are successful and wish to strike out for yourself in a year or two, it might be arranged. Perhaps more importantly, as I watched you cleave Parma's head off his shoulders, I felt your heart was not in it. If you stayed, not only would others hate you, but you would hate yourself. I do not want that for you. Francis is involved in a general sense, but he must give assent. The Queen herself is in some small measure involved and Francis cannot say anything against her."

So, there it is. To trade wholesale killing as part of Drake's crew for the slow death doled out by tobacco and cigarettes back in North America. Perhaps even a plantation thriving on slaves. The beings of the future are not the only ones who have built an empire and gender of death. The choice seems to be between killing people quickly and killing them slowly, bleeding out their money and lives in small increments. Perhaps this is why Isabel says we should go gentle on Suresh.

Raleigh laughs easily, knowing he has me in his palm. "Yes, yes, you must ponder my offer seriously," he states. "You are not cut out for the intrigues of London, Nathan. She is a cruel mistress." When I don't respond, he continues: "Do you know why the servant girl cannot look at you? It is because of the colour of your skin, Nate. No other reason. You could amass fortunes and buy her, heap lavish jewels upon her, but she would still find it difficult to look you in the face. In the New World, your pallor would not stand out against the Indian's. You may let us know at the wedding party. Dress in your best garb, bring a companion, and I will introduce you to the other men who will travel with you. It shall be a merry affair."

"What will you call your new colony?" I ask.

"Virginia," he replies, "in honour of our Queen."

As if to accentuate their point, a neat piece of theatre they have arranged beforehand, the dark-haired girl shows me out, all the while refusing to acknowledge my presence with a look or a smile.

The rain has begun to spit. I lead my horse through puddles of mud, too distracted to ride, my sword trailing sadly beside me. I hardly notice the woman throwing slops out her window before they land in the gutter. The thought of being sent to the New World does not fill me with promise or hope. It is the slops, the dregs of life. I don't know what I truly wish anymore, except that I don't want to be poor. I sit down on the stoop of a house to cry. It is a sudden hot cry, bringing momentary, salty relief. Then I become embarrassingly aware I am out in public. One man, idling some hundred metres away, watches me. He gets closer and through the motion of his hobbled walk and bent frame, I recognize Rawley. That one shut eye which seems to look me up and down behind its closed lid. Like 'court' or 'player'—Rawley/Raleigh—one poor, one rich—punning on each other. Like Duke and Drake.

"How now, Master Nathan?"

He extends his wet hand and I reluctantly shake it. "How do you do, Master Rawley?"

"Are you just coming from the house of Walter Raleigh?"

"Have you been following me?"

He bows a little and winks with his good eye, but the gesture is strained.

"What do you want?" I ask coldly.

Rawley looks up and down the street in exaggerated pantomime to make sure we are not heard. "The time has come, Nathan, for you to do your duty. For England and the world's salvation."

"You wish me to kill Drake?" I ask.

"No, no, Drake is of no consequence to us. He only cares for gold. You have just seen the man you must eliminate."

"You mean Raleigh?" I am stunned.

Rawley tuts and takes a square of folded paper out of his doublet's breast and passes it to me. "You must eliminate the person whose name is written on this slip, do you understand, by any means at your disposal. You are to do it at the wedding of Sir Raleigh's friends and no later. If you fail to carry this out, untold consequences shall be your lot, and that will be the end of you and your friends' story. Understood?"

Rawley shakes his head, smirking. He pats my hand, makes me take the folded-up note. "On the other hand, if you do as instructed, untold rewards could be yours. Our masters have the power to change people's destinies; I believe you have discovered that for yourself? If you have killed twice, it is nothing to kill a third time. I daresay this will even come as a doubled pleasure for yourself once you learn the target's name. Complete this task, your work done, and we may craft any future you imagine. You may be an emperor if your heart desires. Tuck away the paper now or it will become wet."

He saunters away with the swagger and confidence of a man who has lost nothing, neither an eye nor anything else. Yes, my heart desires. I cannot wait until later. Opening the folded piece of paper, I see two words written on it, black strokes lazily slanting through the scratching of a crow quill nib. The black ink begins to soak and run like blood made of crow's feathers. A white piece of paper with two words on it:

Will Shakspear

I fold up the paper again, tucking it into my sleeve.

ISABEL

The day of the performance draws near. Will has become a nervous wreck. He paces back and forth in our lodgings, wringing his hands. He pulls his hair out which sorely needs to be washed. His beard has gone untrimmed for weeks. I thought I had to content myself with a plain dress borrowed from the Rose theatre if Will could obtain it, but now Nathan has offered to buy me something if I go with him. I can ill afford to say 'no.'

The dress arrives. Made of bright red satin, trimmed with goldenrod brocade, it is elegant and simple. Classic enough to feature a farthingale, the dress's sleek lines are modern, its sheen brilliant. The farthingale makes the skirt spread into a hoop. I will have to walk painstakingly while wearing the dress, no doubt. Nathan has also sent pretty blue shoes that will probably hurt my feet but match my eyes. All from Nathan, whose hands have killed and may yet do so again. The dress lies heavy in my arms and I feel guilty holding it. As if I am holding a body in my arms, Suresh's body.

The decision is not really up to me. The play is to be performed in the gardens of Sir Walter Raleigh's house in the Strand—I cannot appear in the garb of a charwoman, a beggar. I wonder if Bess Throckmorton, lady-in-waiting to the Queen and Raleigh's paramour, shall be there? The Queen does not yet know of their relationship but once she does, they will end up in the Tower. Will the altered play be as good as the original? I don't know. I honestly do not know. It will be performed outside so we may enjoy the good weather, take advantage of the sunset which draws later and later these midsummer days. Will Kemp and the others have rehearsed with gusto. Even dear Doctor Dee has gotten involved, overseeing the design of set contraptions.

Will, for his part, frets constantly, changing minor lines and rhymes. He pulls at his beard in frustration. "They call me a beauteous crow," he pouts, "a crow with the borrowed feathers of a swan. They laugh and jest behind my back."

"Who?" I ask. "Do your friends say that?"

"I think it was Nashe that did write it," he grumbles. "Anonymously of course! The coward! The theatre and taverns are filled with cowards. I should have remained a humble actor instead of grousing as a writer. They all want classics, stuff and nonsense they're familiar with, tales of diabolical revenge. Or morality plays."

"Well, whatever happens, Will, it is only a performance. There will be infinite chances to rewrite it and perform it." Curious wording—a slip of the tongue.

He stops pulling at his beard and bores into me, earring twitching. "So much depends upon this performance, does it not feel that way? So many important people are invited. Some say the Queen might appear."

"The Queen—really?"

"Oh, yes," he continues. "They say she and Raleigh have made the beast with two backs. Did you know that? Like Titania and the donkey-headed Bottom in our play!"

"I did know that . . . Will, you shouldn't bite the hand that feeds you." It is only then it occurs to me. Biting the hand that feeds you! It is so obvious—why did I not see it before?

The play, the play's the thing to not only commemorate the weddings of Raleigh's friends but his own. His secret marriage to Throckmorton. Much as I and my efforts must remain hidden within Will's play, Raleigh and Throckmorton must pretend during the performance that they are acquainted and nothing more. He's doing this as a covert celebration for *her*, though it might be the Queen who is the guest of honour. Just like I'm doing this for the memory of my dead father. My yet-to-be-born father who, though I may never return, might yet read me in words.

Or am I doing this for myself? For Nathan perhaps? Or even Suresh? Who is to say? How unknowable we are to ourselves. Keen intelligence provides no fresh illumination; it only highlights ambiguities.

SURESH

He's just an old man. An old man who doesn't know what he's talking about. I keep telling myself that. All this time, I've thought of him as just an enthusiastic and eccentric philosopher with no real grasp of reality or science, a kindly old man who once had friends in high places. I never thought his pamphlet on movement through time would have any successful result. I never thought he could be dangerous.

Now we learn he facilitated the idea of the British Empire, at the very least promoted it. He doesn't feel bad about it either. No self-recrimination, no doubt in his mind. Never has he questioned the results of what he's advanced. I and my family and all of the horrors perpetrated on us are a direct result of what he's suggested, what he's written, what he's thought, what he's pushed for. And Tamils are only a tiny fraction of the Empire. Dee's influence doesn't just extend to the Globe theatre which was what Sullivan cared about. It extends to the entire globe.

I haven't brought this up with him or Jane yet. How does one reckon with that scale of destruction, the imbalance perpetuated through time? One thing I do know is that I can't live here much longer; we either have to find a way to get back home or—I don't know. Thankfully, Dee is out because he's spending his time helping with Shakespeare's preparations. Dee didn't ask me to assist him with the practical effects, and I doubt I'd have helped if he had. There's a chill between us that cannot thaw.

I journey to Raleigh's house on my own on the day of the performance. In the garden of Raleigh's house, there are many guests. Clowns, a juggler, and even a fire-eater were on the stage as I walked in, but now there is a lull in entertainment. I haven't seen Nathan or Isabel yet, but Dee stands with the players who fiddle with the stage. His contributions will be a surprise, I guess. Another surprise of many.

I watch them while they work. The stage itself is a wooden dais near some oak trees with many, many candles set in holders around it. The candles have not yet been lit as the sun is still in the sky, though sinking. Shakespeare is out there somewhere. Francis Drake will also be here. People are talking in hushed whispers about the Queen. Stools and cushions have been placed out for important guests. This is different from the visits to Durham House Dee has described in the past.

I've never seen so many ladies who aren't commoners. Their chatter and the way they look at me, some glancing quickly with a worried expression before pretending they don't see me, others staring openly, some even laughing—it maddens me. They wear colourful silken dresses with bright bows and stripes, gold and lace needlework embroidering grand designs. After spending most of my time at Mortlake cooped up with Dee's family, I find these women both fascinating and hateful. The men have pointed moustaches and beards, their legs are in stockings and their clothing is sometimes as colourful as the women's; what am I doing here?

I'm here because it's important to Isabel. Some men wear long cloaks and garments of black velvet but their necks are surrounded by large, expensive, starched ruffs. None of the other men seem to exhibit awkwardness. If they feel any, they hide it well. Their greetings are hearty, their flirtations with women are coy, bringing out their coquetry and smiles. They slap each other on the back and shoulders, drink from gilded cups. I don't have that capacity, whatever it is, either by genetics or learning. I am too neurodivergent for these finer sensibilities, but I do have feelings and they're simmering.

A heavy, ornate, high-backed wooden chair with much carved design is brought out and set upon the grass, conspicuously empty. It sits in the front row, purple cushion plump and fresh, in everyone's view.

Nathan and Isabel arrive together. When I see what she's wearing, my anger only hottens. He's paid for what she's wearing—she's wearing his money. The red satin dress blazes in the fading sunlight, a fire that's kindling, molten roses blooming. She looks more beautiful than ever, but what did I see in her? She's just another white woman, like all the rest here. She aspires to that which they are born unto. Part of the reason I liked her was that she was different. She wasn't the best dressed or best looking girl in class—now all that's gone. She matches Nathan in his ridiculous embroidered doublet and breeches.

We say our greetings. Isabel swots the grass behind those sitting on stools and then sits down. Nathan clasps his knees and seats himself on the other side of her, staring forward as if to shirk me. I laugh and sit down. The sun flares sharply, then dims, the final burst of a log's fuel, fading light captured momentarily by Isabel's new dress.

181

The stage in front of us stands empty. Neither of them say anything about Isabel's new clothes, or the fact they have yet again arrived together.

"Tell Suresh what you told me," urges Isabel, looking forward, meeting neither of our eyes.

"I got the message from them," he whispers back. "They want me to kill Shakespeare. Not Drake. They want us to kill Shakespeare. I thought it was going to be Drake."

"What are you going to do?"

"They got word to me through a guy I know—they've gotten to people in Drake's organisation. They want us to go through with it tonight. If we go through with it, we have to decide together. We said we wouldn't do anything without talking first."

"This is crazy," Isabel hisses between bared teeth. "I live with him—I'm not just going to let you destroy him. I'll never forgive you, Nathan, if you take any part in this."

"No, I want to hear it," I stop her. "What do we get if we go ahead?"

"Money, I suppose," Nathan replies as if his heart's not in it. "Some kind of unspecified success. On the other hand, if we don't, there's some vague threat we'll be destroyed instead. Perhaps there's a way for you to get your old lives back, return to the future. I don't know."

"Or they could be tricking us. I won't have anything to do with it!" Isabel continues to stare forward, blood draining from her face even as her dress darkens in the twilight. "All I remember is that monster saying I could die, regardless. I don't trust them."

"Raleigh also asked me to join his plantations in the New World," continues Nathan. "Quite separate from the other offer. If I did that instead, would you two go with me?"

"Are you insane?" I stammer. "You do remember I was born in Sri Lanka, right? That I'm Tamil? Our country was colonised by the British and they ruined it forever. Then we were colonised from within by the Sinhalese. I'm not going to help you start a colony! What about slaves? Why don't you go kill some indigenous people while you're at it?"

"I'm not going to kill indigenous people."

"How do *you* know? A real shame—when the colonised becomes the coloniser."

That seems to shut them up. Neither says anything.

As if our talking about him is cue for speech, Walter Raleigh hops up on the stage. He flicks his cloak, claps his hands, and demands our attention.

"There's a story about Raleigh that's apocryphal!" whispers Isabel, her eyes sparkling. "It goes that he once wagered the Queen he could weigh the smoke from tobacco. She asked him to prove it and he weighed the tobacco in his pipe, then smoked it. He tipped the ash into a scale as he smoked, then weighed the ash, claiming the remainder must be the true weight of smoke."

"That's nonsense, scientifically speaking, no better than Dee's rubbish," I shoot back.

"I hope that everyone is having a splendid time!" cries Raleigh, very much in good cheer. "And now—the Queen!" A flourish of coronets and everyone stands solemnly as the Queen's procession arrives. We have to stand up with them and I'm the last to stand, resentfully brushing grass away from my knees. Elizabeth is an old woman and moves slowly. She of course looks nothing like her portraits which show her as young and pleasant. More British bullshit.

Why did I come here, into the heart of all things, the lion's den? Because I followed Isabel, that's why. Now, the Queen is almost sixty and shows it. That's what Isabel is in love with, that's what she'll become in time. The creams and heavy white makeup cannot mask the Queen's age and ugliness. She looks like a tall spindly knotted tree, twisting in the wind. Her face is made of aged parchment, linen creases showing through the heavy layer of stage paint on her face.

She is decked in layer upon layer of embroidery, her bodice made of lush burgundy and velvet, covered in immense pearls, diamonds, and emeralds sewn into the fabric. Large puffs and armbands sit on her sleeves. Ropes of pearls hang off them. She is not a queen so much as a gigantic swinging chandelier, clothed in the colonies. The pearls clack together, making a horrible sound as she walks. Everybody is deadly quiet. The wealth of empire lies upon her body. The swish and clink of her dress, the boorish voice of a bully.

And yet Isabel seems to admire her. The Queen sits slowly, creakily into the large chair placed for her near the front of the lawn. The bottom half of the Queen's dress is covered in ribbons and bows and the farthingale below it is so large that no one can see her feet beneath the petticoats.

Isabel gasps and pulls my sleeve. And then I realise what's made her so rapt. On top of the queen's red wig (her real hair is probably wispy and white) is a simple diadem—a crown. I didn't notice because the rest of her ensemble is so blinding. The diadem is an elegant platinum band with a single emerald embedded on its left-hand side. The diadem catches the last rays of sun and the honey green light it reflects shines upon the faces of the nobles around us. A high collar made of quivering peacock feathers surrounds the queen's neck and in the dark, the feathers' large green and blue eyes seem to watch us.

"Look—over there! On the Queen's head!" whispers Isabel, "do you recognize it?"

Is the Queen one of them? Or did she just merely grasp that along with everything that came her way, simply because she's white and born to privilege? At this point, does it matter?

My migraines come back, full force. Triggered, like a million voices seething in pain and suffering within my head. My head's going to split right open. In the torment, I find a clear spot within my raging feelings and take refuge there. A clean spot to think things over, centre my will. If I have power at all, if my feelings have worth, let me use my will to focus it on the people around me. All their heated ambitions and petty cruelty. Let me with full force direct my anger. Let the British Empire get what it deserves. Nipped in the bud, cut down in its creche. Let it fall. Let it fall. Let it receive its own measure of death.

Somewhere within my seething brain, that temple to all I hold dear, I am heard.

There is a click and the sound of rushing water.

ISABEL

In the ornate wooden chair, the Queen's back towers over us. Everyone else has sat down but I remain standing. It's the only way to properly see over the Queen's wig and watch the play.

The sun is a melted puddle, splitting the clouds into waves of pink. Will steps forward onto the stage as Duke Theseus. I almost don't recognize him at first, so ornate is Will's gold cloak and violet costume with its ruffles and bows. Some boy, playing Hippolyta, accompanies him. My heart jumps into my throat as the dialogue begins.

"Now, fair Hippolyta, our nuptial hour draws on apace; four happy days brings in another moon," recites Will. He is stately, bending his knee slightly, using his shoulder's movement to give the cloak a flourish. He's not bad.

The audience settles, becomes attentive. The beginning of

the play unfolds. Nothing amiss as darkling twilight creeps and night's chill infects the air. The actors speak quickly and get through the early scenes, the ones that require light. Will has finessed the lines but I prompted him. If this has happened hundreds, perhaps thousands, of times in other iterations, is there an original story, a master version? Is there a master to our lives?

Watch the play; I must not get distracted by riddles I cannot solve. Suresh seems very troubled, and that is also distracting. All four Athenians and the actors rehearsing their play for Duke Theseus steal into the woods at night. They find a hollowed oak tree, previously struck by lightning. The actors have moved an actual tree behind the bare stage in Raleigh's garden. Its bole has been hollowed out and its branches twist in the dark as if paralyzed, blackened by the thunderclap of time.

The actors crawl through the hole in the tree to make good their escape from the boundaries of Athens, find themselves transported to the faerie land of Elizabethan England. Then come the faeries. Puck, played as a malicious oaf by the clumsy, boisterous Will Kemp, stamps about the stage. He cannot keep still. Kemp sports clown's clothing with a diamond pattern of black and white. Everybody laughs, including the Queen. Her throaty chuckle rises above the other guffaws which almost seem to part air in order that her gesticulations of mirth might be registered.

Her crown tilts back every time she laughs, reflecting rays of torch light. The boys are seated on either side of me, silent. Nathan seems absorbed in the play, finally giving Shakespeare's production its due, which is good, but the idea that he'd even contemplate harming Will is never far from my mind. I can't tell what Suresh is thinking and that's more worrying. Now Oberon and Titania, king and queen of the faeries, flutter to the stage.

186

The darkness is complete and Raleigh's servants go about, lighting the hundreds of candles that have been set up in the garden and around the stage. Torches held in sconces upon the wall have been alight for a while. Now, in the darkness, they burn brighter. Some of the candles gutter and blow but the air remains still and heavy. Most of the candles still burn. The servants relight them again and again as the play proceeds. Light ebbs and flows. The effect is not incongruous; it provides an effulgent glow that gives the play a supernatural quality.

Well done, Will—and Doctor Dee. The evening blends into time which, haunted, flows into the grove of woods, suggested by nothing more than two trees which stand behind the stage. Everything flickers, not unlike the moment we initially time travelled, descending through the earth behind Leonard Cohen Collegiate. Oberon and Titania enter. They do not enter stage left and stage right but instead, uncurl and descend from the branches of the trees themselves. We do not notice them until they move like winged snakes.

Richard Burbage, whom I saw play Romeo, now plays Oberon. He appears fearsome in a fur trimmed cloak. I think the same boy who played Hippolyta is now Titania. Where Hippolyta was quiet and reserved, Titania is full of spark and fury. She commands her train of faeries and squares off against Oberon. Doctor Dee has designed harnesses and pulleys for Oberon and Titania which lift them out of the trees and fly them over the stage.

Oberon rants and rages, plots and schemes to get back at Titania. They wear diaphanous dragonfly wings which shimmer and glow as candlelight radiates through them. It is excellent. It is excellent.

Even Nathan is transfixed. It truly is different to see the thing played out in front of you. Movement and action. The poetry of the language as it trips across tongues. There is something mesmerising about the production as if it affects our minds, affects time itself. *Is* there ultimate ink animating the poetry of our lives? Puck leaps and hollers about the stage, singing with mad glee, his speech much less refined than the others: *Then will two at once woo one. That must needs be sport alone; And those things do best please me / That befall prepost'rously!*

Now comes the scene where Queen Titania, with the love potion smeared on her eyes, goes to bed with one of the mechanicals: the actor whose head has been turned into that of a donkey's. Exquisite comedy—Titania, who for the sake of Oberon's revenge, has no idea what she's doing, thinks the donkey to be supremely wise and handsome. His large ears, furry snout, and thirst for hay impress her greatly, making the noble, proud queen lust after the donkey even more. People crossing their stations. The Queen and Raleigh? Myself and Nathan?

Once again, focus on the play: Doctor Dee impresses, having arranged a slim bed, by moonlight, to hoist the actors in the air as they lie together. The act of lovemaking takes on a fairytale quality, hanging suspended above the audience, creating a split-level stage that is made of nothing but air.

I hear Queen Elizabeth chortling: "Is that supposed to be me? Is that supposed to be us?"

All chattering and murmuring from the audience stops. Glorianna is obviously much too old and infirm now to make love to anyone, half donkey or otherwise, though she is rumoured to still dance the galliard. So who knows? People are uneasy. Is the Queen offended?

No, she seems to be smiling with her aged linen face, waves her spindly hand to let them know that although she should be insulted, she is quite simply amused. Everybody, including

I'm sure Will, heaves a sigh of relief. The laughing cautiously resumes until it once more drowns out the breeze.

Nathan nudges me and directs my gaze. Drake has arrived with his retinue, and stands towards the back, watching us. Nathan waves but Drake does not return the gesture. It is hard to read the expression on Drake's face in the darkness.

"He won't wave back at you?" I state the obvious.

"I told you," replies Nathan. "I saved his life. He's a complicated man. Stop looking at him."

The play continues. At its end, all the Athenians have returned to Athens. Bottom the actor no longer has the head of a donkey. Lysander loves Hermia again and she loves him. Demetrius still has the love potion in his eyes and so loves Helena, as he is supposed to. He always will. Queen Titania wakes up from her tryst with the donkey and makes up with Oberon in order to have her sanity and rightful mind returned. All's well that ends well. Except it's not. There are so many contradictions woven into this gentle comedy.

A sad and empty feeling steals into my breast. It will be over soon. I will have seen the play during its very first performance, as I secretly intended, but it is not *the* play. It is not *the* play because I am involved. A cool wind blows, guttering many of the candles that are still alight, dripping low with wax. We watch the characters crawl through the hole in the bole of the old oak tree, knotted grooves and bark illuminated by torchlight. Time oozes back through that hole, returning things to normal. Yes, it's sad to leave the realm of faerie and dream where one can fall in love with someone they hate, as if things were not always thus.

Despite my melancholy, the last act is a festive one. The young Athenians join Theseus and Hippolyta to be married so that it becomes a triple marriage. Raleigh's recently married friends, somewhere in the audience, must be rippled with delight even while Bess Throckmorton glows, carrying Raleigh's child. Where is she now, I wonder.

The mechanicals, the players within the play, perform their abominable effort for Theseus and the audience on stage. The real audience roars with laughter, approval, and delight. All that is left now is the speech I rewrote. The closing speech. Will Kemp delivers it, intentionally clumsily, as Puck:

> If we travellers have offended,
> Think but this, and all is mended,
> That you have but rememb'red here
> While these visions did appear.
> And this weak and idle theme,
> Where past is future, not what it seemed,
> Was affected by time's travels, thoughts and intentions.
> Misaligned journeys, timeline's preventions.

I hate my words now that I hear them recited back to me. You can sense the audience, awkward, confused, trying to puzzle them out. They clap slowly, still trying to parse the final lines. Slowly, slowly, they too realise the play is over, is truly over, and begin clapping in earnest. They rise to their feet. Some particularly enthusiastic ones even throw their feathered hats into the air and then have to look for them on the dark garden's lawn for most of the candles are out. It is a hit, a most palpable hit.

Only the Queen does not stir. The last of the candlelight reflects off her diadem and pearls, throwing sparkles onto the grass. Beams of reflected light pulse from her. She *does* possess an aura.

"What did you think, your majesty?" asks Sir Walter Raleigh, curtseying.

"We think, Sir Walter . . . we think it quite bewitching. We thank you for providing it. You know, our head does become fearsome light. We do not know what is story, what is real, what is past and what is present. Who penned this splendid delight?"

Will steps up on the stage sheepishly, still dressed in his Theseus garb. He fingers the stagey crown upon his head which is much more elaborate and gaudy than the Queen's diadem, and scratches his pate where it is beginning to bald.

"You have earned your wages tonight, good man. We expect many more such wond'rous delights from you."

"Thank you, ma'am," replies Will. I've never seen him quite so sheepish. He would be mocking her if we were at home. I think he's humbled by the manners and is unsure of his own gestures. Without warning, he points at me. "I had help, your magnificence. There is my assistant. There is my collaborator, an especially rare woman!"

Everybody turns around to squint at me and I panic. Not just because I'm standing—there is something wrong about this moment, terribly wrong. It is unscripted. I look at Suresh in the shadows, his face a terrain of unmasked rage. The terror I feel is wrong and more frightening for it. I'm left staring back at the audience as if I'm on stage.

Raleigh's house is made of large slabs of stone, decorated with mediaeval motifs and patterns. In the faltering light, all the men and women wear colourful silken apparel with bright bows and stripes, gold and lace needlework embroidering grand designs. The men's solemn faces have pointed moustaches and beards, their legs are in stockings. Those who work for Queen Elizabeth wear long cloaks and garments of black velvet, their heads almost floating upon their large ruffs.

I think of the grinning skull on Dee's work table. Nobody smiles. I should not be here. They look at me with grave faces, pouches and dark shadows beneath their eyes. Every face is utterly serious and lined with confusion and worry. Or is it just me? I look down and see myself dressed head to toe in the most impenetrably shimmering red satin armour.

Where do I remember this from? The most terrifying sense of déjà vu yet. Some kind of trick . . . some kind of trick . . . something is about to happen. I look at Suresh and his teeth are clenched, his eyes pop. The briny smell of seawater assails my nostrils.

The sound of distant explosions; we see light and fire flood the sky. It illuminates the bare stage upon which Will stands. More noises and cries. Men are sent out to ascertain the situation and the news which comes back is more fantastic than the play we have just witnessed.

Apparently, the Spanish Armada has fallen out of the sky.

NATHAN

A swirling portal has opened above London's thatched skyline. More than a hundred Spanish galleons and pinnaces drop out of it, with all the water, rats, fish, oars, masts, sails, and sailors that were sucked up with them. Also, the six fire ships that the English coated with tar and oil to send towards the Armada. Four years ago collapses into the present.

Word comes to us that the worst damage is upon the London Bridge and the Thames, all along the North Bank, the houses and streets that branch that way. The narrow and towering houses of the Bridge are torn off their foundations. The bridge is smashed to rubble.

The galleons, towering castles made of wood, smash upon the ground and river, keel first, splinter into smithereens. Bombs made of wood. Wooden whales, immense dreadnoughts, planks splintering and pouring forth cannons, culverins, men, oars, arms, and powder indiscriminately. Friction and sparks from the impact and the fire ships' sails, tarry cordage, decks still slick and oiled—all spring into fiery balls, spreading their flames to other ships. Powder for the cannons ignites. Explosions everywhere. The lesser houses, made of wood and thatch, easily catch fire.

I can see the character Puck, not the actor but the actual hobgoblin, in the flames as he leaps from thatched roof to roof. Rats, resilient, jump from the ships as they fall and land in the streets, leaping for safe ground. Londoners, moments after seeing the spiral of ships and sea opening above their heads, look down to see a river of rats sweep over their feet, scurry through the gutters and streets as if with one mind. A wave of pink ribbed tails and hissing teeth.

London's rats jump out of the culverts and basements of London's houses to join their Spanish cousins. People are bitten. Others jump out of the way, not that it helps much. The rats move continuously, roiling over everything. We're somewhat protected, within Raleigh's garden in the fortified Durham House, but the chaos will reach us soon enough.

Ships and timbers keep falling, obliterating houses, streets, trees, anything else that lies in their path. Large impact clouds of smoke, splintered wood, and water spread over the city. The ground shakes. Bulwark, rope, mast, and cannon all became one as they fuse into a compressed ball of giant wreckage, falling apart afterwards.

Spaniards that are not killed by the impact have their arms and legs broken. Blood covers the streets. The Spanish horses, those poor noble creatures, are dashed against the ground, forelegs and rib cages broken. From Raleigh's garden, we can hear them whinnying their sucking, piercing, bloodcurdling cries. Men return with reports of the horses' broken bodies and dirt-flanked bellies, still alive, rolling in the debris. Some of the

Spanish soldiers are alive and mobile. Having dazedly put their hands to their heads and stumbling out of the wreckage, they pick up their helmets, rearrange their cuirasses, find a weapon whether it be sword or pikestaff, anything handy.

The rats continue to run over everything. Raleigh's important guests begin to wail. These unplanned fireworks reach us through the swirl of dust and ash. Flames leap over the walls of Raleigh's garden, lighting the branches of his oak trees. Flaming wood falls upon the stage, a fiery semi-circle around Shakespeare, singeing his boots and beard. I laugh as he jumps from the shock.

Licks of flame fall upon the hems of women's dresses and they scream while men, oblivious to their ruffs burning, try to beat their hands against the precious imported cloth. A spear of fire attacks the ornate wooden chair where the Queen sits, forcing her to leap as fast as her feeble bones allow. "What is going on?" she shouts as she stumbles and faints.

So this is what the head warned us of? I finally appreciate the irony, the poetry of our situation: beggars' justice.

Drake turns to the rest of us and attempts to take command. "The Spanish have arrived," he shouts, barely masking his glee. "The Armada is here—a sneak attack!" He can smell the treasure, even through the pain and destruction.

The men, all these earls and lords, gentlemen and captains, come forward, cowed by Drake's enthusiasm. I think about the square of paper, folded, tucked away, with Shakespeare's name written upon it. It makes little sense in all this pain and confusion but little is better than none. He is so vulnerable. So alone. Should I go ahead and stop him? After all, that's the reason I brought us here, is it not? All it would take is a few ounces of pressure applied upon his windpipe with the blade of my sword.

Messages are sent. Horses are called for. People run back and forth carrying pails and ewers, even chamber pots, of water, trying to douse whatever flames they can. I glance again at Shakespeare. There he is, a small man in his ridiculous Theseus costume, fake crown over his straggling hair, fear in his eyes. He's gathered whatever copies of the play's manuscript he can and clutches them to his breast in fear. I could run up to him and wrench them from his hands, rip them up, and throw them into the nearest flames but that wouldn't be enough. He would write again. The message was quite clear. He must be stopped. He must die. If not me, then who?

In the smell of smoke, the noise of flames, I feel the hot metal of the sword's blade by my side. A moment later, a touch of a hand, small and cool, against my fingers. "Nathan, what are you doing?" Isabel. I did not even register she was standing there, nor that I'd put my hand to my sword. More and more, my hand and body react as if they are not connected to my mind, as if I am a machine, programmed by someone outside myself.

Am I a bad person; do I think only of myself?

"Nathan, think what you're doing," she commands, quietly but firmly. Her grasp is tight. I shake it off. "Don't do it," says Isabel. "Don't do it. You're better than that. It's easy to destroy; it can become easier and easier to take a life. But to create, to give life to something, to make life grow and nurture it along, that's difficult. Didn't you enjoy the play—could you create that? If you think your situation with Drake is difficult, think how it must be for Will and the lot he's chosen in life. Have empathy. Understanding."

Suresh stands as if he's been far away all this time but flinches at the word 'empathy.' Have we just become puppets on a stage with our strings irreparably tangled? I hate this feeling, this feeling of not knowing what to do.

Drake suffers from none of this and beckons me forward,

head bent. Hell bent. He is purposeful as always. He tells me we cannot delay and must move beyond Raleigh's walls to confront the situation. Another voice I must obey.

"I have to go," I say to Suresh and Isabel. "Don't shake your heads. I do. Don't make any decisions. Don't do anything till I'm back." Perhaps some action will clear my mind. Perhaps actually doing something that needs doing will bring me back to myself.

SURESH

What have I done? What have I done?

I've criticised Nathan for killing, but the death toll on my own hands is far greater. And yet I'm not sorry. I feel a strange satisfaction, something I've never felt before. Not just for the charred smoke that sticks in our throats, makes our eyes water. That is intoxicating, even though it makes me cough—it is the sound. The sound is a roar, a thousand waterfalls, like Niagara Falls made of fire instead of water, churning in our ears. The voice of the skull, magnified thousandfold, laughing. My heart beats quickly within my chest, feeling warmth—it is pleasurable.

Isabel grabs me by the shoulder, turns me around. "What's wrong with you? You've been acting strange all night. What are we going to do? We have to do something. Do you want to go with Nathan?"

I shake my head and smile. "What *can* we do?"

"We can't afford not to act. This is what we'll do," Isabel's head is down, her voice is low, shoulders raised as she speaks almost into her red dress. "We'll save the play. And we'll save Will. These are Nathan's desires taking hold. You know what I'm talking about. This is his version of 1613, when the Globe burns down. We're not going to let him rewrite history. We have to save the play . . . and Shakespeare along with it."

How wrong she is—if only she knew. "Do you think it really matters that much?" I ask. "That it comes down to just one person?"

"No, I suppose not," she replies. "But for whatever reason, for reasons that might be obscure to Will himself, he is a focal point for this time and age. If we let Nathan or someone else kill him, the whole thing collapses. We throw the baby out with the bathwater, as Sullivan might say."

"One thing that's great about this place is there's no Sullivan. Maybe if we change things, we make the world better in other ways? Maybe we stop England from becoming the empire that rules half the world? Maybe we stop it destroying Sri Lanka and massacring indigenous people?"

She stares at me a long time, despondently glimpsing what I really feel, slowly realising her opinion might not be the only one that matters. Finally, she shakes her head, a frown on her lips: "One thing I know for sure as a woman, if it isn't one group oppressing you, it's another. This may be a bad direction, a bad plot, but at least it's the plot we know, the one we work with."

The sound of fighting in the streets comes closer. Shouts on the other side of the garden wall. A few blocks away, someone's roof catches fire. The fire roars louder as flames shoot upwards. Then the inward crash as the roof crumbles heavily, mass collapsing.

Isabel has to yell to be heard: "It takes a lot to produce a good play, Suresh. A good work of literature stands above empires. Like I said to Nathan, it's easy to destroy. I aim to save these plays. You do what you want but I'm not going to allow them to perish. Make your own choices, I guess." And that's how she makes me feel guilty. She keeps looking aside at the Queen. I can feel what she's thinking: that crown, that device.

Though the fire rages, everyone else shouting, she lowers her pitch to speak with utmost intent. I can hear every syllable and nuance. I can feel her thoughts cleansed by fire. Adrenaline floods my brain.

"Think about your feelings expressed to me," she says, "that time beside the tree." I should be embarrassed but I'm not. "The emotion you expressed in your letter was sincere and beautiful. It was because you expressed it through language, through words, that I could understand what you felt in your heart. Communication—pure and simple. That man (*she points to Shakespeare*), that bumbling oddity whose boots are on fire, is this age's master of communicating the written word, giving expression to thought and feeling. My father would say we come from the tail end of history when communication falls apart. When literacy regresses to infancy, to limitations inherent before the Renaissance happened. We don't know how to write a letter expressing our most personal feelings. That confidence, that vulnerability. We hate ourselves and each other for it. But somehow, by our own bumbling, you brought us back to the moment in our language's history when it begins to grow in earnest. When our language's arms and legs lengthen, when the head and heart enlargen. Our society's puberty. The birth of the modern English language."

The birth of your society, I want to say. But words fail me.

"We have to save those manuscripts," she adds quietly. "It is our duty."

The intensity and passion of her words echo the burning heat of the flames. How can she be so sure? Despite everything, despite not wanting to, I feel the folds of my heart open. Like a rose after rainfall, I begin to colour and draw towards her again. The heat is no longer just a physical phenomenon.

"Okay, I'll save the manuscripts if you want. And I'll talk to

Dee. I suppose I must. He'll know how to save and transport Shakespeare, so that Nathan nor anyone else can get to him. What are you going to do?"

She fumbles and turns away. "Thank you, my friend. I'm going to try and get back the crown from the Queen's wig. It's our only way out of here."

NATHAN

I exit Raleigh's garden cautiously, hand upon my sword, looking for my horse. The scene outside is madness, the complete opposite of the play we've just seen. Maybe Shakespeare made veiled allusions to war and discord but here, the theme is very real.

Horses stamp and squeal in the stables. They pound their hooves and rattle their stalls, sensing confusion and destruction. I find my roan mare and saddle it, comb my fingers through its mane to calm it as best I can. I stroke its neck and offer a piece of apple which it eats even while maintaining panic in its eyes. All the while, I think of Isabel upon that lawn with Suresh, and her experience with the horse after seeing Shakespeare's previous play. There are going to be a lot more dead horses when all is said and done. Whatever I'll encounter outside will be a hundred times worse than a bear garden.

I understand how my horse feels. Swinging myself gently into the saddle, I coax the animal out and tighten the reins so we can wade through the destruction. The wooden wreckage of galleons and houses is everywhere. The Armada has been washed up by the tide of time. Beams from houses lie burning into the masts of ships and their fluttering sails. Clouds and columns of smoke rise as if the mouth of hell has opened into the city. Flakes of dust and rubble float all around us. The horse and I choke upon them as we push forward. Coughing, eyes watering, I raise a sleeve to my face and Shakespeare's death note crinkles within.

Survey the scene for immediate threat. Poor people, nobles, merchants, run down the end of the Strand. The last of the rats scurry behind them. Fights between Spanish soldiers and English yeomen. Commoners pitch in. Those who haven't left their houses boil pots of water and oil to pour onto the heads of Spanish soldiers below. One noble has dressed both himself and his horse in suits of armour and stands at the end of the street with a longbow and arrows stuck in the ground. What they used before gunpowder came along. As the Spanish advance, he picks up arrow after arrow and using his full frame to draw the great bow, looses them upon the advancing band of scattered soldiers. Few find their mark. When one does, a man clutches his chest or neck, then falls down with a choking sound.

Fish, still alive, flop in the street. Water sloshes around us as if the Thames has oversurged her banks. Broken bodies of horses lie within the water, trying to raise their heads, glimmers of desperation looming in their large, terrified glossy eyes. This is the end. A young mother lies prone, knees tucked against her chest, making a sucking sound that's more animalistic than human. She cradles a swaddled infant. There's blood on her legs and skirt but somehow, she's found the strength to hold the baby above the water that swirls around my horse's hooves. The baby, wrapped in a shawl, miraculously does not cry. The mother raises the baby up to me as I ride closer to look down at them. I think of Isabel and what she says about "not throwing the baby out with the bathwater."

"Take it," the woman pleads as she struggles for air, "save my only child." Tears run down her face. An only child, like myself and Isabel. The mother's look so grievous it melts my heart, so grievous it would melt Rawley's heart. The baby is whole and alive. What am I supposed to do with a baby? It begins to cry as we trot around it, a soft mewling sound as if the baby hasn't

200

quite accepted that its mother will no longer cradle it against her breast.

The horse naturally stops and bends its head. I lean down and take the baby, holding it safe and protected as a pigskin. My own mother doesn't exist yet and I feel hot tears fighting their way out of my ducts. Not saying anything, not wanting the mother to see me cry, I turn away and hold the infant against my shoulder with one hand while holding the horse's reins with the other.

The woman turns inside herself with a moan of despair and allows herself to pass out. Her chest stops heaving, her body slumps, and the waters wash over her. I stay to witness her last moments, but must move on. Drake instructed me to watch for soldiers that we know and there is no sign of them.

The large house to the right is in flames but the small cottage beside it has escaped, unharmed. Its smaller and lower roof means that it has avoided the fires that blaze on either side. The occupants of the large house are handing each other pails of water, refilled from the street, before throwing the water against the flames.

For some reason I can't explain, I stop here. I dismount and cautiously knock on the door of the smaller cottage. A maternal instinct pulls me. A woman in a nun-like wimple answers. She is older and stout, bent over as she shuffles. Cracks in her skin and puffy cheeks make her eyes squint but as far as I can tell, there's no malice or greed there.

"Will you take care of this child?" I ask.

My request, without preamble or explanation, seems absurd. But in the moment, with the havoc and destruction around us, the woman understands. No excuses or bartering; she reaches out for the swaddled child which, amazingly, has returned to silence within my arms.

"It's the trot of your horse, not you," says the woman, reading my mind.

I give up the baby and it begins to wail fitfully. The old woman hushes and rocks the child, then urges me away. Was the baby a boy or a girl? Within the roar of the flames around us, the sneering laugh of the skull repeats: "Ask us not our gender, for we are the gender of death."

The horse whinnies frantically. I'd better not stress it anymore.

Leaving the horse untethered by the old woman's house, I walk through the flames and smoke. A dog whose fur is on fire yelps and runs across my path. "Admiral Drake's men!" I yell. "Admiral Drake's men! Where are you?"

"El Draque! El Draque! Aqui! Venga aqui!" I draw my sword and wheel around to see the owner of the Spanish voice coming at me through the smoke. Before I think, my arm extends, stabbing, again and again. I am a windmill, I am a lever pushing against the world; the sword is an extension of me, finding flesh. He falls just as my shoulder explodes in a burst of pain. The arm smarts and spasms with blasting shock, like a thing beyond my control. Is that the clatter of my whole arm or just the sword hitting the ground?

Blackness, as my legs go from under me.

ISABEL

The Queen has fainted and lies upon the burnt grass. Suresh and I walk around her in order to hunt for manuscript pages which lie scattered. Others are distracted but there are too many people watching the Queen for me to act upon the crown.

Some of the pages have burned. As I try to pick one up and put out the embers at its edges, I see it is a charred and torn first page. *A Midsummer Night's Tyme*: am I at this point saving

202

Shakespeare's reputation or my own? The first fifteen lines have burned away. They refer to Theseus laying siege to Hippolyta's people, the Amazons. He has burned and pillaged their land and taken her prisoner, and now the same thing happens to us: our city is burned and pillaged.

As flames and havoc abound, I finally understand why the audience at the Rose theatre could stand in mud for hours on end, listening to the most refined poetry, the greatest artistry, then go to the bear garden and see livid dogs tear into a horse's flesh. The writing, its heated emotions and rivers of blood, echoes the emotions and appetites of these people. The blood life of this city is constantly in roil—whether the stimulus enters through the brain or the eye is of little matter. The Elizabethans are a people whose hearts beat like a war drum, living a state of constant alarm. This is why they string up beggars and thieves; there are not enough gibbets to satisfy the bloodlust. These are my ancestors.

Could Suresh be right? Is there any point to gathering the last of Will's pages and joining him? Will has shed his Theseus costume and attempts to mat out the sparks and burnt patches of his blue doublet. The slashes of silk have burned first. Some of the fire must have leapt onto his face, from the evidence of his singed squirrelly beard. I cannot resist being cliched: "No use worrying about your beard when your head might be chopped off, Will."

I hand the remaining pages to Doctor Dee and Suresh who have joined us. "Whatever you do, you must not let this out of your sight. Go with Will to our lodgings and rescue whatever else you can. Take all papers and notes, no matter how rough or incomplete. Save them all. Will, it is time for you to return to your wife and children!"

"Why? What are you going to do?" asks Will, his curious eyes hovering in their deep sockets, sensing something greater than the conflagration around us.

"You have to go now," I urge. "If you are to continue writing, you must escape the chaos which is to come. You must especially use this time to think out your ideas, what it is you wish to say and how to fashion it. Come up with things wondrous and new. Go! It might already be too late. Our lodgings are cheap and who knows what has now burned down? You must save what you can."

"Come, Will," says Dee tiredly, sensing Suresh's cold silence towards him. "We must tend to our families. This is a young person's world now."

"Suresh, you go with them too," I add. They will hang him quick as lightning if they discover him with me, given what I'm about to do. The only reason I can even attempt it is because I'm white and female. I understand how unfair that is.

"Be careful," replies Suresh. He understands.

"Whatever they say of me, Will, remember that I helped and praised your writing. That I loved working for you. Use your unerring sense of people's character and glean for yourself in time who I am, and what I did."

Men. My life has always been directed by men. Once they leave, once I am on my own, I turn my attention to the Queen. Blankets have been found and brought for the Queen to lie on. She is still unconscious. Many of the soldiers and nobles have gone. Those left still battle the blaze in confusion.

The branches of the oak trees continue to burn, dropping crisped and withered bark upon the stage like crooked matchsticks. The stage will soon catch fire. Two women attempt to carry the Queen far from it before it erupts in flame. Raleigh's house is largely made of stone but will it withstand the fire? And where is Raleigh himself? Is it only we women who are left?

I help the pair who have placed the Queen on the ground near the walls of Raleigh's house. The stone is hot so we cannot go inside. I take the Queen's pulse. It's steady.

"What are we to do?" asks the tall, willowy woman in her plum coloured dress. Her companion seems permanently panic stricken.

"Go! Get some water and a cloth." I try my best to sound calm and authoritative. They seem uncertain but when I flash them a cold look, the women reluctantly leave.

Now, quietly, quickly, I must pry the crown free from the Queen's wig. Ah, so that's why it didn't fall off when she fainted. It's sewn right into the wig itself, along with the pearls. The wig is attached to the Queen's head but I can't tell how. I try to prise the diadem free but it is intricately held in place by the crocheted strands of the wig's hair.

Only one thing to do—I yank it forcefully but the whole wig comes off. The Queen's wispy white hair falls onto the ground in strands. It is thin and adds even more years to the aged face. The Queen wheezes in her sleep, vulnerable and exposed. Her cheeks tighten, the lips pucker. Rings of black makeup frame her eyes. Those fearsome eyes are closed and the tongue is silenced but there is still something ancient and terrible written in the parchment of her face. A mysterious and severe expression. I cannot decode it.

Her wispy hair is pure white, the colour of melting snow. Imagine what she must have looked like when she was young and fertile, my age. A formidable and athletic beauty, a great prize to be won. Unlike other women, she has not bowed to the pressures around her. Is it right to take her property thus? The Queen twists her mouth again, becomes once more the old, withered woman.

I think of Ms Sullivan and her red hair, shot with streaks of grey. An urge to smash the Queen's face overtakes me. All I'd have to do is pick up the crown and smash that parchment to pieces. Tear that ancient and terrible paper. The feeling is overpowering; where does it come from? This reliquary of an age, sleeping in shock upon the lawn, must die.

Very slowly, very carefully, I count backwards from twenty. I think of the Shakespearean manuscripts en route to safety with Suresh and Doctor Dee. Why am I holding back here? Sounds and intense cries, getting closer, bring me out of myself. Sweat runs down my face and soaks my dress. Get the crown. *Get the crown.* That is the only thing that matters. Before the women come back.

Where are those women? I pick up the wig. The sound of the fire melts and flows like water. It gushes. How much time has passed? Pull away the crown . . . that's all that matters. I pull at the gingery strands of the wig. It breaks my nails. Only with great effort do the strands come loose. A clinking of pearls. Suddenly the immense dress, the gilded chandelier before me on the lawn, ripples and comes alive. A weatherbeaten and withered hand grasps my wrist. The other seizes the wig. The parchment has awoken.

She sits up. The Queen is a towering, spooky tree. Her voice is burning timber. "Women, subjects!" it cries, "This one assays to steal our crown."

The women find us and congregate, stand in a semi-circle, flank us.

"Treason!" screams the old and wretched Queen. "Treason! This traitor is in league with the Spaniards!" The women crowd me—a flock of gaily coloured songbirds in dresses profligate with satin and bows. Everything is disconcertingly hushed. Moments ago, I could have run, escaped across the stage. Now everything is afire. The trees smoke into glowing embers. The oak with the hole hollowed out in its centre melts into char. There is nowhere to run. Nowhere to escape.

"Treason!" screams the imperious voice. "She was trying to take our crown!" Farthingales tighten around me. I have never felt so powerless. I drop the wig and crown and issue a silent plea to Nathan within my mind. So many other things have happened in conjunction with the crown and thought. And communication. At a loss, I don't know what else to do. I feel guilty, not wanting Suresh, only Nathan. This is what he's built for. I think of us playing Chopin, side by side, in the music room all those years ago, my hand in tandem with his. His fingers dancing across keys. I play that same tune upon my heart.

NATHAN

"Nathan! Nathan! Come help!"

Set to the sound of piano notes.

Jerks me out of sleep. Who said those words and where am I?

I lie on the floor in the corner of a dark cottage; a small room that is hot, yet in the grate, there is no fire.

It comes back to me. The sounds of fire raging outside these walls. Outside, it is night and I can hear yelling as people continue to put out flames.

My right arm hurts, especially below the shoulder. I cannot move it at all.

The arm is bandaged and held against my body by a make-shift sling, consisting of rags. I try again to move the arm but can only jerk it a little. Even that hurts a great deal.

"Nathan!" There is the voice again. I listen closely. Does it sound like Isabel? A picture of her forms in my mind. Isabel as I last saw her, wearing the shimmering red dress I bought for her.

But now I cannot hear her. How much time has passed? Her words were echoey and distant, emerging from darkness.

They rang with fear. Where is she? Presumably still at Raleigh's house. I must get there. I sit up. The dull throbbing in my head grows. Now the room begins to spin.

A candle is lit, throwing light into the room. "What are you doing, my soft lad? But you'll hurt yourself if you don't lie down." The older woman in the wimple. She cradles the baby against her shoulder. The baby is quiet again and does not cry. Perhaps sleeping. That is good.

"I have . . . to go," I say. The words come slowly and with great effort. "Will you help me up?"

"Not now," replies the woman. "You need your rest. Stay still."

"What happened to me?"

She puts the baby down into a basket lined with a shirt, and looms over me. "I heard a thunderclap in the street and then your horse began to rear itself, making frightful noise. You were down on your back, some yards away, when I found you. The trail of blood from your arm was still fresh so I tore an old tunic and tied it. My husband, when he was alive, occasionally served as a soldier. Dragging you inside without hurting you was difficult. You have my neighbours to thank for that—they paused dousing their fire, and carried you in."

My temples still throb but I begin to string thoughts together. "I don't suppose you saw my sword?"

"I did not see anything."

"Do you have any arms? Something that belonged to your husband?"

The woman shakes her head. A suspicion enters her eyes, a distasteful resignation. She wants to argue but can tell there is no point. A coldness that was not there a moment ago fills the room. "There's a pistol, old and rusted. I don't have any powder or shot."

"Good. Retrieve it for me, please?" Like the Duke's pistol, now on Raleigh's wall.

"What shall you do with it—it should only be effective as a club," she scoffs.

"Better than nothing. Just get it for me."

She fetches the pistol. I have no real experience with firearms but even I can tell it is useless. "Stuff it into my waist," I instruct her, "then help me get to my horse."

The baby begins to wake and cry as the woman helps me struggle to my feet. Searing pain runs down my side every time the bandaged arm moves, and even when it doesn't. I focus on the baby's crying: it isn't the keen wailing most babies usually make. More a kind of mournful lowing, an infant's dirge. It is a smart baby. It knows what kind of world it's born into.

She helps me into the saddle of my mare. Through clenched teeth, I bear the pain. I must bear it and make myself as comfortable as I can. My right arm, my throwing arm when I played football, as useless as the firearm. The arm I hold a sword in, the arm which should pull the reins, the arm I eat with.

Clasping the reins in my left hand, I lean my body backwards to try and achieve stability. The woman untethers the horse and it rears up, glad to finally be free and moving again. With each movement and jostle of the horse's hooves, a fresh searing jolt gallops through my right arm, down my side, and into my rump.

"I don't even know your name," I say to the old woman, looking ridiculous as I try not to double over.

"What does it matter?" she replies. "You shan't need to know my name where you're going."

Yes, what does it matter? "Take care of that baby in there," I whisper softly, nodding my head in deference to her age. She deserves it.

I lean back as much as I can during the painful ride through the smoke and water to the safety of Raleigh's house. It's night but with everything ablaze, there is no lack of light. No shortage of things to see either: broken men and horses, soldiers and citizens fighting in the streets, smoke everywhere.

People and rubble covered in ash and dust. Grey soot rains from the sky. Civilisation's graveyard. The end of Elizabeth's peaceful reign. It isn't even clear who's fighting whom. Londoners fight each other for scraps of food or souvenirs from crumbling houses. At the same time, others work in tandem to beat out fires and help those in need. No good or evil, simply madness.

I concentrate on Isabel. The distance to Raleigh's house is not far. I've aged lifetimes by the time I reach it. The old trees in his garden are still ablaze, mostly liquid tar now; they sizzle rather than flame. The stage has smouldered and split into planks.

Isabel is seated on the grass along with the Queen and many women. Suresh and Dee and Shakespeare and Raleigh are nowhere to be seen. I instinctively realise what's happened. She sent them off before I could make up my mind what to do with Shakespeare. I scoff at the realisation, the pain in my body momentarily forgotten. Shakespeare is gone but Drake is here. It seems he found his men after all and they were caught by a column of Spanish soldiers. As I ride into the garden, the Spanish have Drake and his men lined up against the wall and are about to execute him with an arquebus that must still work.

Isabel and the other women sit in a group around the Queen, forced to watch. Seeing Isabel, I remember the plea, the piano tune. She is surrounded, a captive among the Queen and her ladies. They in turn are captives among the Spanish. Where are Admiral Howard and Rawley in all this?

I am too late for Isabel. But perhaps I can save Drake. Let me at least try.

Mustering all the composure I can, I cry: "Stop! Lower your weapon!"

The soldier holding the arquebus turns around, still holding his gun level against his chest. I can see the stubble, the hairs of an almost short beard on this man's face. His large lips as he licks his mouth.

"What are you playing at?" asks Drake, puzzled to see me swaying atop my roan mare.

I transfer the reins to my bandaged hand with as much grace as I can muster. The horse instinctively remains still. I could dig my heels into its flanks and make it rush into the Spanish soldiers but the charge would probably destroy me as well. With my broken and bleeding arm, I certainly could not control it.

The pistol is empty but it is the best thing I have. It is still night and perhaps the light from the smouldering trees isn't enough to show that the pistol is old and rusted. It would be purely a theatrical gesture, like something out of a play. A feint. It occurs to me again that a play is also a strategy for football players. The English language—what a strange thing.

Spots dance in front of my eyes. My mind vaults and my body sways. Must not get sloppy or distracted. I pull out the pistol and wave it ambiguously before aiming it in the general direction of the soldier with the arquebus.

"Execute them, sir!" cries the Queen, cold fury in her voice.

"No!" cries Isabel, directing her gesticulation towards me. Confusion is sown. Raleigh comes out of hiding. He and Drake's men seize the moment and rush the Spanish soldiers. Do I squeeze the trigger or not? Do I have the stomach to kill again? And whom do I kill?

It only occurs to me later: there is no shot in the pistol. My mind is no good. The trigger is too rusted. There is no shot in the pistol. Instead of a shot, a folded square of white paper falls out of my sleeve and flutters to the ground. All I hear are the men rushing forward as I am dragged off the horse before the pistol falls from my one good hand. My right arm spasms in pain and my body hits the ground.

SURESH

Three days. It takes three days to fully deal with the damage we've wrought. Some of the fires still burn. The initial carnage is over and pockets of London are in substantial ruin. Shoreditch to the Strand and especially the areas around London Bridge are most affected. We are lucky much of the fleet landed in the Thames, which is clogged with wreckage.

More damage has been done to the Thames embankment than the sprawling city around it. It's the theatres, shut down, and forbidden to conduct their commerce within the city limits of London, that are ironically unscathed.

The Queen herself is recovered and well—the palace of Whitehall and the Westminster area in general are unaffected. Doctor Dee has heard she has retired to her palace of Greenwich in the East. She doesn't wish to see the smouldering flames or the wreckage, the bodies strewn in the streets. The blood and bodies and timber of the Spaniards lies mixed with those of the English. Dee and I walked around. You cannot tell which parts belong to whom. In the midst of all this destruction, I slowly begin to not forgive him exactly, but understand him a little perhaps.

Mostly, we are told to stay indoors but Drake and his confederates have plundered without setting foot off dry land. Now that they've gotten used to the destruction, some are even rejoicing, calling it a boon from heaven. They're arguing the vast and shattered timbers of the Spanish galleons can be used to rebuild London's houses.

Even Nathan, laid up at Raleigh's, profited second-hand though he could not take part. The Spanish executioners were themselves immediately executed. Nathan always comes out on top. They found the note that fluttered out of Nathan's sleeve and all it said was Will's name. Ambiguous, but not enough to place him under suspicion. Not like Isabel, who is very much under suspicion and jailed in the Tower. The only thing delaying her interrogation and torture is the current crisis. Nathan's upset at myself and Isabel for not including him in our decisions. Not having waited for him, acting on our own once he'd left. He will not talk to me. Yet he came back for Isabel, and in doing so, probably saved us all. Even I have to admit that.

Dee has been able to ascertain where in the Tower Isabel's being held. Despite her extensive knowledge of history and literature, she has ended up the worst off. She is confined to the Cradle Tower. Dee tells me that the tower looks out from a very high rampart onto a moat of water surrounding the Tower complex. It doesn't have the nice accommodations of the White Tower. Dee tells me that when Elizabeth was confined to the White Tower during her sister Mary Tudor's reign, she could bribe the warders and have one's friends bring comforts and materials such as books, food, and tools for crafts—needlework or carving—to pass her time. I feel we must do the same for Isabel but Dee is reluctant to try. He has much to lose and moreover, a family to think of.

They've interrogated Isabel somewhat I'm sure, but she's

probably stuck to a simple story: she knows nothing. She simply wanted the crown because it was pretty and it had called out to her. After a fashion, this is truth. We can only vaguely guess at the invisible strings pulling our puppet lives; it's a miracle we've lasted this long. And it's all my fault. It's all my fault and I must do something about it. I think of Isabel. I think of her and we have to find a way of bribing the guards. We must get past them.

ISABEL

I pace back and forth in my cell, still wearing the beautiful but burnt and torn red satin dress that Nathan bought for me. Back and forth. Back and forth.

I sit down on the hard ground because my feet are killing me, listen to the footfalls of the guards outside my cell. It is more room than Will and I ever had but the confinement is torturous. The warder moves around. I hang on to the echo of his voice and the footfalls of others but I must not call out to him or bother them too much. They get upset when I do that. Get myself into greater trouble. I get up, again pace back and forth.

I also hear the caws of crows and the warbling of pigeons who fly up from the Thames. The authorities evidently do not know what to do with me. It is only because they are otherwise occupied with London's destruction that I have been granted a reprieve.

On my fourth day here, I am visited by Suresh, Doctor Dee, and Sir Walter Raleigh. Either they bribe the warder to gain admittance or use Raleigh's authority; I am not sure. Nathan doesn't come with them and that makes me sadder when I should only be happy to see my friends. They bring food: cheese, bread, and oranges, much like what I transported to Will after visiting Mortlake so long ago. How did things ever get so bad? We had adapted; we had it under control. I'm too hungry to reflect too deeply on the past and wolf down the bread and cheese immediately—it tastes much better than the slops they feed me here.

Suresh has a very long face; sorrow hangs on his frame like a cloak. "Don't worry, Suresh," I croak, "whatever you feel, I'm feeling it ten times worse." Even the sound of my voice in my ears startles me, forcing an involuntary shudder. My hair, normally smooth and tied back, straggles in knotted wisps about my shoulders. I wish Nathan was here.

"Your hair's starting to look like Ms Sullivan's," says Suresh. "If you're not careful, you're going to end up unmarried like her." I laugh, despite myself.

"I must have lost weight. Do I look horrible? The skin is all blistered and cracked on my hands." My lips have also peeled though it's only been a few days. They have yet to empty the bucket for my waste; the reek in the cell embarrasses me.

"How now, Isabel?" asks Doctor Dee lightly. He sits on a stool that the warder has given him. He sits apart from Suresh who stands beside Raleigh as if Suresh is using Raleigh to separate himself from Dee. Everything has fallen apart.

"Were you able to save Will? The papers?" I ask, wishing to draw conversation away from me.

Suresh nods. "We saved most of the manuscripts but Will won't go. He insists on being here in 'this most exciting time in the city's history.' Your lodgings, north of the river, were fine by the way. He's using the 'lockdown' time to write new work."

"Lockdown?" Suresh's use of the term, so evocative and pointed.

"It is the rats you see," explains Dee. "The rats are even worse than the Spaniards. The plague has returned. The rats poured out of the ships and joined the rats of London in one large swarm. Emboldened them, you might say. More than a few people were bitten. Many of our acquaintances are removing themselves to the countryside. Will's own players will tour to put on performances, but he will work on writing new plays."

"That is good," I mutter. At least some good came of everything. "They must have told you something of what's going on, Sir Raleigh? What really goes on, I mean."

Raleigh appears uncomfortable. He's known for his silver tongue but hasn't said anything. He shifts uneasily in his large leather boots. As Captain of the Queen's Guard, he will have to question me formally soon enough and I gather it will not be gentle. Raleigh takes a couple of shillings out of his purse and hands them over. I look at the money dumbly, wondering what good it will do me now.

"From Will," says Raleigh, "your share of the pay for helping him. He says he does not wish to see you again. You will understand, of course, that he shall want to distance himself as far as possible now." Now, I have not only lost Nathan. Will wants nothing to do with me. I nod. Does Will truly believe I'm some sort of nefarious mountebank or spy? After all our discussions about writing and life? I'd cry but I am all out of tears.

Raleigh crouches down and stares at me intently. It's hard for him to crouch in the long boots and they creak stiffly, the smell of oiled leather momentarily cutting through that of the waste bucket. His sword clanks against the flagstones loudly, making me once again think of Nathan. He strokes his beard which juts out over his ruff. "These men have told some pretty and fantastic stories," he says, "but then I remembered the substance of Will's play, and that you did help him finish it. I thought of your Athenians who cross time's river, and the fancies began to conjoin in my addled brain. I've sailed far myself but never have we thought of crossing the tides of time. If you do not wish to see me again—and in a very different manner—tell me something I can believe. No falsehoods now; I do not wish to throw away my Queen's trust for a pouch of fanciful lies."

So they've explained more than I hoped. There's nothing to be done for it now. Raleigh's a sly one—who knows what he'll do with the information. "You're secretly married to Elizabeth Throckmorton," I say, "whom others call Bess, lady-in-waiting to the Queen. You have conceived a child together. That's who the play was truly for, wasn't it, or at least the wedding ceremony? Yourselves?" I lean into my words to give them emphasis. Raleigh immediately goes white. So, I am right.

"Put yourself in her shoes, Raleigh," says Dee quietly, indicating me with his forefinger, "none of them belong here. It is no good harbouring one at your house and allowing the other to rot in the Tower. We must help her. We are privy to a great and rare privilege; we must help them all." Suresh winces at the irony of Dee's words.

"It's akin to witchcraft," whispers Raleigh. "Worse even. You can see how this will be perceived, Dee—you attract the most dubious companions."

"She has not used her knowledge for anything except to try and find a way out, back to her own time," urges Dee. "Can you blame her? The only one that has ascended is your own charge, Nathan. The forces of Time have tried to kill her. Kill all of us, and failed. We have somehow survived and for this, we must be grateful. You must use your influence to help. You *must* do the correct thing."

"What can be done?" whispers Raleigh. The footfalls of the guard outside resume. We wait for him to pass. "To know the future, what must come. Dee, I know you have performed many Actions but this is strange, even for yourself. If we take the risk, Nathan must leave with them. It is paramount. They do not belong here."

This is a dress rehearsal for the interrogation to come. The birds are our audience; they coo outside my cell and nest on the ramparts, they strut on the roof above. Even the mice and rats which run over the floor have more freedom than I do. And soon, they will possess more longevity. When the men have tortured me, ripped all the secrets out of my tender brain and lacerated my flesh, they will lead me out to the executioner's block. The hooded executioner will lay a heavy axe against my exposed, malnourished neck. Unless Raleigh does something.

"The crown's the key," I venture, "The Queen's platinum crown with the transistor or the emerald or whatever you wish to call it. Can you get it for us?"

"How would I do that?" asks Raleigh, alarmed.

"Your Bess. She must have access to it. Could you not ask her to steal it away for us?"

"No, that will not do. She is in enough trouble, especially if you know about us. Who knows what you shall spill once they put you to the rack? No, for that reason and that reason alone, I shall help you escape but you must also take Nathan with you. Far from here." He strides over to the corner of the cell and feels around the bricks in the wall. Some of them have become loosened by the reverberations and shock from the recent catastrophe.

The mortar has crack lines in it. Like loose teeth, a few stones wobble at Raleigh's touch. He withdraws a large iron spike, almost like a very small crowbar, flattened and sharpened at one end, from his pouch, and a ball of twine. So, he obviously was prepared but needed convincing. He's slippery; no wonder he and Nathan get along.

He shows me the items, then hides the spike and twine in a corner. "Use this," he instructs, "to loosen one of the stones. Chip away at the mortar slowly and steadily over the next two days. In time, you will be able to move one of the larger stones. You then use it to smash the lock on the door to the roof. You understand me?" He points to the door in the roof of my cell which can be reached by a narrow ladder set against the wall. I'd never thought of using it to escape because reaching the roof simply means coming out on the ramparts of the fort. It is a small rampart, from what I'm given to understand, and there would be high walls on either side of me. Surrounding the wall is a moat, chilly air, and of course the terrible fall into the water below.

"What could I possibly do then?" I ask Raleigh.

"Then you tie the twine around the spike, securely and carefully, and throw it over the water. Your friends must help with the rest."

I look at Suresh who is trying to put on a hopeful face. "We can do it," he smiles. "We just need to get the crown and then get you out of here."

But we'll never get the crown. Raleigh will never compromise his wife.

"If we can find some way to steal the crown, Doctor Dee and I will examine it," continues Suresh. "The crown we saw on the night of the play is modified; it has no leads and may not work. That's another problem. Doctor Dee and I will have to smelt something using his laboratory. I can maybe use the remaining parts of my cellphone."

"Okay . . . " that's a big if, "and then what?" I try to gird myself.

"Take no longer than two days at most to chip away the brick. When you have it loose, you'll be ready to escape." Raleigh's voice trails off towards the end, as if even he doesn't quite believe in his own plan.

"I'll be waiting for you," Suresh declares a little more forcefully. "We'll have the crown by then, hopefully wired up and ready to function. There's still so very little we know about how the technology works." I look at him. Is he putting on a brave front or is he as emotionally out of tune as ever? Does he not realise how bad our situation is? If I were him, I'd probably be entertaining thoughts of saving my own skin. And yet, more than ever, I don't want to be abandoned and left here to be tortured, then killed.

"When you have loosened a brick, you can break the lock on the door like Sir Raleigh says," continues Suresh. "Eat and sleep in the meantime so that you are well rested. Once you're above, on the wall, throw the spike and twine over the moat and the outer wall. I'll be waiting there with a rope which we'll tie onto the twine and then you can haul the rope back over the moat."

I nod for him to go on.

"Then comes the difficult part," he says. "You have to climb hand over hand across the rope to safety."

The difficult part? It's all difficult. But the image of my broken body rotting away in the ground flashes through my mind. My blood flowing across the executioner's block. And that is how I make my mark in this century. No more than a stain. I must believe in Suresh. There is nothing else for me now.

"I wish I could stay here inside, with you," Suresh blurts, suddenly. "Caw like one of the crows when you're on the wall, and I'll caw back." He stares into my eyes and clasps my fingers. My face and hair are filthy. A filthy shipwreck stuffed into a red satin dress. My eyes move away for I cannot look at his face.

"I'm going to get you out of here," he says.

WILL

It is difficult to write amidst chaos and confusion. Our lives have been brought to a standstill. It is even harder to believe that Isabel is any kind of spy, though people say it must be so.

If she is a spy, she acts more convincingly than any player I have met, more convincingly than any person I have met, and yet, what advantage to foreign powers could be served by living with me? None at all. She was truly passionate about writing for the theatre. In writing, it can be hard to discern what is true and what is not, but she truly seemed to love that which we accomplished together. It pains me to cast her off. What her true story is, I will never know.

The last thing I expect to receive is a letter directly from her. I expected news of her death before I expected a letter. Curiosity gets the better of me and I break the seal on the covering, open it to discover a fairly uninteresting letter, written in a large hand with much spacing between the lines. It smells faintly of oranges and reads:

Dear Will,

Thank you for the two shillings you have spared me from the proceeds of the play. I thought it performed exceedingly well and your production captured the spirit and whimsy of the plot. I think that once the present difficulties are over and attendance at the theatres returns, it will prove a profitable play, one you should mount often.

It is your own mirth and ingenuity that have provided the heart and soul of it. Though I attempted to help, it was you all along. You have something rare and therefore, you should not give up your pursuits to expand the English language or our understanding of human nature. To write well and truly is perhaps the most difficult and rewarding endeavour a person might engage in.

Yours in earnest,
Isabel

It is a sweet sentiment but impersonal, does not sound like the woman I know: the demanding and precise Isabel who, in exasperation, argues with me. Why did she send it? I am about to drop the letter into the fire, as I should have nothing connecting her to me after the events at Durham House, but as I hold it against the flames, the faint smell of oranges wafts over me again. Are there oranges in the room—has one rolled into some nook or cranny after I played with it weeks ago? It should not smell sweet; it would be rotten. The paper, momentarily forgotten, warms by the fire, browning. Letters, more brown than the paper, slowly crisp upon it between the lines I have just read. There is a secret letter between the lines, brown sugar only now revealing itself:

> *This is written in secret, using the extract of oranges, in case they read it. Come visit me, if you do not hate me already. You may want nothing to do with me and I promised myself I would not disturb you, but despair over my situation has gotten the better of me. Do come visit if I have been of any service to you. It was never about the money. They will kill me; I am sure of it. If I don't want to die, I must try and escape. Even then, if by miracle I am not killed, I will never see you again for I must flee London.*
>
> *I bribed the warder with the two shillings given to me. He is a stupid but agreeable man. He will admit you and not report it if your visit is brief.*

Well—this is most intriguing. And a tempting proposition to boot. I know it is dangerous and that I am told to have nothing to do with her or her situation, but I am curious. Whatever her story, I may gather details to use in further plays. Even the visit to the Tower might prove instructive. It will give me a chance to survey London after the ruin. It may even give me a glimpse into the nobles and their twisted and ruined lives.

The slow walk towards the city's centre allows me to think and ruminate until I come to the radius of destruction which only intensifies, the further I walk. Large numbers of dispossessed people make their way slowly in the opposite direction. Others lounge around listlessly, huddled over fires on the heath. How many are in towns they have never seen before, with acquaintances or relatives they hardly know?

The wreckage is still being carted from the river as I get to town. Bodies are being burned along with cast-off timber from the wrecked houses. No time for burials unless you are one of the rich and can afford the time and luxury of a lavish ceremony. The stench of burnt flesh hovers over the city and will not disperse. Can this really be the work of sorcery and nefarious spirits as people are saying? Did the ships truly fall out of the sky? Who saw them fall? I only remember worrying about the conclusion of the play, that it should sufficiently tickle the nobles without incurring their wrath. I was looking down instead of up.

Again, I look down as I stumble through my thoughts when my feet inadvertently trip over swords which have been laid upon paving stones. People have set up makeshift stalls along the Thames, selling items they have scavenged or outright stolen from the wreckage. This is expressly forbidden as all properties belong to our sovereign Queen; all spoils and booty are supposed to be diabolically tinged. However, people are desperate and will flout the rules. The city fathers have larger fish to fry. Though it is easy to gossip about the occult and the evil eye, the heart of mankind is sensible of what it does, seeks to make sense and truth of understanding, although expressing that truth is a vastly different matter.

I stop to examine the wares. Combing through a pile of

swords and halters and soldiers' jerkins, things that have clearly been pillaged from dead soldiers' bodies, I am struck by something that flashes at me, gleams with platinum light. I pick it up and look at it. A single, elegant band of platinum with two trails attached to it. Not a crown exactly but I have seen something like it before—what is it? And then, it comes back to me—the Queen, our Elizabeth, was wearing something very much like this. Hers was a diadem, polished and holding a green stone, not red like this one. This one's exterior is muddy and briny; and what are these two things which trail from it?

"How much for this?" I ask.

"For that?" says an old man, wrapped in a sooty blanket, staring shrewdly at me, grinning through missing teeth. "Half a crown if you like. Half a crown for a crown!"

"This isn't a real crown, and you know it, sir! This does not look like precious metal and besides, is filthy with seawater. Where did you get it?"

"It's Spanish treasure, sir, as true as any you'll find. Three shillings then and that's a fine bargain. What do you want it for? Fit for a king, that is."

"I want it for a theatrical costume. The one we use is shoddy and gaudy. The simplicity of this is appealing, but it's no treasure. I shall offer you one shilling and not a penny more."

He looks comically in both directions, away from me, a gesture worthy of Will Kemp, supposedly to make sure no one's watching but truly for my benefit, and whispers "sold."

A little further, before I reach the Tower, the thought of trying on the new prop makes me pause. After all, I should see if it fits and what it looks like. I make my way down to the water's edge and try on the "crown." It fits perfectly. I gaze into the water and . . . the emotions and images that come rushing to me! Within the grey roiling waters of the Thames, I see visions of things impossible: stars and vistas as bright as the heavens, animals as fantastic as those from the Bible or mythology, many-headed dragons and basilisks and serpents crawling out of the caves of Hell. I see cities and empires rise and fall, as mighty as London, mightier even. Two lovers entwined around the bark of a tree ripe with fruit, a colour I know no name for. I see the sea's spume crash into the shore of an unnamed land with Herculean force. Armies clash like waves against each other on ancient plains with large shields and spears, their skin sunburnt, heads lost in flashing helmets adorned with colourful plumes. I see stallions snort and eagles soar. And myself, like Jove, in golden raiment flying through the clouds, presiding over a fleet of ships that circumnavigate the globe. Myself the monarch, the emperor of everything. No longer a beauteous crow but a giant eagle or a roc. Nothing that can be imagined is beyond my power.

I see all of these things and more, quickly, terribly, flashing through my mind, reflected in the Thames' waters. The power and desire so seductive. Suddenly, I feel the compulsion, the urge, to rip the crown off my head and leap into the water. To leap headfirst, descend beneath the swirling currents, and embrace all of those fantasies. For, the certainty there is no afterlife comes to me. But I may have it all, all that I see, simply by leaving this impoverished life and embracing that beneath the water.

The crown almost makes me jump, and no one stops me. No one cares. My death would only be another insignificant detail in the horrendous catalogue of the past few days. The wreckage of galleons still floats in the river; people tarry to fish anything they might use out of the soup. The rubble of London Bridge and the houses once built upon it all around us, clogging the water's flow. Decapitated heads, black with pitch, have been freed from their stakes and bob upon the river. Some seem to look up at us, pleading as if they have merely misplaced their bodies, imploring us to help them find their absent torsos beneath the water, while others sink, only to be pushed further downriver.

Enough! I tear the crown off my head. Enough of this madness. Why would I wish to jump in the river and add to the death toll? What is this urge and whence does it come?

At the Tower, the warder is hospitable, as if he expects me. It is exactly as Isabel said: he has a ruddy face that is agreeable and is both benign yet stupid. It allows him to be a happy man.

Even the catastrophe has not jolted him. His prattle unceases: "A playwright, are ye, and the woman who's imprisoned? A shame she's a traitor, and so young. Strange what the women do when you're not looking. My wife goes in for the theatre but I don't understand what she sees in 'em. You pays your penny, stand around, a lot of people shout, and then you go home, cold and tired. Let me tell you, real life, especially what comes through the Tower, is what's interesting. If you put me on your stage at a penny a head, I'd tell some real belters!"

"No doubt you would," I reply. It is quite obvious he's drunk. Isabel's money, the fruit of our labours, has poured spirits directly into his veins.

"For what's the difference between them nobles that come through here and myself?" he continues, entreating me with a command performance. "Why, we shall both go to the same place under the ground which people stand on, commoners and princes alike. The only difference is they that come here shall, more often than not, arrive there sooner than myself. First class lives all the way; first class speed into the ground. No thank ye, I'd rather take the slow coach."

"There is a lot of wisdom in what you say."

"Aye, make no mistake. A simple life and a great deal of tolerance shall speed one well enough, if ye catch my meaning. I will outlast the rats and the monarchs and be happy doing it. Now, you may visit her but do not tarry long, sir. I must ask ye: what is it that ye be carrying, is it real gold?"

"Oh this?" I turn the fishy diadem around in my hands, "surely not. It is a stage crown, made of board and paint. See this 'jewel'—it is no ruby."

"Ah, yes, I could see that instantly. I have been in view of many riches myself. I could see the difference but others might not. Shall I hold it while you talk with the young lady?"

"Oh no, that will not be necessary."

"Then I suggest you hide it under your clothing. Not for myself, you understand, but it may prompt others to speak. Rumours are thicker than arrows lately." He lets me into the cell, and even gives me a stool to sit upon.

Isabel is huddled against the wall, hair falling in tangles over her downturned face, as she clasps her knees with trembling hands. When she looks up and sees me, shock and joy wash over her face. "I didn't think you'd get my letter," she cries in a tearful voice, "or if you got it, I didn't think you'd come."

"Isabel, I was not sure I should, but I had to find out whether the rumours are true. You did not have to write your secret missive in orange juice, you know."

"Why is that?"

"I'm sure the warder is quite illiterate."

"Oh!" she laughs madly. "This place. All the suspicion and paranoia! I will never truly understand this place; I am not from here—that is true—but I am no spy. It is all just fancy, Will."

"You are not going to tell me where you are from?"

She shakes her head. "Weren't you the one who told me that mystery is of utmost importance?"

I laugh. "Touché!"

She blushes. "Do you really believe that I could care about something as fickle as espionage? I lived with you. If you do not understand a person's nature and character, what hope is there for the rest of us? I just wanted to see you one last time. Before I make my departure one way or the other. I did not want you thinking the worst of me."

"Well, if I am truthful," I begin, and stroke my chin, "your forthright and passionate ideas about our play . . . I feel guilt as I receive the credit. You did bring forth novel ideas I had not credited before. It is a difficult thing to write a play, to balance all the components just right, it requires a deft touch. I hope you may pursue the practice wherever you end up, and that it is an easier affair than it is here." Her blue eyes stare back at me, probing, watery, as if she almost wishes to talk and divulge her secrets, but of course she does not. Whatever knowledge she harbours remains unperturbed and locked under those watery irises.

"It is you who must persist," she finally says. "I know it. You shall produce miracles."

She seems assured, though despondent about everything else. "Why, do you have other plots in mind?" I ask tentatively.

"Will, I do not think this is a good line of discussion," she shakes her head. "You shall work on your own from now on. It is enough to see you one last time and thank you. I know you shall make good."

"Is there something we could have improved in our play?" I ask, not quite ready to leave, still puzzled by her origins and intentions.

"Well—if you are asking me honestly . . . "

"I am."

"You could yet write stronger women's parts. Women are the same as men. We are not separate species. There is a lot more that is similar than different. There is a lot more that is universal than different."

"The play is driven by women, with strong characters to boot. Helena, Hermia, Titania . . . "

"Titania is forced to sleep with a donkey," she says without humour. "Helena and Hermia fight in the mud for our amusement. They are there to be torn down and mocked for mirth. Women players cannot even play the parts which represent them. I know this is not your fault but you *can* write parts that are more in earnest, that are more serious. Your own queen is a woman, is she not? And now she might take favour to you even as she throws disfavour on me—I don't know, it doesn't matter what I think, does it, in the end? You do what your instincts dictate. Something will work."

She becomes despondent again. "Look at this, what I found," I pull out the diadem from within my doublet to show to her. It sparkles in an odd way, still exerts its strange pull upon my emotions like a tide.

As her eyes catch the gleam of the metal, her disposition changes. "Where did you get that?"

"I bought it, Thames side. People are selling off wreckage. It is not gold of course, it is much too light. And this is not a gem. The man selling it had no other Spanish treasure, only weapons and halters. It is waterlogged and dirty but I thought by cleaning it, we might use it in our costumes for either Oberon or Theseus. It is better than a pasteboard crown. I then remembered our Queen wore something like it and your trying to filch it. Can it all be coincidence?"

"Will, listen to me, I need that. No, it cannot be coincidence that you found it. I do need it. It is not jewellery, it is worthless to you, at least it is worthless in the way that you think. Oh, I know I am not making sense but I need it. You must give it to me. It once belonged to me and my friends. It has brought us much trouble. If you give it back, our story here will be finished and we may leave. Won't you please, for a fellow writer, allow her to finish her story?"

"There is a lot you are not telling me."

"There surely is." She keeps staring at me, her blue eyes wide.

"Very well, I cannot pretend to fully understand you but I believe there is veracity in what you say. Truth be told, the object disturbs me." She nods in agreement. I reluctantly hand over the briny diadem, its two trailing parts tangled together. Even now I feel a pull and want to hold on as she grasps it. I wish to fight her for it.

My fingers finally let go as sense returns and my feelings ebb. My only wish at this point should be to reforge my life as a playwright, perhaps to see my family sooner than later. That is paramount now, that when I see them, I have money to give. I must stay the course.

"I shall never see you again?" I ask uncertainly.

"I doubt it, Will. In this case, the less you know, the better."

SURESH

Doctor Dee and I take our final ride down the Thames. Each piece of wreckage in the water feels like the exploded shrapnel of the trust and affection I once felt. It's certain this is the last time I'll see him. This is probably for the good. I sit as far apart in the boat as I can. The boatman stands between us, oblivious to our disagreement.

This morning, I ate nothing after sleeping fitfully. My stomach has shrivelled to the size of a prune. I didn't say goodbye to Jane or the children and they didn't say goodbye to me. Perhaps this is their way of indicating their home is still open, come what may. Perhaps this is their way of indicating they are done with me, just as I am done with them.

Near the centre of town, we pass a gibbet with rotting bodies hanging from it. No matter what changes, the gibbet endures, carrying out its function. I fancy I hear the creak of their ropes as the bodies swing, necks tightening, but of course I can't. Just my imagination.

"It is like the river Styx, is it not?" proclaims Dee loudly. "What are you thinking, Suresh?"

I look him directly in the eyes for the first time. I debate whether to not say anything and simply leave it at that. Sometimes Isabel is wrong; communication is not always better. "Are you sure you really want to know?" I ask.

He nods his head.

It's complicated with the boatman between us so I must talk around the thing. "How could you recommend the expansion of the British empire? How could you do that and also put me up, purport to be my friend? All your talk about the colour of my skin and your acceptance of me. How can you be the same person who sees no problem with the idea of slavery and empire?"

He stares back at me, rattled, quickly masks his expression with annoyance. Surely my feelings can't be that surprising to him. He gazes into the distance, beyond London, and coughs into his hand. "We are an island, Suresh. We have to preserve ourselves. If we do not, we will be swallowed by other powers. One must eat if one does not wish to be eaten."

"I was born on an island too," I reply angrily. "And we never tried to conquer anyone else. Well, the Tamils didn't. The Sinhalese just tried to swallow us. But we got along until the British devoured us and left chaos in their wake. Trust me— you cannot justify your appetite through size—it is nothing but greed. Pure and simple rapaciousness."

"There is no point crying over spilt milk, or rueing houses

after they're built. You judge me with the arrogance and ignorance of youth," he proclaims, miffed that I should question him. He's the one who asked for my feelings. "But I never judged you. I only found you interesting and did all I could to engage you. You repaid me by dismissing me as an old man, all of the knowledge I had endeavoured to learn and master as rubbish. You think I didn't know but I just let it . . . " His voice trails as he looks away again. So he knew what I thought all along.

"I didn't think you'd encourage the British domination of the world," I counter, giving vent to the fury simmering in my soul. We discuss as if it's already happened though it does not bother him. "You have the blood of nations on your hands."

"If you say so. It's the first time you have actually bothered to discuss the matter with me. And yet, you were happy to ask for my help, my money, my lodging, for the food from my children's mouths. I did not begrudge you anything."

"Except the survival of my race." That finally earns the attention of the boatman who turns around with a mystified expression. We say nothing after that, grateful for his presence between us.

"I embraced you in the spirit of knowledge," hisses Dee over his shoulder as we disembark at Durham House. "You are still asking for my help."

"In between my cleaning your chamber pots! Tell me again how I was lucky to land with you instead of becoming the Queen's groom of the stool? Like the way I trusted you with the draft of my letter to Isabel—you gave it to her without even telling me."

"I was helping you," he stammers weakly. "Jane and I thought you needed a little help putting yourself forward. You needed a push, that's all."

"A push? Now, who's condescending? I wasn't your pet; I was your experiment."

It is my first time back at Raleigh's since the events on the night of the play. We walk past scorched walls and burnt trees. The stage that once proudly mounted in the garden is char, the grass around it blackened. The smell of soot still cloys to the air. Inside, Raleigh leads us to Nathan who lies on a couch, nursing his fractured arm. I walk around Nathan as he lounges, his arm in splints on a pillow above his head. Both helpless and hopeless.

He wears a silk embroidered doublet and hose slashed with gold silk, for display and boasting, a ridiculous peacock, as if that makes up for his incapacitation. He stares at us, right through us, exhales a grunt that could be either greeting or warning.

Dee coaxes Nathan to talk, bringing up Isabel's plight.

"How is she?" asks Nathan, as if he doesn't know.

"We came all this way to accompany you and she's the one paying for it," I say. "You've come out lucky. I don't care if your shoulder's busted up. You always come out lucky. We're here because of you." I'm speaking loudly now, almost shouting.

"Help you? Why should I help *you*?" He sits up with some effort, pain declaring itself on his face. "Last I checked, I was the one who saved you . . . and Drake. And you hadn't even listened to my request to wait until I was back to handle Shakespeare. You decided without me."

"Grow up! Don't you ever think about anyone other than yourself?" I ask. "I hate you so much. You're fucking pathetic. I could gouge out your eyeballs with my thumbs and you couldn't stop me."

That got his attention. "Me? You're the one who's pathetic— you follow me around like a stray dog, hoping I'll be your friend. And I was your friend, as much as that was possible. You're creepy and weird. Now, you've insinuated yourself between myself and Isabel. If I wasn't laid up, I'd teach you some manners."

233

"What has happened to you?" asks Dee. "It is as if you were looking to fight with everyone. Nathan is your friend."

"Yeah, we're friends when it suits him," I reply bitterly. "When he needs something and has nowhere to turn. When he needs to hand in an essay, or he'll fail the class." I walk over to Nathan as he raises his good hand to shield his face. It's no use. He's as helpless as a kitten; I press my thumb against his wound. He howls in pain. Not knowing how to fight, I grasp him awkwardly for my black robes are long, and give him a bear hug against which he squirms, biting his lip, holding back pain.

"Let's go," I say. This has been coming for a long time. "Let's rumble."

I pull him off the couch, still clasping him, so we roll onto the floor. I want to put my hands around his throat but he slithers out from under me. Dee, old and weak as he is, grabs my robe and pulls it as best he can. Raleigh pulls us both apart with a finality that stops the conversation. Raleigh's arms are strong. My knees are scraped and my clothes are dirty.

"You try this when I'm better," Nathan snarls, teeth clenched against the pain, "and I'll kill you."

"You're not going to be killing anybody again, ever," I hold my ground.

"You cannot stay here," booms Raleigh, speaking over us both. "I have helped as much as I can, for Dee's sake. Now you must leave. You are both making things worse for me and you do not belong here." He firmly picks Nathan up and places him back onto the couch, plumps the pillow before sliding it under Nathan's head. "You will never fit in with the soldiers, Nathan. Injury or no, you had better go and as soon as possible; my house cannot be a sanctuary for you."

Even I can hear the resignation in my voice, defeated. London has worn us down. "Isabel's going to die if we don't help her." I rub my elbow. "Don't you care about her?"

"Of course I care!" shouts Nathan. "I saw them torture that thing in the Tower. I know what happens there. We could have all secured our destinies, but you two dropped the opportunity. It's ruined now."

Isabel's face, framed by auburn hair, comes into view. She will be executed. That auburn hair will be separated from the rest of her, permanently. Just another head upon another pole in this horrible place. What will that final look on her impaled face convey? Will it be an expression of despair, forever recriminating? Because I could not act? No, I *must* do something.

Raleigh comes to my aid, sort of. "Master Nathan," he lulls in his steady, grave, melodious voice: "you cannot stay here but you may voyage far away. I still offer you employment in my colony abroad if you wish—many a man starts his life over in the New World. But you must help your friends first. They do not belong here any more than you do."

"I didn't come all the way over here just to go back, the slow way," Nathan replies bitterly and begins to cross his arms, but soon realises he cannot. "Okay," he cries with sudden exasperation, as tired, exhausted, and heartbroken as I am. When did any of us last sleep? "It's better than nothing at this point, I suppose. You'd better tell me of this brilliant plan of yours. How on earth are we supposed to free Isabel?"

ISABEL

I use the iron spike, slowly and sparingly like Raleigh suggested, to chip away mortar around the stone. The work must be done carefully, mostly at night, when the guards' footfalls echo less and less often, and their voices can no longer be heard.

Finally, the large stone pries loose and I feel cold air through the opening. The aperture is only large enough to fit some fingers through, but no matter. I can hear the wind and see the sky. A pinprick of hope beams into my cell. More importantly, it gives me a sense of when day turns to night. It is the night that I need. The remaining time is spent eating the rest of the bread and oranges to regain my strength.

The last orange has some mould on it. I roll it around the cell and think of Will. It is strange to think that I got so used to living with him, working with him, talking to him. My father and Ms Sullivan built him up so much that the effect of talking with him, once I was used to it, could only be humdrum. Not even disappointing but worse: routine and ordinary. But now he is gone, he and his mythical self become conjoined again in my mind. He is once more a vessel for the plays he will write. I hold the platinum crown in my hands and think of him. He begins to glow, radiate, as he did before.

I attempt stretches and push-ups. It is difficult. I carefully replace the stone that is loosened and hide the spike and twine behind it. The evening of the second day draws. I must play the final gambit, regardless of whether Suresh will show. Because there are no other options.

Once the twilight bleeds into night, I make my move. I loosen the stone and look through the opening, confirming that it is indeed the darkest night outside my tower. A draft blows in and I once again hear the cawing of nearby crows. Practising cawing myself to see if I can imitate the sound, I become satisfied I can execute an approximate call. I have cut off part of the twine by wearing it down against rough stone and now use it to tie the crown to my thigh, hidden by my dress's skirt. The crown is light and I can feel it pulsate against my leg, willing to attach itself, almost communicating through my skin. Urging me on. I climb up the narrow ladder and balance myself at the top, bash the lock with my stone. It takes less effort than I'd anticipated—it's an old lock and its metal is corroded.

Now I carefully replace the stone in the wall. Fishing out the rest of the twine and iron spike, I tie one end of the twine to the spike and then coil the whole thing about my arm. Hiking my skirts up, I climb the ladder once more, push through the door in the ceiling, hoist myself onto the ramparts.

The moon appears from behind a bank of clouds. The cold, wet stones of the tower are bathed in ghostly light. I can see over the walls into the still black water of the moat. It contains a murky reflection of the moon and clouds drifting over it. I can hear the water gently lapping against the stone. The drop must be something like seventy feet, a hundred even. My neck will break. Then the crocodiles that are rumoured to live here will rip me to pieces. One of the guards told me the Queen is supposed to have exotic animals living on the grounds, lions even. Was he pulling my leg? It takes a long time for my body to stop shaking, due to fear.

When I get hold of myself, I see the far wall, beyond which lie the wharf and freedom. If all is not lost, Suresh is on the other side of that wall with a long rope and a ladder. God, I hope he's there for I cannot see over the wall. To my right is a glimpse of London. Tower Street and Thames Street stretch away. Further away lie the remnants of the bridge. It's in pieces and the destruction only spreads north and west from here. The houses that once towered over the bridge lie demolished. The Thames embankment on the north side will not recover for many years.

In the dark, I see the crushing glow of fires amongst the ruins of once proud houses—roofs and walls thrown into gutters, nothing left except waste and debris. Hulls and wreckage from boats still float upon the Thames' strangled tide. Curved shapes that might be rotten corpses or animals wash against the shore.

The moon goes back behind the clouds and sight is taken from me. No time to grieve, but to act.

Unwinding the twine from around my arm, I approach the edge of the battlements and caw with all my strength. Some of the birds nesting amongst the stones around me become startled and fly away. Hearing nothing, I caw again. Then it comes. There it is. A very faint cawing, off register, unmistakably produced by a human voice.

I can't see anyone on the wharf so if Suresh is there, he must be in the shadows. Heaving the iron spike with all my might, I throw it across the water. It's too dark. The line and spike fly away from me. A loud clang and the twine drops. Damn. It's dropped too much. The spike has not made it over but has instead clanged against the near side of the wall.

Slowly, patiently, so as not to lose the spike, I hoist up the twine, hand over hand, fist over fist, feeling the weight of the spike at the bottom. It's a little wet but I haven't lost it. Quickly, dry the spike against my dress, retie the knot to make sure the spike is secure. Then, concentrating and projecting on the other side of the wall, lob it again with even more force. It sails from my hand like a cannonball shot to the rafters; my arm almost wrenches from its socket. The spike flies with such force that the twine threatens to pull me off the tower, into the moat.

Luckily, the battlements stop me. Success! The twine lies taut and stretches over the water. The line falls at a very slight angle as it extends to the far wall but there is not much difference in height between the walls. I still cannot see anything. I wait.

Finally, the cawing sound again. Suresh! I pull on the twine. I pull and pull, careful not to go too fast. Eventually, the end of the twine comes back. The spike has been replaced by a heavy rope. I haul in the rope, pulling it over to the jamb of the door I've climbed out of. I tie the best knot I can through the large loop where the broken lock once rested. Three knots, then a fourth. This rope must be as secure as possible.

Now comes the difficult part. I have to climb onto the edge of the battlement, then grasp the rope and climb hand over hand to the far wall, my legs dangling over the moat. The darkness is a blessing. I can hear the black water rolling quietly below me as I launch into space. The rope is rough and thick. My hands feel small but the rope is large and steady. Its coarseness burns my palms.

I am weak; the rope sways the further I travel towards the centre. What is that movement below? What floats? Are those a couple of pale reptilian eyes? No, don't believe it; I'm not going to be eaten by a crocodile. Let's think of titles to distract me as I inch forward: *Pride and Prejudice*, *The Once and Future King*, *King Lear*, *Vanity Fair*, *Wuthering Heights*, *A Christmas Carol*, *Alice's Adventures in Wonderland* . . . the rope burns my palms and my legs dangle. My hands are tired and my body becomes heavier. The muscles in my arms burn. My elbows and shoulders are lacerating shards of pain. What other books can I think of? Dickens. Shakespeare. Austen. *Think. Think. Think* . . . no titles will come . . . *A Midsummer Night's Dream*. But that doesn't count. That title doesn't exist anymore. It is now *A Midsummer Night's Tyme*; all wrong. I've screwed up. The crown speaks, communing with my leg. Doesn't speak exactly but soothes my troubled mind. It doesn't matter if I have a block and cannot remember book titles. Nothing matters.

None of it matters. I might as well let go of the rope.

SURESH

What is she doing? What's taking her so long? I stick my skull-capped head over the wall: "What are you doing? Hurry up!"

When Isabel finally replies, her words come between sobs: "I

239

don't have the strength." I've never heard her like this.

"I'll heave you over if you can give me your hand," I shout.

"I don't have the strength to keep going," she moans.

It dawns on me. She's wrestling with whether to give up. Stuck in the middle between panic and despair. What if she does let go? What then? "If you want, I can climb forward and meet you?" I cringe. I didn't think of this. In my haste, I didn't think of all the possibilities.

"Don't be stupid. Then we'll both die."

"Nathan's here," I whisper, "he's standing, holding the ladder at the bottom of the wall." I hate myself for saying this—will I be upset if his presence revives her? The thought of him compelling her when I cannot. I should be at the bottom of the ladder and he should be at the top.

"What?" she yells.

Without thinking about it anymore—I know thinking will only freeze my resolve—I roll up my sleeves and slowly, hand over hand, begin inching towards her. The rope strains with our weight. Don't look down. Don't look down. The strain upon the muscles in my arms is immense. My legs flail in the air. She looks up, sees what I'm doing. It sets new fire to her efforts. Her head raised, her body comes alive and energy shudders through her arms. I can feel her revive through the rope. She ignores the pain and inches toward me.

I grab her quickly by the waist as soon as she reaches me, to communicate I won't allow her to fall, but we can't stay like that—I need both hands. Quickly letting go, and moving as fast as I can, I lead her back towards the wall. With my last muster, I hoist her onto the top of the wall. We sit there, still clutching the rope out of fear. Her body shakes. I try to put an arm on her shoulder and then realise my own body is heaving and my fingers twitch without my being able to stop them. We wait, allowing cold air to wash over us.

"It's good to see you," I say, "in the free air."

"We're not free yet," is all she can reply between gasps.

We finally get up, let go of the rope which is tethered to a post on the wharf. The ladder stands against the wall with Nathan at the bottom. We caw towards him to let him know we're coming and then, using the rope to hoist ourselves over the top of the wall, rappel down. It's a lot easier than going up, more dangerous too.

I allow Isabel to rest her feet on my shoulders from time to time. She's still shaky but her strength comes back to her. I can feel her heart pumping blood through her feet.

"Nathan's here," I mumble.

"You said that." The clicking uptightness in her voice is back.

When they stand face to face, there's such electricity between them, so much that I'm not sure if it is love or hate or something else I cannot identify. The charge makes my own tussle with Nathan seem like a playful conversation. I could live to a hundred and never have that with her.

"We've all got to move or we're going to be caught," I urge them out of their locked stare. "They'll have sounded the alarm. If they catch us, we all go to the executioner's block together."

"Wait a minute," says Nathan, "wait a minute." He looks at Isabel, then me, then back to Isabel. "There's something we have to settle first." What's he on about now?

"What?" asks Isabel.

"You have to choose," says Nathan, flatly. He's not menacing or condescending, or even proud. Not even competitive. This is him showing vulnerability, I guess. "You have to choose between myself and Suresh. We both like you. That's plain. You have to choose once and for all." The wind goes out of Isabel's sails. Her face takes on the same expression it did halfway across the moat. Caught in the middle. She turns around and walks away, then comes back.

She puffs out her cheeks as if she wants to blow us far away from her. Her voice goes small. "I care for both of you." She takes both our hands. "I care about you both. I want us all to be friends. I want to return to the way things were."

Nathan shakes his head. "It's too late for that. We're not the same people." With one arm swaddled, he looks both tragic and absurd. "Things just aren't the same anymore. Too much has happened. You have to choose: me or Suresh. It's that simple."

Isabel turns around and gazes into the Thames. The moon has come out again and its reflected rays illuminate the river's deep currents and wreckage. A mist and stink rises from it. Time is a river that brings only sadness and pain. As Dee said when quoting Heraclitus to me: "You cannot step in the same river twice."

"Why should I have to choose?" cries Isabel. "Why do I make all the hard decisions? Why don't you two date each other if you're so eager to date someone? You can hold hands in the moonlight, plant soft kisses as you go skipping down the street!"

"It's okay," I say, to stop her tirade from becoming even more shrill. "Things have changed. You two knew each other before I met either of you. You have a bond that's greater. I understand. I'll take myself out of the equation."

"What are you saying, Suresh?" asks Isabel, her voice quavering.

"I've changed so much since we've arrived here, I don't understand it. I hardly recognize myself sometimes. You two figure out whatever you need to. I'll give you room."

I walk away and turn my back but it's impossible not to hear them.

"If you feel that you have a right to be upset at me," Nathan states, "and keep in mind you ended up in the Tower because of what *you* did, I'll go to Raleigh's colony. I don't care. I'll start again."

"Why on Earth would you do that?" whispers Isabel, exasperatedly. "I acted in the moment because it was the only chance to get a crown back for all of us. Look!" Curiosity gets the better of me—I look over my shoulder to see what's going on. She has reached under her skirt and with a bizarre flourish, unties something from her thigh. What is that? Is that the—no, it can't be!

"Look what Will found among the wreckage being sold in the streets!" she cries triumphantly. "He was going to use it as a stage prop. If this isn't a sign, I don't know what is. We must return home, to our own time."

"There isn't anything for me there. I'll never be able to play football again or do anything that makes me feel good, not with my arm. It's not just that. I'm a loser there. No one takes me seriously. My father doesn't love me and my mother's angry all the time. Here, at least, I feel like a grown-up, my own man, something—the air feels different, like it's harsh but has possibility. It's better for me. You two go ahead."

"Are you sure?" asks Isabel, "don't you want to see your mother again?"

He shakes his head. "Everywhere I go, I'm trapped. Here, at least, I have the chance to try and write my own destiny. I'd rather venture to the New World here than go to Japan in your time. I'll take things as they come."

"My foolish idiot," Isabel whispers softly, and strokes his chin.

"My second mom," he replies.

I turn away again but can see them out the side of my eye. They're kissing. "Be careful then," she whispers, pausing. "Be cautious and careful." He cups her face with his good hand. Before they can kiss again, a coronet blasts from over the moat.

243

Shouts and cries are heard.

"That's them!" urges Nathan. "You'd better go. Suresh, it's time to cut the rope."

Nathan hands me a dagger and, with some difficulty, I cut the rope and it slackens.

"Nathan, are you sure?" Isabel asks one last time.

"I'll stay and deal with them," he replies. "Don't worry about me."

They've forgotten about me but there is no time for jealousy. Nor do I feel things as keenly; she still matters to me but not in the same way. Why was I so infatuated at one time? I take the crown away from Isabel and hold it up against the darkness. It glows pellucid green. Amazing that the wires and contacts are still attached. I trace my finger through the grime coating the metal. We are fishes and this is the hook that will pull us through the waters of time.

Isabel looks back at me, acknowledging how impossible it is that we should find it again. "It's like the story of *A Midsummer Night's Dream*," she says. "We thought we brought the story with us, either to save or destroy, but we were the story all along. It's looped around to pick us up."

I place the platinum band on my head and give one of the contacts to Isabel which she presses against her temple. We intertwine fingers and stand beside each other, say goodbye to Nathan. For a moment, he looks like he might speak or change his mind, but he just stands there silently, dagger in his hand. The cries of the guards intensify.

The waters of the Thames continue lapping. The crows above are cawing. The moon comes out, shining. I place my free hand against the circlet and concentrate hard. I send my alpha waves into this thing, this time machine, this particle accelerator, this mystery.

ISABEL

"Think and focus," encourages Suresh. "Remember the exact moment that we left. Concentrate on the school. Sullivan's classroom. The poster of The Globe on Sullivan's wall . . . remember it all."

I try my best to do as he suggests, to concentrate, to reinforce his memories with my own. Hopefully our different impressions will fit together like a jigsaw puzzle, take us back precisely to when we left. With nothing changed. But it's already changed, hasn't it? We're returning without Nathan. If we returned to the day before we left, would we find Nathan there? Would we find copies of ourselves—our previous drafts?

The ruby transistor on the side of the crown lights up, the glow increasing until it becomes an effulgent fire above Suresh's head. The glow spreads and encompasses both our bodies like some supernatural aura. Nathan's jaw falls slack in wonder and this is the last I see of him.

Our bodies shoot up into the sky. We don't enter the ground like before. Instead, like a couple of Elizabethan Mary Poppinses, like Dorothy in *The Wizard of Oz*, we rise. Looking down, we can just see Nathan with his shaggy hair and sling, one arm immobilised and the other holding his dagger, peering up. He's gone. We rise over the Tower walls like some gigantic bird, with wings half black and half red, conjoined heads half brown, half white, flying over the wharf.

Soldiers run down both sides of the Tower's complex. Soon, they'll surround Nathan. If he doesn't fight, perhaps he will fare better than us and depend upon his connection with Raleigh. We rise above the Thames River bobbing with the wreckage of our time here, the flotsam and jetsam of human beings and the strife they cause.

We rise even higher and see the destruction spreading

outward like a spiderweb north of the Thames, as if we are looking at the cracked screen of Suresh's cellphone. The stone embankment is broken. There is destruction all along Thames Street, roads of carnage, time's hellish map imposed on the mighty city.

Rush fires burn idly but we are too high to see the people huddled around them. Will might be down there, in our lodgings, writing. Dee also.

How could these events not affect them? There's Temple Bar and The Strand where Raleigh's house still stands, its tiled roof sooty from flame. There is Westminster and Whitehall. We can see Shoreditch and Southwark. In my mind, I can see the theatres. People might yet flock to them once again. All is not necessarily lost. Poetry frozen inside manuscript pages as if encased in ice: The Rose, The Curtain, The Theatre, The Swan. And even the bear garden, even the bear garden. How could I ever leave this place?

"Are you thinking about the exact time we left?" Suresh has to shout above the wind to be heard: "12:59 PM."

"I think it'll be a miracle if we can get back to the right year," I shout back. "Why do we keep going up? Are you sure this is how it works?" And, as if in response to my question, we suddenly plummet, falling faster and faster into the Thames.

SURESH

Rough-hewed timber presses back against our knuckles. It is wet and black with the ocean's spray, slick with oil. We are wet and cold.

At the same time, fire rages around us.

We are no longer above the Tower. The ground, which is splintered and rotten, is made of wood which seesaws about us. We have to lean our bodies in close to the wood so as not to be thrown by the rocking motion. Small things scurry all around us. It is hard to speak.

Our descent—sudden is not the word for it.

"What have you done?" Isabel screams at me. "This isn't Leonard Cohen Collegiate!"

I gaze back at her. My face must show how dumbfounded I am. I don't have an answer. My courage and resolve, so newly discovered, have left me. But I'm still wearing the slim platinum band with the two contacts trailing from it like wisps of hair. There is no explanation for what has happened. We slowly get up and look around, holding each other for support.

We are in the middle of the sea, upon a ship. Darkness and water surround us as far as the eye can see. The darkness is made light by the burning of many ships. The smell of tar and the noise of flames surround us. Perhaps there is land in the far distance.

Between us and land lies a vast flotilla of galleons. Ancient ships with massive bulwarks and staggered levels and huge decks and promontories, rising out of the water. Ornate wooden skyscrapers, bobbing on the ocean, weighted down and rigged with large sails, lined with many oars. In the dark, we can see people scurrying about, clambering up the ropes. Their faint cries come in, off the wind.

Where are we? What small things scurry around the deck? The reason they run, the reason we can see the immense flotilla, arrayed out in its indomitable crescent, is because our own ship is on fire. We are at the prow but the aft and mid deck are covered in blazing tar. The small, quick things scurrying around us are mice and rats. There are many of them and now, with the ship burning, they rush about in furry streaks of panic ahead of the flames. In a swarm, they jump into the water.

Isabel too realises what is happening. She screams. Not

because of the mice or the flames—because we are living the beginning again. We are caught in a loop. That whirlpool which exists in time as well as water tries to suck us in. There are five other warships, equally deserted, their decks and masts aflame. Slowly, we make our way towards the Spanish Armada. We feel the flames at our backs as our clothes are tattered.

The sense of déjà vu is overpowering. Sickening. I feel the whirlpool coming, as if spinning from within our heads.

"Take the contact! Take my hand!" I yell over the flames' roar. "It's trying to take us to the beginning of the story, to start again. We've got to counteract it!" We grab contacts. We grab hands. The fire spreads behind us. The six English ships, black with tar and ablaze in the night sky, drift towards Calais, where the soldiers on the Spanish galleons quickly try to cut their anchors and break away.

Now I can see that not all of the other English ships are deserted. The one closest to us has three people on board, leaning against the rail. They must have blended into the darkness and rigging before. I raise my hand and wave it in the night sky, shouting, but it is too hard to hear over the roar of the flames; was that us?

I concentrate hard and focus control. I think of Ms Sullivan's class, Shakespeare, and A Midsummer Night's Dream. But it is too difficult. What are we doing here? After all we've been through, I still cannot understand. What is time? Perhaps it is no more real, less real even, than the mind. Is time like the water around us? In the way that all the water in the world is linked? There was no water on the Earth in prehistoric times until it crashed onto our planet from outer space; that is a piece of knowledge I learned once. That thing which constitutes the greater part of ourselves is an alien visitor: think of all that water immigrating to Earth, frozen, on asteroids, seeking asylum after an interminable journey through space, integrating over time, determining the course of life.

Is time like water, then? And our minds the tide? Or is our mind like water and time the tide? Is it like the fire around us, with time the warmth? Can AI from the future actually see time, see it for what it is devoid of our tripping minds, or can they only manipulate it? A Google doc constantly being rewritten, as the head suggested? The thought is chilling. The idea that we are just the umpteenth revision, the latest version. That there are so many versions of us, unknowable to each other and ourselves. Completely lost. Space-time so worn and frayed with each rewriting it is threadbare.

I am paralysed and cannot gather my thoughts. No alpha waves. The maelstrom begins and the platinum band is ripped off my head. It flies upward, into the air. Isabel and I grasp at the contacts and wires.

Isabel, in a daring move, lets go, jumps up into the air, catching the crown with one hand. She brings it down, crouching, holding onto it for dear life. "Not this time!" is her cry.

The water begins churning around us. A whirlpool is being created out of the sea, the waters roil and tempest. The wind picks up even more and rages, almost blowing the flames away. A typhoon rises from the water.

"It's too hard to put the contact on properly or think!" I scream into the raging wind.

"Look at me," she screams back. "Do what I say and just hold onto the crown. Do you understand? Hold onto the crown! . . . No, better yet, hold onto me. Let me do it!"

She clutches the platinum circlet with bone white knuckles while the flames recover, burning against us. I let go of my contact, then gingerly place my hands around her as if we are dancing.

"Tighter!" she screams. I wish I could relax. I press tighter. The farthingale below her dress is large and bustling, like a blown-out umbrella. I can just place my arms over her waist. How tiny she is, pressed against my body. She always seems so much bigger in my mind. I place my cheek against hers so that I can speak into her ear.

"Now close your eyes and concentrate." She grips the circlet and seems to be concentrating her thoughts into her fists. I can feel her heart beating faster and faster. Her chest heaves in and out and in time, bellows in unison with my own. The circlet begins to glow its greenish ethereal warmth and the ruby transistor pulses with life.

I open one eye and see her transformed. The whirlpool, the vortex from the sea is almost upon us but we rise above it. Her clothes are destroyed. I can see her flesh through the farthingale. Isabel's whole body, supple and arched, glows green like the crown. Looking beyond her dirty auburn hair, her blue eyes, her scowling mouth, I gaze deep within her lungs where the alveoli work furiously, pumping pure oxygen into her bloodstream. I can see the blood shoot out from the ventricles of her heart into a thousand capillaries, circulating back through the veins. I can see her glorious tendons and muscles jointed to that delicate curve of a skeleton, pearl white in the night's moonlight shine.

Her thoughts dance an agitated hopscotch of unseen ideas and terrible notions. Books and characters and insights and language wash back and forth like waves. She is all these things and more. She is more idea than reality, more dream than flesh. She is made of water; she is made of time; she is made of ideas; she is made of everything. All this time, I thought maths and physics to be some perfect universal language that spoke life's truths. Truth that transcended our petty lives and planet. Yet these feelings, these impressions, these ideas flowing through her like water—they are just as perfect. Just as brilliant a way to understand the universe, perhaps even better. So unique, yet so changeable, fathomless, mysterious.

I hold on to her as best I can.

ISABEL

Words, words, words.

Books, books, books.

Thinking about time is the wrong way to go. Suresh is doing that, and that's what keeps us trapped in a cycle.

Let me work through stories instead to get back to our own place in them. A beginning, middle, and end are necessary. Can I construct a whole continuum out of printed words?

I try.

Get back to what we know—memories and impressions created by words.

I think of the first conversation I can remember. I am three and my father is swinging me around by my arms. I ask him to do it again and again. I think of going to the library, first with dad, then on my own, bringing home armfuls of books.

That first time I took home abridged interpretations of Shakespeare's stories. Will's stories. I loved them so much. Afterwards, I read each of the original plays one by one: *Othello*, *Macbeth*, *King Lear*, *Hamlet*, *The Tempest*. It took me years and at first, it was very difficult. I think about each of these stories and their protagonists.

The writers my father made me learn about and read. It became the only thing during the pandemic: so suffocating I hated him, and by extension my mom for allowing it. Then he died. No, don't think about that. Stay with the writers. Major seventeenth century authors after Shakespeare's time:

251

Johnson, Pepys, Dryden, Marvell. All men. Think of the women that come afterwards: Jane Austen, the Brontës. The favourite books and authors who have special place in my heart: *Wuthering Heights*, Jonathan Swift. The Romantics of the late seventeen hundreds: Blake and Wordsworth and Coleridge. Mary Shelley!

Think back to everything I have read by them: every poem, story, and play. All the feelings I experienced as a child: the characters and plot twists that entered my brain and flowed through my heart.

We fall into the sea churning below us.

In my mind, I swim through the Victorian era and think of Dickens and Oscar Wilde and Lewis Carroll. Step by step, page by page, I move us through time, inching towards the twenty-first century. Time becomes words and words become time. There is no difference.

I am made of words and we float in a sky of text. Suresh and I swim in a sea of paper.

I don't know if we talk or if we are wet but we hold on to each other. We are no longer built of atoms or molecules, but thought and language. It's hard to know where he ends and I begin. Step by step, word by word, we move through the centuries. All of the universe's possibilities and creations, those formed, forming, and non-formed open to us. Is this what Will experiences when he goes into one of his late-night writing fugues? The sea of possibilities open to him through language?

In the twentieth century, there are so many choices, so many books I've read that the paths twist and vary. There are *The Once and Future King* and Beatrix Potter. There are *The Wizard of Oz* and Dorothy Parker. There are JD Salinger and Harper Lee. And then there are all the Canadian writers I know and love: Margaret Laurence and Alice Munro, Michael Ondaatje and

Mordecai Richler, and then of course, there is Leonard Cohen. Leonard Cohen, whom our school is named after.

We pass through the world's seas and oceans, never letting go of the crown. Suresh can feel what I'm thinking and I can feel his thoughts. We combine minds and think of Leonard Cohen as I guide us up through the water and into the ground. Up through the fundament and into the topsoil, right to the land around our school. Leonard Cohen Collegiate. We focus on the day we left and the material we had studied. *A Midsummer Night's Dream.*

Let us meditate on the question of Helena's predicament. Let us remember the quotes we identified. Let us think of the play's characters and their attributes. The earth encompasses us now. We rise through the grass and dirt, dark as poppy seed, propelling upwards.

We feel the roots and the earthworms and the pebbles and the minerals and the water. Organisms glow phosphorescent as they slowly eat the mulch. We can taste the saline and the salt in the taproots and the fibres that spread all around us. We move up through the taproots until our essences spread through the network and ganglia of tendrils, rising through the birch tree trunks in the ravine behind the school.

Somewhere, a lone heron stands upon one leg in the burbling water and cries out.

We rise through the tree trunks and the branches, spreading out into a thousand glorious points, leaves shooting and crumpling in the brisk vernal sun. We become paper, floating down through the air, wave after wave of words, raining down upon the quivering fields.

We come to upon the grass near the racetrack, our clothes completely shredded and useless now. The large crow stands in front of us upon the grass, caws once, then flies away. Suresh

looks at me in my red satin dress, broken spokes of my farthingale poking out. I look at him in his old and musty black robe
cut to tatters, skullcap long gone.

We are separate again.

We hold onto the platinum crown with strained knuckles.
"Want to let go of it?" he asks. "You first." Finally, we relax our
hold and place it on the grass between us. The intense platinum
glow slowly diminishes and the blinking transistor goes out, its
energy seeping into the ground.

Dreamily, steadily, we collect ourselves.

My heart slows to a normal beat. It must be just after we left.
Students are still streaming out from the school. Some of them
look at us strangely. Oh my God, we're really here.

We are really back!

Nathan is not here, of course. Why did I still hope he would
be? Neither is the traveller whose device we stole. It is ours
now—we are the travellers. We lie on the grass and look at
the heavy clouds scudding above us. Only a few seconds have
passed since we left, and our sojourn took its time in months,
but I feel it's been years. It's been four hundred and forty
years.

The long grass ripples between our legs. Time, also having
rippled, solidifies. There is another century, another eon somewhere far, far below us that we can no longer fall into.

"What shall we do with the crown?" I ask. "We can't take it
around with us."

Suresh sits up, elbows on his knees, hands around his chin,
not talking for a long time, just allowing the place with its grass
and buildings and breeze register upon his consciousness. He
can no more believe we're back than I can.

"Dee would bury manuscripts in the grounds around his
house," he says. "In the middle of the night so no one could see

him. We could go down into the ravine, where there's cover, and bury the crown there—somewhere only we could find it. For the time being, anyway."

So that is what we do.

SURESH

I doubt we'd be able to tell anybody about what happened even if we wanted to. If we drift apart, she to her interests and friends and I to mine, we will always have this one big thing in common. The memory of this lost time together, unique in all the world.

"What do you think happened to Nathan?" I ask.

"I don't know."

"London burned down. I still don't believe it."

"It would have burned in 1666 anyway," muses Isabel. "There would have been a great fire causing London to be rebuilt. Now they'll just do it earlier."

"So nothing's really changed?" As close as I came to her, as deeply as I could glimpse into her body and mind, she acted on her own without considering me. She always acted alone, as much as Nathan did, more even. She rebuilt our timeline so we could return to the present, flitting her way through the white writers that she liked, the classics canon. She only cared about what she liked and wanted. We're no different than when we left. She has rebuilt the status quo.

"Well, we'd better get out of here," she says reluctantly as if she can no longer read my thoughts, but can still smell their flavour. "Let's go inside the school before they close all the doors, see if things are the same. Let's check our lockers. That'll give us some idea."

We dust ourselves as best we can and walk towards the school. When I get to my locker, it takes me a few tries to remember my lock's combination. Weird. To use it after all this time. The wheel clicks reluctantly as if stuck, as if resenting me for trying to pry treasure from its grasp. I fiddle and fiddle and finally get the lock open. Things look normal, as best as I can remember.

"It looks like yours anyway," states Isabel, echoing my thoughts.

The smell of tobacco smoke cuts harshly through the air, then the words: "Isabel? Suresh? What are you doing?" Sullivan's voice! It screeches at us from down the hall. What is she doing here on a Saturday? Encountering her is the last thing I want. "And why are you dressed like that?"

Yes, it's her but the differences are noticeable. She's older for one thing and has a nervous tremor. Her face shakes a little at regular intervals while she holds her cigarette, almost finished, high between two fingers. The smoke circles around her weathered face and clings to her hair. Most of the red has disappeared from her curls; they are now almost entirely grey, except for the ends stained by nicotine. She seems kinder, or at least more subdued, as if she's older than our Ms Sullivan. The cigarette is jarring, though it seems to mellow her out. Wearing a mocha cardigan, satchel briefcase in hand, she is oblivious to me. Why isn't this equally awkward for her; why isn't she upset at me for having livestreamed her on TikTok?

"Ms Sullivan, you're smoking!" stammers Isabel. "And in school! Why are you smoking—it's really bad for you?"

Sullivan drops her cigarette butt on the floor and grinds it out with her shoe. "Oh Isabel, don't tell me you subscribe to those conspiracy theories. It's just a harmless vice, allows me to get work done and keeps the weight off. You'll be doing it soon enough."

Isabel and I look at each other, puzzled. Now that we think

about it, the smell of lingering tobacco was in the air even before Sullivan arrived. Her arrival just accentuated the harshness of it over the briny reek of our clothes. Sullivan now draws attention to us: "It's me that should be asking why you're both dressed like that," she ponders. "And why do you look so rough?"

"Oh, we're rehearsing for a school play," Isabel stumbles in reply.

"What play?"

"Not a whole play. We're going to try and do a presentation in front of the class—present a scene for extra credit," I say, my excuse not much better. "You wouldn't have a copy of the play with you, by any chance?"

"But why do your costumes look so destroyed? Is it a post-modern thing?"

"Why are you here on Saturday?" asks Isabel, changing the topic.

"I thought I'd come in to get some planning done for the anniversary," replies Sullivan, still parsing us out. "Did you want a copy of *Midsummer*? That's what you're rehearsing?" She fishes in her briefcase and pulls out a dog-eared, well-worn copy of the paperback and hands it to me. It has a different illustration than the one I remember. Now there is a fairy on the cover holding a timepiece, instead of Bottom with the head of an ass. The title is *A Midsummer Night's Time*.

I show it to Isabel and she flips to the back and reads Puck's closing speech:

> And this weak and idle theme,
> Where past is future, not what it seemed,
> Was affected by time's travels, thoughts and intentions.
> Misaligned journeys, timeline's preventions.

Isabel clucks her tongue and closes the book, giving it back to me. "It sounds so wooden to me now," she says wistfully, "I thought he'd change it." Turning to Sullivan, she asks, "Are they still trying to get rid of him from the curriculum?"

"Who?"

"Shakespeare, of course."

"Shakespeare?" asks Sullivan in surprise, lifting her glasses. "Why would we get rid of him from our curriculum? We celebrate his birthday every year. It's coming up. I don't think we'd get rid of him!" She laughs airily, then speaks with concern: "Are you two alright? Should I phone your father?"

"My father?"

"Look, if something's wrong, I should phone Adrian. He'll be worried. I can take you home."

Big breath. Big breath. When Isabel can finally speak, it's everything she can do to deliver her words in a flat, even voice. Command performance: "No, it's alright. We'd best be going home now."

"Okay, but if you need me to . . . " Sullivan trails off. She bites her tongue before saying the rueful word "teenagers" and shaking her head. I don't know how, because the crown is far away from us, but I'm able to pick up on Sullivan's thoughts. I didn't understand her at all before we left. Now I do; I can sense the outsides of her feelings, as if the gap between our ages has closed considerably.

"Just tell me one thing before we go," says Isabel in that same dispassionate voice. "Do you teach Nathan this semester?"

"Nathan who?"

"Nathan Shimura," replies Isabel.

Sullivan shakes her head, still dumbfounded. She puts her briefcase on the ground and takes out a red pack of cigarettes and shows it to us. "I smoke Nathans. That's the only Nathan I know." Her tremor subsides as she calmly withdraws one of the cancer sticks from the box and places it in her mouth. She gives the box to Isabel while she finds her lighter, pretty much offering Isabel a cigarette without saying so.

I look at the small box over Isabel's shoulder. It is scarlet with a white circle on the front. Stylized imperious yellow letters at the top spell "NATHAN'S EMPIRE." Within the white circle is a cartoon man's head. As Sullivan flicks her lighter, the acrid smell makes me remember the skull: *don't ask of us our gender, for we are the gender of death.* The mascot on the cigarette pack looks nothing like the skull. In profile, it looks a bit like the Washington Redskins football team mascot, except the lips are smoking a cigarette. Isabel flips the box over to reveal no surgeon general's warning, no photos of diseased gums or rotting teeth, only a pattern of red Tudor roses.

Isabel hands me the box and I gaze at the front again. The head has a large earring in its ear and an even larger feather in its long black shaggy hair but it's impossible to tell what ethnicity it is—it's not indigenous exactly but it's not white either. Then I notice the jaw, the firm jaw. Is that . . . ?

Isabel is as startled as I am.

Nathan, what have you done?

Sullivan takes back her pack of cigarettes and, shrugging, places it in her briefcase. Smoking and slightly trembling again, she leaves. I root around the bottom of my locker and come up with some old gym clothes I've never seen before. Nothing for Isabel though, I'm afraid. "Okay, I'm going to go get changed in the washroom. Wait for me?"

"Of course. I need you now, more than ever."

That catches my surprise. "Why?" Doesn't she want to get home and see her dad, now alive?

She throws her arm around my shoulder and kisses me

nervously on the cheek. "Because we're not *home*. Perhaps we never shall be. We are truly through Dee's perspective glass now. We have poached more than Will ever could. Maybe it will always feel this way. We are words pried from our pages. This is not the place we left and I don't know what my dad will be, who he will be, what I will be once I get 'home'—will you go there with me? You're the only thing I have left now of the old world. Everything else is counterfeit. I'll do the same for you. With your family."

Her words sink in. She should be more excited, but she is right. We are both filthy with the past and all we have is each other, that's what she's saying. Now I understand. This is not the way I wanted her, nor do I truly want her anymore. Not at the cost of the whole world. Somewhere, somewhen, the AI skull is laughing. After the relief of coming home, we are duped, lost forever.

We will never completely relax again. Perhaps we could do something with the crown but no . . . it would be dangerous, it would be yet another revision, it would only throw us further from our homes. And neither of us can take the crown home for who knows what awaits us there? It must stay hidden in the ground for now, a problem for another day. Isabel feels it, knows what I'm thinking. She shakes her head gravely. Was it worth it? Was it all worth it? Did we kill Shakespeare after all or did we save him? Did we win or lose?

We shall never know, I suppose. And all the writers Isabel thought about, channelling us to this time, this reality, are white—every one of them—we have lost more than we won.

There is something new between us but it has a price. I smile bitterly. "Of course I'll go with you. I hope what we find will be to your pleasing."

In the washroom, I exchange my shredded robe for the track

pants and t-shirt and hoodie I found in my locker. They smell, their smell foreign to me as if belonging to a doppelganger's scent, but are less likely to raise eyebrows than the black robe which still reeks of London's filthy, sooty air, the destruction of all those homes and galleons.

It's strange to feel track pants and a t-shirt, grey ones at that, not black, rubbing against my skin after so many months, so many lifetimes.

ISABEL

Even if the revision is for all intents and purposes nearly identical, it's going to take time getting used to. In the end, we can only move forward a day at a time, an hour at a time. If we found the strength to make our way through Elizabethan England, we can do it here.

We should be grateful for the things we have, those that have stayed the same. And that we're still here. That we have a place, and parents and families even if they are not our own. We shall have to discover them anew.

"I'm glad you're here, with me," I tell Suresh once he emerges from the bathroom. I'm so used to seeing him in black robes that I almost don't recognize him. His t-shirt hangs baggily off his shoulders.

A bus arrives at the bus stop on the corner. The way I remember. We don't get on it. There is something different about it. I cannot say what or spot the differential detail. Just something different. A crack felt in an otherwise perfect vase. Just a hair's width off.

Perhaps it is not the bus itself. Perhaps it is something about the sun, the way it shines through the clouds which are more pink than usual, or the way the warmth filters through the spring air, a bit too hot for this time of year. It is in the air and the moments that scatter between the leaves. The knowledge that time and the universe are not what we thought. "Why does time even have to exist at all in the first place?" I wonder. It's a stupid question but I can't help asking it. "Why can't things just stay the same forever? You and me. Our friendship. The way things were before the stranger brought the crown to us. Why do things change?"

"That's what I was trying to ask all this time," he answers slowly, "ever since we had to leave Sri Lanka, I've tried to answer that question. But if time hadn't moved forward, I'd never have known you. It is only through time that we know and understand one another."

I allow him to continue. "Time gives us the gift of living life," he adds. "Doctor Dee liked quoting Heraclitus: 'you can't step in the same river twice.' Neither you nor the river are the same. He also liked to say 'may you live in interesting times'—and I replied 'but aren't all times interesting?' *Isn't it our lives that make them interesting?*"

I squeeze his hand. What a gift it is to have friendship. We walk down a suburban street that branches off from our school, and the people watering their lawns on a Saturday afternoon stare at us. Our hair is mangled and hideous. We reek. My dress is shredded as if I'd fallen into the gears of some machinery.

The lawn waterers only see two weird and surly teenagers. They keep staring and we glare back at them.

"Friends?" I ask, looking at Suresh inquisitively.

"Friends," he replies warmly.

We continue walking, our future as mysterious as an unwritten page.

DISCUSSION QUESTIONS

1. Do you think Shakespeare should be taught in high school? Why or why not? To what extent?

2. The novel eschews traditional numeric chapter headings in favour of rotating protagonists to narrate the story. Why do you think it does this?

3. When figuring out the framework to tell this story, the author smashed different genres together. He thought of it as *Shakespeare in Love* meets *The Terminator*. What are the benefits of combining genres, and mixing high and low culture?

4. Isabel tells Suresh that she only intends to use Suresh's pdf to nudge Shakespeare in the right direction. Is she being truthful? In what ways is her relationship with Shakespeare informed by her relationship with her deceased father? To what extent does she replicate the way her father treated her when dealing with Shakespeare?

5. Puppets and puppeteering crop up numerous times during the narrative. Discuss the implications.

6. Mirrors, mirror images, and reflections are a recurring motif in the story. How do they relate to literature and social media? How do they relate to the idea of performance in public and private spheres?

7. Other characters muse on Nathan's mixed ethnicity, even though he might not be consciously aware of it himself. There are suggestions that his biological father might be black or mixed or perhaps indigenous. Does Nathan code switch as a habitual practice without realising it? What are the implications in relation to his decision towards the end of the novel?

8. In an episode of *The Office*, a visitor tells Michael Scott: "secret secrets are no fun / secret secrets hurt someone." All three protagonists carry secrets within the narrative. Discuss the way they handle their secrets and whether this is healthy or not.

9. One of Shakespeare's plays is titled *All's Well That Ends Well*. Is that the case with the end of this novel or is it more ambiguous than that? How so, and why?

10. Is time something that exists in and of itself or is it something purely psychological, a set of relationships between events, something in the mind? Are the events in this book the result of causality or something else? What exactly is the nature of time?

ACKNOWLEDGMENTS

Thanks to Nurjehan Aziz and MG Vassanji and Peggy and Kaitlyn and Sabrina and everyone else at Mawenzi! My gratitude to Heather Mawby and Kumar Sivasubramanian for reading early versions of this manuscript and giving honest feedback. My thanks especially to Ivan Cooper for reading a later version and using his prodigious knowledge of British history to inform me what was plausible and what was not in Elizabethan society.

Thanks to Alan Moore for introducing me to the figure of John Dee in particular and the idea of revisions in general. Thanks go to Chris Zeichmann for his support and friendship. Special thanks to Julian Dwyer for his great work on the cover. And last but not least, thanks to Wayne Johnston for his generous blurb on the back and the wonderful books he has written.